ISTORIA BOOKS
presents

Dragon Lady

a novel by Gary Alexander

This book is a work of fiction. Characters and places are either made up or, if real, used fictitiously. Any resemblance between fictional characters and real people is entirely coincidental and not intentional.

Get on the Istoria Books mailing list!
Subscribers learn of special limited-time-only discounts. Sign up at the website where you can also view other Istoria Books titles:
www.IstoriaBooks.com

Copyright 2011 Gary Alexander
ISBN-13: 978-0615675763
ISBN-10: 061567576X

Cover design by Amanda Kelsey of Razzle Dazzle Design.

Our numbers have increased in Vietnam because the aggression of others has increased in Vietnam. There is not, and there will not be a mindless escalation.
                              Lyndon B. Johnson

We learn from history that we do not learn from history.
                         Georg Wilhelm Friedrich Hegel

The 803rd Liaison Detachment did not exist. Anybody who served in Vietnam knows that it could have.

Chapter One

In Seattle, Washington, on Thanksgiving, November 25, 2010 at 5:12 a.m., I died peacefully in my sleep, my loving fifth wife at my side.

Happy Fucking Turkey Day.

Medical science, bless their collective hearts, takes death personally. They kept me clinging a bit too long. I was quite ready to check out.

Months earlier, as they prepared to roll me into the MRI that found the thing causing the headaches, the thing that was to kill me, they asked two questions I'd expected:

1. Are you claustrophobic?
2. Do you have medical insurance?

They asked one I hadn't:

Do you have any metal in your body? A steel plate in your cranium, a pin in a hip?

I had to think. It'd been years.

Decades.

Yeah, as a matter of fact there was. Pointing at a half-inch-long indented scar in my left forearm, I told them about a chunk of iron in there, the size of a grain of rice, compliments of a Vietcong satchel charge.

In 1965, when I'd awakened from the anesthesia at Clark Air Force Base in the Philippines, the surgeon had told me they'd removed all the foreign material but that fragment. They'd left it alone because it rested beside a major blood vessel. It wasn't worth the risk of going after, the risk of nicking the vessel. They'd warned that it could shift. In almost a half century, I hadn't felt it.

The MRI folk reminded me that the M in MRI stood for magnetic. They said the shrapnel might be attracted. They said I might feel a slight tug.

Sure enough, I did.

When they rolled me out of the machine and its blaring electrical hum, I couldn't stop jabbering about that old war. I couldn't. They'd heard of Vietnam from their fathers and grandfathers, who'd either participated in it or dodged it. No, I said before I went any further, don't get the wrong impression. I am not a war hero. I am anything but. I was a shirker, a malingering goof-off slacker extraordinaire.

I was assigned in Saigon, I babbled on, far from the paddies and the jungles and snipers and shit-smeared punji sticks. I was attached to a bizarre outfit of paper shufflers whose mission is classified to this day.

The shrapnel was a result of being at the wrong place at the wrong time. I was a helluva lot luckier than my best buddy. I came home vertically. He didn't. He had a junkyard's worth of metal in him, I continued babbling and then was bawling like a baby.

They patted my arm, as if I were a live explosive, saying, "Now, now, it's all right. It'll be fine."

But it wasn't all right. It would not be fine. Two days later, I received a call to come back in. *As soon as possible. Please.*

A neurologist showed me the bad news, a series of photographic slices of my gray matter. Even I could distinguish the growth that didn't belong. It looked like a golf ball. The neurologist went on to explain in layman's terms why there was nothing that could be done. My golf ball had roots he could see but I couldn't.

I went home to die.

Always a voracious reader, I dove into Vietnam, a subject I'd avoided for years. I read and read. The numbers staggered me. The consensus for U.S. dead in the Vietnam War (1960-1975) was 58,199. When I began my Vietnam tour in 1964, there were half that many *live* GIs in-country.

Sally, my bride of less than a year, was incredibly supportive. She was one of the two great loves of my life. Sally was a tall, graying blonde, the antithesis of my other, my Vietnamese Dragon Lady.

Sally and I took what we thought was going to be one last trip together. We went to Washington, D.C. and visited the Vietnam War Memorial. The Memorial doesn't look like much from a distance. It's long and black and low and shiny and V-shaped. The power is up close and personal, when you see it gridlocked with names of 58,249 (am not gonna quibble over a difference of 50 names) dead, when you see older men taking rubbings of a buddy's name, tears streaming. These were big burly guys with beards and white hair. These were guys who would not whimper if you had their private parts in a vise.

Back home, I read and read and read. They say my year in country, 1965, was a pivotal year. Politically and militarily, we could've gone either way. We could have declared victory over counterinsurgency and the godless communists, saying that we'd won their hearts and minds to boot, and packed our bags. We could have done what we did--that is, "stayed the course" to the tune of 500,000-plus troops, 58,000-plus of them needing only one-way tickets.

A historian wrote that Vietnam was our first war with "amorphous" battlefronts. In previous wars, the lines were clear-cut. When I was a kid during Korea, growing up in the Pacific Northwest, the newspapers had maps and dotted lines, the good guys on one side, the bad guys on the other.

But in those papers, the comic section was the front section to me. My passion for adventure comics developed at a young age. I couldn't wait for Sunday's, four entire pages in color.

Tarzan and *Buck Rogers* and *Joe Palooka* and *The Lone Ranger* were okay, but the niftiest by a mile was *Terry and the Pirates*. There was a crackling sexual tension between Terry Lee and his nemesis/femme fatale, the Dragon Lady. I instinctively knew this before I knew what sexual was.

My flesh-and-blood Dragon Lady and the Dragon Lady in print represented a lifetime of tingling fantasies and wet dreams and masturbation and erotic memories. One drunken night, I confessed my kinky obsession to Charlotte, who shortly thereafter became my second ex-wife. My Dragon Lady hang-up was also instrumental in costing me Lea, spouse number one, and Marcia, number four.

Mum had been the word with Sally till a week after my diagnosis. I told her that she ran second, a very close second, to my Dragon Lady. Why I told her, I'm still unsure. It was needless and cruel. I guess I didn't want to take anything with me.

Sally handled it well. No tears, no silent treatment, no hissy fit. An advantage of being terminal is that your indiscretions are taken in stride. You are easily forgiven.

That magnetic tug in my arm tugged at me to put down what follows. In The Land of the Living, I was not introspective. My nature was to lead with my mouth or a fist rather than with my brain.

These days, I am on my best behavior.
And I have all the time in the netherworld to write.

Cordially,
Joseph Josiah Joe IV

Chapter Two

Saigon 1965

"Lookie, Joey. A gift from God," said Ziggy, a man of almost no words and an atheist to boot.

These days you'd call it a crime of opportunity, but then it was a miracle. Strapped onto a United States Air Force flatbed truck stalled in the other direction was a GE air conditioner for home and office, brand-spanking-new in its box, a sacred offering on a pedestal.

That air conditioner was a perfect chance for Ziggy and I to score brownie points with the captain. Just in the nick of time. As usual, we'd been in the doghouse, skating on thin ice, stepping on our own peckers whenever we laid a foot down. We were duds. We were malingerers. We were serial screwups. We had not subscribed to can-do. We had not gotten with the program.

Saigon was a steam bath. It had two seasons. We were in the blue-sky humid-hot season. The other was the monsoon humid-hot season.

The netherworld I referred to, where I am nowadays, formally designated as The Great Beyond, is a stunning contrast. We have the invariable climate of a suburban shopping mall, with elevator music playing every lounge-lizard classic imaginable, day and night, presumably for all eternity. There are times that I yearn for Saigon climes, for *any* uncomfortable extreme. Typhoons, blizzards, flash floods, hailstorms, you name it.

Anything that kept you cool was scarce in 1965 Saigon. Window air conditioners were scarcer than scarce. What was available on the black market was third-hand garbage that had been passed along like a cheap whore.

Traffic wasn't budging. Bicycles, cars, wagons, trucks, cyclos, armored personnel carriers, scooters—nothing was moving. Heat waves and tailpipe smoke boiled up, mixing with the odors of incense, food, flowers, sewage and intrigue. There was a throbbing, noxious din of sputtering exhaust, shouting and horn-honking. Whoever had named this town the Paris of the Orient had done so long, long ago.

Ziggy squeezed out of our taxicab, lumbered to the flatbed, and proceeded to undo the buckles securing the a.c. unit. The airman driver opened his door and began raising a ruckus. I hopped out of the taxi and kicked his door shut.

I shook my head as kindly as I could and said, "Don't do something you'll be sorry for. I am sincere about this."

Wide-eyed, he said, "What the hell is this shit?"

He was an airman second class, a two-striper, nearly as low on the totem pole as us.

"It is what it is."

"You can't."

"We are."

"I don't believe this."

"Believe," I said. "I am sorry."

"Fuck you."

"I really am sorry."

"My ass'll be grass."

"No, it won't. In this traffic, you have ample time to think up a story. Tell them we were Vietnamese gangsters, masked and armed."

The poor bastard sized me up, then Ziggy through his mirror. I'm no ninety-seven pound weakling. Kick sand in my face and one of us will be hurting. But when you look at Ziggy, the first thing you wanna do is fork over your lunch money.

Ziggy went six-four, six-five and was cone-shaped. I hadn't an inkling what he tipped the scales at. If he was of a mind to shave his chest and back, he'd need a lawnmower.

Ziggy looked as if he should have become extinct during the last Ice Age. And Ziggy was the most brilliant person I would ever know, before and after my dying day.

The Sunday funnies out of a stateside newspaper were on the seat beside the airman.

"You have your folks send them to you, too?"

He nodded morosely, drumming his fingers on the steering wheel.

"What's your favorite?"

No reply.

"C'mon."

He sighed. "*Dick Tracy.*"

"Yeah, Tracy. Pruneface, Rhodent, Tess Trueheart, all his supporting characters, they're good too. My all-time favorite's *Terry and the Pirates*."

He shrugged.

"All it'd take in Vietnam is ten Terry Lees. Parachute them in and we can all go home in a month," I said, laughing.

The airman did not laugh. He did not answer. I didn't think he and I were going to have much of a conversation. Which was just as well. I couldn't confide in him that *Terry and the Pirates* was my favorite comic strip because of the Dragon Lady, and my obsession with her and with her flesh-and-blood counterpart.

I'd had an average number of girlfriends, some serious, some not. Some dumped me, some I dumped. I had never truly been in love, not until my real-life Dragon Lady, whom I knew existed but had not yet met.

Ziggy lifted the air conditioner onto the top of his head and walked off as if the carton was empty. The airman glared straight ahead. This was a scared kid wearing a wedding ring. He was drawing three hundred dollars per month, including family allowances. Smart kid, too. No way was he gonna sacrifice life and limb for a piece of government property, which he also was.

We heard a terrible shuddering *ka-boom*. Everything and everybody froze for a second, as if there'd been film breakage in a movie projector. Even the automotive fumes seemed to hang in midair globs.

The Vietnamese stuck in the tie-up looked knowingly at each other, as did Ziggy and I. One of two things had happened. General Curtis LeMay had dropped a nuke on Hanoi, as he was itching to do. But the *ka-boom* came from downtown, so it was the other.

We *knew* the Vietcong had bombed the U.S. Embassy. Rumors in Saigon spread faster than the clap. The word had been out for at least a week. Everyone and his brother had heard the stories, except, apparently, the people in charge of preventing it.

Another lively rumor was that secret negotiations were underway to admit South Vietnam to the Union as our fifty-first state. Absurd as it seemed to me, this rumor was gathering momentum, gathering it quickly.

Nineteen-sixty-five was early in the war, prior to Uncle Sam shipping over any young male able to fog a mirror to prop up the Vietnam domino. It was ten years before North Vietnamese tanks rolled into Saigon, before Saigon became Ho Chi Minh City.

In 1965, crewcuts and madras shirts reigned. Now, in The Great Beyond, aided by the perspective of time and an undemanding regimen, I look at 1965 as a Bohemian Vacuum between beatniks and hippies.

It was the Year of the Nonconformist Void.

It was the year that Joe Namath signed a gigantic four hundred thousand dollar contract with the New York Jets. It was the year that Spaghetti Os and Slurpees hit the marketplace. It was the year that young guys emulated the Beach Boys. It was the year of Selma and Watts. Churchill died and Malcolm X was assassinated.

Gas cost thirty-four and a half cents a gallon. The Dow Jones was under 1000. The year 1965 was two-thirds of the way to 2000 A.D., when we thought we'd be getting around like the Jetsons.

How innocent 1965 was. It preceded the Tet Offensive, My Lai, Vietnamization, light at the end of the tunnel, Kent State, Watergate, unindicted coconspirators, Patty Hearst, emission controls, the Silent Majority, the Moral Majority, Chernobyl, The Falklands War, Iran-Contra, AIDS, SARS, the World Wide Web, the dot.com craze, Y2K, hanging chads, 9/11, Enron, Paris Hilton, Sarah Palin, and the proliferation of consultants.

In 1965, Vietnamese would still stare at us and our round eyes. Ziggy was a sci-fi lover, with a fanatical preoccupation with the planet Mars. We could've been Ziggy's Martians, we were such novelties.

While the adviser bullshit was coming to an end and we were taking over the fighting, if your number was up, you were as apt to have a barstool blasted out from under you as catching a North Vietnamese bullet between the peepers.

We were unable to stuff the box into the little cream-and-blue Renault taxi as is. To make the air conditioner fit, Ziggy ripped the cardboard off like he was peeling an orange. Half the people on the street did the airman's see-no-evil. The other half gawked, not sure what they were seeing.

That's what this war did for you.

Gave you fresh experiences every single day.

Chapter Three

After Ziggy and I installed the air conditioner in the window behind Captain Dean Papersmith's desk and cranked it up full blast, the captain closed his eyes and smiled blissfully. He fluttered his pockets and flapped his shirt against his bony chest. He cooed like a pigeon. Until now, the only man in the outfit with an air conditioner was our commanding officer, Brigadier General Whipple, and his machine was unreliable.

"Private Joe, Private Zbitgysz, I may have misjudged you. Good work, men. A number one, can-do job," Captain Papersmith said. "I know resourcefulness and possibly heroism was involved, given the nature of this hellhole city. By the way, did you hear? The VC blew up the U.S. Embassy. A terrible shock. It caught everyone by surprise."

Ziggy and I let our jaws appropriately drop. As I did so, I was distracted as always by the photographs on the captain's desk. The one in the large gilded frame was a professional color portrait of him and his horse-faced wife and their two children, a sullen boy, who had juvenile delinquent written all over him, and a grinning girl, who already knew the score. His missus wore a pearl necklace and a bouffant as tall as Marge Simpson's would be.

Mrs. Dean (Mildred) Papersmith was an heiress in a clan that manufactured drawing instruments and technical products. Their cash cow was the slide rule, in which they ranked second to the venerable Keuffel & Esser. I'd owned one of Mildred's family's slide rules. For my one disastrous quarter as an engineering major, I'd had to purchase one.

Little did Captain Papersmith or anybody else in 1965 know that in a decade the pocket calculator would relegate the slide rule to a Smithsonian relic. It would obliterate his better half's family firm and trust fund, a circumstance that would cause the good captain to suffer yet another nervous breakdown.

◆

Please allow me to pause here for a moment. I apologize for the boldface type and the italics. It won't happen again. I have to explain a few things before we proceed. It's extremely important that I do (at least to me) and that I have your full attention.

I am not clairvoyant, I am not Nostradamus. I am not predicting the future from 1965. I am in the future, in The Great Beyond, or rather, from your point of view, in the present, speaking at the very instant you are reading this, whenever that might be.

The loose definition of "the great beyond" is the afterlife, life after death, and so forth. Which is precisely what The Great Beyond is.

Is it Heaven or is it Hell? Beats the hell out of me. Thanks to the psychological games They play with me, one day it's one, the next day the other.

I do know that The Great Beyond is a municipality. Whether it's a town, city, county, state, nation, continent, world, solar system, universe or galaxy, I do not know. The people (?) who run this place are probably capable of building a chain-link fence around infinity, so their accomplishments and capabilities are limited only by my imagination.

I've already mentioned the non-stop elevator music ("Lady of Spain" now playing) and the San Diego climate, but I've broken the narrative flow of this yarn long enough. The travelogue will continue later.

◆

Tucked into the picture frame of the all-American household was a Polaroid snapshot of the captain's girlfriend and the woman of my dreams. My Dragon Lady had been inserted as if she were the captain's car or favorite pooch.

Thus far, sadly, the Polaroid was the extent of my relationship with her. I alone knew her as the Dragon Lady. Beginning then with her inaccessibility, she'd break my heart again and again, till it was a heap of shattered china.

My Dragon Lady didn't wear the red metallic gowns with high collars as did her comic-page namesake in *Terry and the Pirates* (like the panel I kept in my wallet, nestled next to a rubber and, figuratively, my heart), but rather the traditional Vietnamese *áo dài*, a long silken tunic split at the sides, worn over loose pants.

Unaccompanied by her cartoon counterpart's long ivory cigarette holder, she projected an innocence that I didn't swallow for a moment. She was lovelier than the infamous Madame Nhu, sister-in-law of South Vietnam's late president. My Dragon Lady made the Mona Lisa look like a hound dog. Her cheekbones were higher than the Chrysler Building stacked atop the Empire State Building. She seemed to be gazing beyond the photographer, presumably Captain Papersmith, straight into my eyes.

She was satiny soft and as tough as a hardware store full of nails, a contradiction that simultaneously gave me goose bumps and a hard-on. I'd looked and looked for an ideal complement to her visage, a tinge of cruelty in her eyes or at the corners of her mouth, and had found none. But nobody was perfect.

To be so obsessed by a combination of a Sunday comic and a low-resolution photograph was by any definition a psychological illness. I accepted my malady then and I relish it from my present aerie. If I were a sick puppy, so be it. The last thing in the world I wanted was the services of a competent shrink. To be cured would be unbearable.

As I continued staring, Captain Papersmith snapped his fingers. "Yoo-hoo, Private Joe. Are you with us?"

"Yes sir."

He glanced at his watch. "Where have you men been today?"

We shrugged in unison.

"The air conditioner requisition does forgive you for being unaccounted for much of the day. However, I have an important mission for you. It has to be accomplished ASAP."

Where we'd been was avoiding our duties and settling a bet. I'd told Ziggy about a book I was reading on U.S. presidents, on how George Washington had not pitched a silver dollar across the Potomac River, but supposedly a stone or a penny across the smaller Rappahannock.

"It's lore," I'd told Ziggy. "In the category of chopped-down cherry trees and wooden teeth."

"Fucka buncha lore," he'd rebutted. "Anyone can toss a dollar across a river."

I'd said, "Oh yeah?"

He'd said, "Yeah, we got this river here that's a pissy-ass little river."

"Like Cuba's a pissy-ass little island? Ask the Bay of Pigs survivors."

"Who said shit 'bout some island?"

Well, off we'd gone. In this day and age, we could plead Attention Deficit Disorder for this sort of meandering stunt. Back then it was 24-karat goldbricking.

We'd ridden a taxi through downtown Saigon to the skinniest part of the Saigon River, which was still awfully wide. Ziggy wouldn't've thrown a silver dollar even if we'd had one. We weren't that flaky. He did fling a flat rock that skipped a third of the way out. Not a bad effort, but I won the wager. We were headed back to the outfit by way of a couple of bars when we'd come upon the air conditioner.

"We were out being heroically resourceful for you, sir," I said. "Resourceful heroism is time-consuming. Sir."

Our company clerk, Private First Class A. Bierce, almost smiled. He sat in a corner, in the shadow of his massive manual typewriter, quietly listening, absorbing all. PFC Bierce had a poker face and a receding hairline. He had a hint of south of the border in him, like Fernando Lamas.

He had a semi-famous name, too, although he didn't know that I or anybody in the United States Army knew. Bierce worked long hours at the keyboard, but I never saw his work. To a man, we left him alone. Veteran soldiers knew that you did not make an enemy of a company clerk.

Captain Papersmith raised a delicate hand. He had a pencil neck and pale, translucent skin you could see veins through. He was not young, thirty-five years of age at the very minimum. His background was as classified as our duty station, the 803rd Liaison Detachment.

He said, "Indeed you were resourceful, but cease the sarcasm, Private Joe. I do believe that the air conditioner requisition indicates you're ready to assume more responsibility."

"Yes sir," I said warily. In the army, "more responsibility" translated into a dirty detail.

Ziggy didn't say anything. Ziggy didn't speak unless spoken to and sometimes not then, unless you got him going on Mars and Mariner 4's approach to and imminent arrival above the Red Planet. The builders of that satellite guaranteed that, once and for all, Mariner 4 would separate Martian fact from Martian legend, an assurance that tied his stomach in knots.

"Stop pouting, Private Joe. I don't understand you men, Joe and Zbitgysz. There are two of you, replacing one. Am I overworking you? Is the supply room such a burden?"

Ziggy and I had replaced former Supply Sergeant Rubicon, who had received a compassionate reassignment to Fort Lee, New Jersey. His German war bride, widow of a Wehrmacht lieutenant killed at Stalingrad, had turned out to be the forty-something lawfully wedded wife of an SS officer who'd been stationed at Buchenwald. Simon Wiesenthal had recently thrown a net over him in Argentina.

I'd eavesdropped on Sergeant Rubicon as he'd pled ignorance to a chief warrant officer from the Criminal Investigation Division (CID) named R. Tracy.

Besides having a name from the funny pages that hung around his neck like a five-hundred-pound albatross, CWO R. Tracy bore an extremely strong likeness not to square-jawed Dick, but to Lee Harvey Oswald. The days since November, 22, 1963 must've been hell for him, the poor bastard the object of wary stares and the butt of endless jokes.

I'd liked Sergeant Rubicon and believed him even if CWO Tracy hadn't. He was especially devoted to his stepdaughter, who'd been a preschooler during World War Two. She'd had vivid memories of "airplane skies," which was her term for B-17 raids, hundreds of the bombers visiting at a time. Rubicon had hoped she'd someday get over her nightmares. I did too.

When Rubicon had said his piece, CWO Tracy had looked up from his notes with an Oswaldian smirk, saying nothing. Yeah, Rubicon had gotten a ticket home, but then what for him? The next day, the 803rd was without a supply sergeant.

"Is it a burden, Private Joe?" the captain pursued.

I gave the one acceptable answer. "No, sir. Not a burden."

"You will also assist PFC Bierce with clerical duties as I see fit. Bierce works like a dog."

Our official MOS (Military Occupational Specialty) was Duty Soldier, so "more responsibility" of any ilk could be piled on us. In effect, we were coolies. But Ziggy and I as clerks? That was a crock of guano. The captain was laying a trap.

I looked at PFC Bierce. Pretending to ignore us, he carefully scrolled more paper into his typewriter. The incommunicative Bierce was a mystery man in many respects, materializing at the 803rd from parts unknown.

He had replaced Specialist-4 Cleon, who'd been surprised in the latrine by our super-patriotic executive officer, Colonel Jake Lanyard. A transistor radio to his ear, SP4 Cleon had been masturbating to Hanoi Hannah, North Vietnam's equivalent of Axis Sally and Tokyo Rose.

I'd listened to her, too, to her *Hi, GI Joe. How are you? It seems to me that you are poorly informed about the going of the war, to say nothing of a truthful explanation of your presence here to die or be maimed for life.* She didn't sound particularly sexy to me. My image of Hanoi Hannah was closer to Ho Chi Minh than Jayne Mansfield. But to each his own.

Colonel Lanyard did not drink, smoke or chew. I knew zilch of his love life, here or stateside, but I doubt that he consorted with women who did drink, smoke or chew. Ultra-clean living lent a high level of self-righteous intolerance to the colonel. His only known vice was that he had no known vices.

General Whipple had overheard the enraged Colonel Lanyard bellowing at Cleon, calling him, among other things, a degenerate and a commie punk. His intervention had prevented Lanyard from blowing PFC Cleon's head off with the .45 that was on his hip day and night. The colonel did manage to get Cleon convicted of misdemeanor treason or some such and sent to Leavenworth to pound rocks.

I wasn't sure where Captain Papersmith came from either and what he did here at the 803rd besides bossing us around. He called himself the company commander and detachment adjutant. His primary duty seemed to be reviewing paperwork and sending it up and down the line.

Which brings me to our 803rd Liaison Detachment in general. My dictionary defined "liaison" as communication between different groups or units of an organization. To "liaise" was to effect or establish a liaison. A "detachment" was a small unit, created for special duties.

I was unable to detect any duties, special or otherwise, in the Fighting 803rd, nor any communication or useful activity whatsoever. And what of the previous 802 liaison detachments? Had the original crossed the Delaware? Had one established liaisons at Antietam and Belleau Wood? I'd researched the unit's history and found no history, let alone any active "liaison detachment," should there ever have been such an animal.

Anyway, why were we commanded by a brigadier general and a bird colonel when we were few, doing little?

The 803rd's Annex across the street was the key. Had to be.

Our personnel jackets were on Captain Papersmith's desk. He knew exactly what he had in us. I was a draftee who'd get out the same way as I came in--as a slick-sleeved private. There was a drinking-on-duty incident and an altercation with a sergeant. My military downfall was my temper and my big mouth. In the army, insubordination was worse than being an atomic spy.

My parents summed me up pretty well as a misfit with alcoholic tendencies who didn't want to be anything when he grew up, should that miracle occur. I was a college boy, a professional student. In the space of six and a half years, I'd earned fewer than two years of college credits in any specific discipline. I changed majors like I changed underwear. The Selective Service System had finally lost patience with my academic buffet and invited me to take my draft physical.

I was the diametric opposite of my brother, Jack, who had flown through undergrad work and was a doctoral candidate in aerodynamics and fluid mechanics. I suffered mightily in comparison. In addition, my mother and stepfather taught mathematics and English, respectively, at a junior college. My family had the three Rs covered. To call me a black sheep was to insult the species.

It's sad that I can't return from The Great Beyond to counsel myself. I sure as hell could've used my wisdom.

Ziggy had more than his share of problems, too. He was a high school dropout and an enlistee who'd been on the ragged edge of a Section Eight from the day he'd raised his right hand. He'd been promoted to PFC and demoted to private more times than Carter had pills. He should've had zippers on his sleeves.

Ziggy had been hauled before a judge for some offense or another. The judge had let him pick between the jailhouse and the recruiting station. It was routinely done in those days. In 1965, there was more of that flavor of patriotic zeal filling the ranks than the Pentagon cared to admit.

Ziggy and I had one thing in common. Nobody wanted us. My original MOS was cook. Ziggy was an ammo loader. The army had sent me to cook's school, where we prepared pots of greasy stews that reminded me of witchcraft and cauldrons. They'd taught us to cook spaghetti that was crisp and bacon that was not. Ziggy had no formal education in ammo loading.

Neither of us had found our assignments vocationally appealing. This must have showed. They had us pegged as jack-offs who could get you killed, either poisoned or blown to smithereens before Victor Charles had an opportunity to take a lick. We'd bounced from here to there, winding up at this puzzling organization, most likely at random.

As the 803rd's duty soldiers, we cleaned the latrine and mopped floors. In our supply room duties, we humped tons of mimeograph paper and file folders and carbon paper and adding machine tape and punch cards and correspondence to the door of the mysterious Annex. The punch cards arrived in bricklike packages. If they'd been actual bricks, we'd handled enough of them to build a medieval cathedral, flying buttresses and all.

"If you typed, I could assign you duties less menial," the captain went on.

I could hunt and peck, but Ziggy didn't know which side of a Remington was up. Biting the hook, I quickly lied, "We do know how to type, sir. Fifty words a minute, though we're a little rusty."

"I wasn't aware," the captain said.

Ziggy piped up, "Sir, I don't know how to type."

I gave Ziggy an elbow. You never knew when that prodigious brain would jump out of gear.

The only instance in which you ever ever ever volunteered in this man's army is if they asked if you typed. Typists were scarce, and if you said you could, truthfully or not, they invariably sat you in front of a typewriter in a warm, dry place.

Volunteering for anything else, forget it. I'd learned that the hard way in a morning formation during basic training at Fort Ord, California when a sergeant with a clipboard had asked if anyone had a driver's license. Several suckers, me included, thinking ahead to an easy day behind the wheel, had raised our hands and spent the rest of that easy day driving a push lawnmower on the parade grounds.

"As you were, Zbitgysz," Captain Papersmith said. "I say you're typists, you're typists. They're Specialist-4 E-4 slots, men. The sky's the limit if you behave and apply yourselves."

We were private E-2s, so the captain's limitless sky had a fairly low ceiling, but I remembered when I used to be a PFC E-3. It had been a nice two weeks. Then I'd coldcocked that sergeant.

"Yes sir. Thank you, sir. What Private Zbitgysz meant was that we'll be outstanding typists after we knock off that rust and limber up our fingers."

"As you men are aware, the enemy is escalating the war. Consequently, because of our rapid buildup to counter communist aggression, various matériel and equipment is in short supply."

Saying "the enemy" as if he'd been in hand-to-hand with Victor Charles.

"Yes sir."

"Senior officers require transportation when they require it," Captain Papersmith went on. "Colonel Lanyard, for instance. A man of his rank has to submit a request days in advance for the use of a motor pool Jeep. That's outrageous."

The captain reported directly to Colonel Lanyard, the one person in the 803rd who wore a uniform. Colonel Lanyard nominally reported to the commanding officer, Brigadier General Whipple, a reservist and a research botanist prior to being called up. General Whipple rarely ventured from his office, which resembled an arboretum. He himself joked that it wasn't an office, it was a terrarium.

We were on Hong Thap Tu Street, a few blocks from MACV (Military Assistance Command, Vietnam) Headquarters, in a hand-me-down building from the French. The stucco came off in gooey slabs, the floorboards creaked, and the red tile roof was scuzzy green from mold. The 803rd Liaison Detachment smelled like the Foreign Legion had garrisoned in it.

Outside Captain Papersmith's window, I could see our Annex building, which dwarfed us. It was an old warehouse, with windows painted black. Construction was going on inside. You could hear the sawing and hammering. Whatever they were doing in there, it hungrily gobbled electricity. Unreliable local power was routed in by wiring that looked like a tangle of black noodles. Auxiliary generators hummed day and night.

The Annex was totally off-limits to us. Colonel Jake Lanyard had told us this the day we'd reported in, under threat of court-martial and reassignment to an infantry unit in the Delta, where we'd be up to our chests in malarial water and vipers and guerrillas.

"This is not an order," he'd said solemnly. "It is a promise."

I saw an army bus stop in front. Annex personnel began filing aboard. They were bussed in every morning, bussed out for lunch, bussed back in, and bussed out in the evenings, often late, to and from Tan Son Nhat Air Base where they were billeted in secured quarters.

The Annex was peopled by oddballs. That much we knew. These days you'd call them nerds or geeks, but then they were oddballs. They wore wrinkled civvies that didn't fit right. They were clumsy. They had bad haircuts and big asses. Their glasses were as thick as telescope lenses. The oddballs were said to hold the rank of warrant officer.

We had oddballs in high school. They belonged to the radio club and didn't play sports. The jocks picked on them and called them homos. I don't think they were queer. I don't think they disliked girls. They simply didn't notice them or know how to approach them if they did.

The 803rd Liaison Detachment oddballs were good-spirited as they got on and off their buses. Whatever the hell they were doing, they seemed tickled pink to be in the army, in the middle of what was shaping up to be a bona fide war.

I had to again wonder: As you got smarter and smarter and smarter in college, did you go around full circle and start over as the village idiot? I wondered that out loud once to my mother, stepfather and Jack. I'd directed it at Jack, who'd skipped three grades but couldn't tie his shoelaces until age nine. My family was not amused.

Our oddballs were sent paperwork as thick as phone books. It came from DoD and DA, and CINCPAC and USARV and USOM and HEDSUPPACT and USIS and COMUSMACV and USMACV and MACV. The papers were sealed inside envelopes marked TOP SECRET CRYPTO.

Whoever came to the Annex door and signed for the stuff was careful not to give us a peek within. The oddballs were off-limits to us, too. Even to say hello to. But I knew that someday my curiosity would get the better of me.

"Private Joe, get your eyes off the Annex personnel and listen to me. As I was saying, a full colonel has to submit—"

"Yes sir, outrageous."

"Requisition of a Jeep outside channels, is that feasible?" Captain Papersmith asked.

We were apparently finished on the subject of typing, clerk-typist status having been dangled as bait.

"Sir, does the colonel require a Jeep now?"

"By the ingenuity you men displayed today, it strikes me that you have alternative matériel sources."

The captain was correct about Jeeps being in short supply. The buildup was accelerating beyond the ability to support it. From econ classes, I recalled the supply and demand curve. In 1965 Saigon, the curve was bent sharply toward demand.

If the captain wanted us to steal a Jeep for the colonel, though, I wish he'd spit it out. But Captain Papersmith wouldn't say shit if he had a mouthful.

"Alternative matériel sources, sir?" I asked.

Digging at his chewed fingernails, the captain said, "Outside of official channels. Unofficially speaking."

"Is this what you mean by 'more responsibility,' sir?"

"Are you being smart with me, soldier?"

"Sir, no sir. Just want to confirm the facts."

"There are no facts. We aren't having this conversation."

"What conversation, sir?"

Ziggy laughed and Captain Papersmith flinched. Ziggy's laugh sounded like a truck backfiring.

Red as a beet, Captain Papersmith said, "That'll be all. Dismissed."

We whipped salutes on him and headed out to follow orders we hadn't been given.

Chapter Four

"The captain, , he acts like boosting a Jeep is im-fucking-possible," Ziggy said contemptuously as we climbed into a taxi. "Joey, they're the easiest rigs anywheres to hot-wire. A monkey with a screwdriver'd be taillights down the road in sixty seconds flat."

I had no basis to disagree. Although I lacked Ziggy's criminal background, I felt at home as a member of the Alternative Matériel Source Team. I was in the Zigster's good hands.

Ziggy, incidentally, was the only person to call me Joey, a diminutive I didn't recollect hearing from family or friends even as a small child. I was not one to whom warm and fuzzy nicknames came naturally. Inevitably, four of my five wives came to refer to me with other four-letter names.

Ziggy and I were an odd couple before *The Odd Couple.* We'd bonded before "male bonding" came into usage. Our bond was our mutual alienation from most people and institutions. Call it unhealthy if you like, but it worked for us.

Me? Who am I?

While we're in the taxicab, slaloming in the maniacal traffic, it's high time we get an autobiographical brief out of the way.

I am the late Joseph Josiah Joe IV, last of the Joe line.

My family tree is rather peculiar, an asymmetrical arrangement of dead limbs.

We can trace the Joes back as far as the Civil War, to Gettysburg, where Josiah Joseph Joe Senior was felled by dysentery or some other shit-borne disease. In the Spanish-American War, charging up San Juan Hill with Teddy, Josiah Joseph Joe Junior was sliced in two by a cannonball. During World War I, the first Joseph Josiah Joe was cut down by machine-gun fire when he lifted himself out of a trench to fetch coffee. Joseph Josiah Joe II bought it at Guadalcanal, courtesy of a Jap sharpshooter hidden in a palm tree. When I was nine years old, my father, Joseph Josiah Joe III stepped on a mine at Inchon.

Are we seeing a pattern?

My family and I sure as hell were. My predecessors were awarded posthumous Purple Hearts. No heroics, just atrocious luck. Accordingly, my Vietnam going-away party was grim. I regarded it as a retroactive wake and said so, suggesting that we should've had an ice- and beer-filled coffin with a Purple Heart dangling from it. An aunt and a female cousin cried. My stepfather gazed at the ceiling and shook his head, not for the first time. My mother glared at me and my gallows humor.

In bleary bravado, in a vain attempt to undo, I said, hey gang, no sweat. I have no intention of carrying on the tradition. I was confident that I was returning home in one piece, as the sole surviving Joe J. Joe.

As you'll see if you have the patience to continue reading, I was almost wrong.

The taxi let Ziggy and me out at Tan Son Nhat Air Base's main gate. The war had transformed Tan Son Nhat from a drowsy tropical airstrip to a tent city and perhaps the world's busiest airport. Jets flew in and out, day and night, shuttling troops to and from home, predominantly from. We scouted the USARV compound for Jeeps. The pick of the litter was parked next to a mess tent, behind a metal storage container. It had decent tires and not too many dents.

The container had such a dinky padlock that Ziggy said they were asking for it. He snapped off the lock with a rock. There was a lot of crap in it, but we found a case of Spam and a dusty M-14 rifle with five full clips.

Headed downtown, I drove the Jeep while Ziggy read one of the sci-fi magazines he was never without. The cover of this issue featured Troy Donahue's twin. Troy was in a tin spacesuit, firing his ray gun at a seven-hundred-pound side order of potato salad with claws. I was a voracious reader, but sci-fi passed a light year over my head.

To continue on me. In life I was a nondescript white Caucasian of middling height and weight, average in all mental and physical respects except for scar tissue and the number of times my nose had been set.

The fisticuffs started in the second grade with wordplay on my name: Jo Jo with the underarm digging and call of Tarzan's Cheetah. I was not one to take a joke when I was it.

I matured from playground skirmishes to saloon brawls, where I quickly learned that when you're hit over the head with a barstool, it didn't bust into kindling like they did in the movies. And when you're thrown through a window, you came out the other side bleeding. In my twenty-four years as of 1965, I had given and received a banquet of knuckle sandwiches.

Years later, Janelle, Wife Number Three, encouraged me to enroll in anger management classes.

"Why?" I'd flippantly responded, on my sixth or eighth or thirteenth beer. "I already know how to get pissed off."

Janelle had not been amused. I eventually grew up in my 40s, finally admitting to myself that my carload of insecurities made me such a hothead. I gave up the sauce, too, but by then Janelle was long gone.

In the realm of identifying features, complemented by injuries from the Battlefields of Stupidity, I sported an unsolved mystery on my body. At Fort Ord, where I'd attended Basic Training, I'd also matriculated in AIT (Advanced Individual Training)--which, for me, was cooking school. A week prior to graduation, on a dark and stormy payday night, I went out and had a drink or ten or twenty.

I remembered two things that occurred that lost evening. I remembered barhopping in San Francisco. I remembered wanting a Piet Mondrian tattoo on my arm.

My last college major had been art appreciation. I'd fallen hard for Piet Mondrian's intersecting perpendicular lines and primary colors. A Mondrian was a happy marriage of beauty and simplicity. A classic Mondrian was the order absent in my life. His *Composition 1921* was my druthers.

I was not and am not wearing a Mondrian. Instead, I've got a map of Montana on my left biceps. It is an outline of the state and an X marked in the southeastern portion, approximately at Billings, Montana's largest city. I'd awakened in an alley with a sore arm and there it was.

I had neither a recollection of the tattooing, nor did I know why Montana was on my arm rather than

Composition 1921. I'd never been to Montana and was fairly certain that Mondrian had not in his illustrious career painted a map of Montana. People frequently asked if X was my hometown. I did not shame easily, but I often dressed in long sleeves, even on warm days.

I always enjoyed the drive into downtown Saigon, a little breeze always welcome at 10.45 degrees north latitude. The city was flat, and the nicer parts were leafy. Tamarind trees arched out to provide shade. The French had built wide boulevards to remind them of Gay Paree. We were bound for Saigon's toniest and fleshiest district, toward the cathedral, the opera house, and expensive hotels, including the historic Continental Palace and the ten-story Hotel Caravelle, toward glitzy Tu Do Street, where goods and services offered by shops, bars and whores sold at a premium.

I glanced at street names on the signs: Truong Minh Giang, Cach Mang, Cong Ly, Nguyen Hue. To facilitate translation of the Bible, French missionaries had Romanized the Vietnamese language, all the better to flog the love of Jesus into the savages. I was as fond of missionaries as I was of a colostomy, but I had to admit that their work had made it a helluva lot simpler for us to get around when we didn't need to deal with Chinese-like calligraphy. Chicken scratchings, if you will.

Zealots have an extremely difficult time adjusting to my new homeland, The Great Beyond. Missionaries where I am twiddle their thumbs, frustrated to the extreme. They had smugly presumed absolutes--paradise for themselves and eternal damnation for us heathen sinners. Since we've already checked out of The Land of the Living, they have nothing to promise their sales prospects. The televangelists, the 1-800-SENDMONEY types, are in a constant frenzy. Their cash flow has

37

stopped flowing. We do not have money in The Great Beyond, nor need money, but that is no consolation to those old boys.

We passed a theater with a poster of Sabu on it. We passed a cathedral that wouldn't be out of place in any occidental city. We were passed by a massive 1956 Buick crammed with Vietnamese teenagers.

We came to the American Embassy. It was smack-dab in the heart of town, on narrow, crowded streets. Big building, big target, a nightmare to protect. It was a hollowed-out ghost. There wasn't an unbroken pane of glass.

The attack happened on March 30, 1965, so early in the war that to most it didn't seem like a war at all. It was a different story if you were standing here looking at what we were.

We'd heard that the people who'd followed procedure and hit the deck at the first sound of trouble—gunshots by guards in this instance—had survived. Those who'd instinctively gone to the windows to see what was going on had received the brunt of the explosion. They'd been pierced by glass shards, as if clawed by tigers. Charlie had double-parked a Citroën packed with a couple hundred pounds of *plastique*.

The area remained sealed off, crawling with trigger-happy ARVN troops and American MPs. We didn't stick around.

Our destination, Bombay Tailors, was on Tu Do, Vietnamese for "freedom." It was Rue Catinat under the French. In the unified communist Vietnam now, it is Dong Khoi, or Street of Simultaneous Uprisings, also known as the Street of Simultaneous Erections. Some things never change.

Mr. Singh, Bombay's proprietor, was in.

"Gentlemen, it has been too long."

Mr. Singh was the hue of milk chocolate. He had jittery eyes and a blinding smile. He was immaculate in blue slacks and a shirt as white as his teeth. He spoke clipped colonial English and could sew you a suit that fell apart in the second cleaning. His expertise was in money-changing and black-marketeering.

Nobody but nobody, from the top brass on down, changed money at the legal rate of seventy-three Vietnamese piasters per U.S. dollar. Nobody. MACV generals sent their drivers out with their many dollars.

You changed downtown for 120 to 130, depending on how close to payday it was, the higher number the day before, the lower the day after. The East Indians ran that show, and Mr. Singh's rates were as competitive as anybody's.

"Got goodies you're gonna love," I told him.

"I anticipate eagerly," Mr. Singh said, peeking under the blanket we'd laid over the back seat.

Though he wasn't too thrilled about the lunchmeat, he swooned at the rifle and ammo.

Yeah, I was a goldbrick and a dud. I would have been voted Soldier of the Month when the Mekong River froze over. But I was no traitor. No one hated commies more than I did. In the hands of a real soldier, the M-14 was a solid, reliable weapon, but we were phasing out the 14s in favor of the M-16. The VeeCee and NVA used the AK-47 the Russkis gave them, a weapon some claimed was superior to the 14 and 16 combined.

Mr. Singh wouldn't be selling this junk gun to the Reds, who'd laugh in his face while slitting his throat. It was destined to wind up in the hands of a wealthy Saigonese who wanted firepower around the house, and who could blame him?

"Mr. Joseph, I have a special treat in store for you."

Which meant Singh had decided how he was gonna screw us. He led us through a bead curtain to a back room. He reached inside a lacquered table and said, "Mr. Joseph, I recall that you expressed concerns regarding personal security for yourself, did you not?"

I'd once mentioned to Singh that I felt naked without any protection. I hinted that a stiletto would feel comfortable in my pocket in case I had to do close-order drill with a VC sapper or an angry bar girl.

"Is there anything you don't recall?"

Mr. Singh smiled, his hand still in the drawer.

I played it cool, saying, "Ziggy and I figured on booze and cash. Fifty bucks minimum and a gallon of Johnny Walker Black Label, our favorite flavor of Scotch. Whatever else is icing on the cake."

I looked at Ziggy, who nodded, his neck creaking.

Mr. Singh pulled out a tiny little Browning .25 caliber automatic pistol. It was as cute as a button. In its holster, it would be no more noticeable in my pants pocket than a wadded-up hankie.

He commenced negotiations by making a face at the Spam. "This is a pork substance. As you gentlemen are two of my dearest friends, I shall endeavor not to take offense."

I couldn't take my eyes off the peashooter. As I was the principal negotiator and weakened beyond repair by desire, Singh knew he had us by the short hairs. I settled for the popgun, a half-gallon of Johnny Walker Red Label--a lesser brand than Black--and a fat wad of piasters that added up to the grand sum of seven bucks.

On the way back to the 803rd, we stopped at an Esso station and slipped the pump jockey those piasters to paint over the Jeep's old markings and stencil on 803 LD.

If Ziggy was pissed about me giving away the farm to Singh, selfishly caving in because of the .25, he didn't say so.

His focus was on his sci-fi magazine, probably at the section in the story where Troy was obliterating an invading armada of the potato salad critters. The closer Mariner 4 got to Mars, the less interested Ziggy was in this planet. A sci-fi yarn could be set anywhere in the universe.

The planet Mars, relatively speaking, was right around the corner from us. Mariner-4 was bringing reality and escape together for him. I hoped it wasn't gonna be a head-on collision. His sci-fi was Ziggy's greatest of escapes.

My reality was the twelve months I was spending in Vietnam. That was the standard tour. Then it was Back to the World, the Land of the Big PX, the U.S. of A. You didn't have to extend unless you wanted to. I had four months left. When you hit one hundred days to go, you were entitled to ownership of a short-timer's calendar. Everyone counted the days before boarding a Boeing 707. Ziggy, as of now, had eighty-five and a wake-up, but he couldn't care less. I'd had to buy his calendar and maintain it for him, for Chrissake.

We got back to the 803rd, gone a mere three hours. When the captain saw what we'd parked at the curb, he looked at us as if we walked on water. "Men, I'm putting in papers to immediately elevate you to private first class."

I thanked him as humbly as I could manage. As happy as I would've been to be promoted, the clerk-typist slot was foremost on my mind. As PFCs, we'd be booted out of the 803rd sooner or later. It was inevitable. I did not wish to be helicoptered into the godforsaken to hunt

Victor Charles and for Victor Charles to surely reciprocate.

I wanted a clerk-typist MOS on my résumé. I wanted to be where Charlie would have to barge into my clean, dry office and fire a round through my Underwood to get me.

"Thank you, sir. I request that you send Private Zbitgysz and me to typing school so we can improve our skills on the job and become improved soldiers and lighten PFC Bierce's burden."

Bierce didn't look up, but his clickety-clack-clack ceased.

"Out of the question, Joe. Haven't you been listening? We're mobilizing on a comprehensive wartime footing. We have to sacrifice and do the job that best serves our country. You're on permanent special assignment."

"What kind of special assignment, sir."

"Whatever kind I see fit to assign you," he said. "In appreciation of your efforts to date, take the rest of the day off."

I had a brainstorm. "Sir, the Jeep."

"What about it?"

"Sir, it is the colonel's Jeep, is it not?"

"So?"

"Well, sir, I thought that if before turning it over to him, you might care to avail yourself of it for any mission you so desired. It was your foresight that began the process."

"True," he said thoughtfully.

"If there is *any* special assignment in which you are taking a field leadership role and it's convenient to have transportation and a driver and an assistant, Private

Zbitgysz and I hereby volunteer. Discretion is guaranteed."

Ziggy grunted in confusion.

Colonel Lanyard yelled from his office, "Papersmith!"

Up the captain popped like a jack-in-the-box. As he scurried down the hallway, I pocketed his Dragon Lady Polaroid. If Papersmith swallowed the bait, I'd be seeing her in person soon.

We heard heavy trucks brake at the Annex. We went out and saw that they were escorted by Jeeps. MPs piled out of Jeeps. They formed a perimeter around the trucks. I thought that they were dropping in to grill Ziggy and me about our day's activities, but they paid us no attention whatsoever.

They were babysitting as oddballs unloaded boxed air conditioners from the trucks and rolled them into the Annex on handcarts.

One after another after another.

Chapter Five

The following morning, Ziggy and I went in early. I finished writing a letter home and left it in the mail room, which was in a corner of the supply room. The versatile PFC A. Bierce would pick up the mail later on.

My feeble, prosaic correspondence:

> *Dear Mother and family,*
> *Having semi-wonderful time, am glad you don't have to be here. As a member of an elite alternative matériel resource team, I'm doing special assignments, but can't discuss them as they are classified, as is the military organization to which I am assigned. I have enhanced my personal security, so I'm as safe as anybody over here can be.*
> *Cordially,*
> *Joseph J. Joe IV*

The distance between Mother and me was greater than the seventy-four-hundred statute miles between Seattle and Saigon. Our formality was a long story, which I'll explain as we go. It was in retaliation to Mother's coolness, or perhaps she'd retaliated against me; it's unclear how and when it escalated in earnest. We'd been remote since my time in her womb--she'd joked that I'd kicked her black and blue, and had been a long, painful delivery. I sensed she'd suffered postpartum depression ever since.

To be honest, my behavior since I'd been weaned had strained our relationship. Stepfather very recently leaving Mother for a younger woman had not perked up her or her prose.

While I haven't encountered her in my afterlife surroundings, I know she's here. Mother preceded me by twenty-two years, victim of a stroke. I expect Mother to be in a burb, not too awfully far from me. Mother and I will connect in The Great Beyond. Time is not of the essence. When we do cross paths, we shall cling and hug and cry. I know we will.

I suppose I'll bump into Stepfather too, as chronology is the only demographic I can discern. I don't anticipate seeing Joes I and II. No ladies in hoop skirts, no men with powdered wigs. Nor folks decked out in loincloths or chain mail or togas.

According to our busy rumor mill, the afterworld occupies separate levels, partial century by partial century, as if floor by floor in a department store. Housewares on Six, Seventeenth Century on Nine, in that vein. As in Vietnam, the grapevine is proving to be the most reliable media.

I have to believe these stories, although I am unable to participate in the chitchat.

And why can't I?

Let me back up a bit.

If your conception of The Great Beyond is running along conventional lines in terms of leadership, forget it. There is no St. Peter pulling sentry duty at any gate, pearly or otherwise. Please be assured, too, that I did not arrive after paddling up the River Styx in a leaky kayak. I simply materialized where I am, wherever that is.

God? A big, cranky bearded guy in a robe, flinging lightning bolts? Haven't seen him yet and am not anxious to.

I'm in a middle-class subdivision on a cul-de-sac. I'm the center home of three, in a split-level identical to the other two, right down to the beige-and-blue paint scheme. I rattle around in what must be eighteen-hundred square feet of space. Our infrastructure can use work. I have lawn and landscaping care that I never see, but they are lousy edgers and miss too many dandelions. My patio sliders stick and there's peeling paint in the third bedroom.

My kitchen takes up half the ground level. With its granite countertops, stainless steel appliances, and copper cookware hanging above a center island, it's far too upscale for the neighborhood.

Food is provided and mysteriously replaced when consumed. If you can call it food. The freezer compartment is crammed with TV dinners. The pantry is floor to ceiling with army MREs and the earlier C-rations which we had when I was in. The Cs include delicacies I'd had to eat such as ham and lima beans and chicken and noodles. The only appliance required for meal preparation is the microwave.

I have a two-car garage but no car. I have not seen a motor vehicle in The Great Beyond.

I have cable television with 8,720 channels. All except three are snow and static. I tune in any of the three, and five minutes later I want to throw a chair at the fifty-two-inch HDTV screen.

Channel 82 is an afternoon talk show that runs endlessly without commercial interruption. It is as banal and excretal as any I'd ever seen. The hosts work in shifts and are all the same. They smile and ask cutting-edge questions that are stupid beyond belief ("How do you feel now that you're dead?"). There is one topic: Vietnam. Their guests range from U.S. generals to LBJ to Ho Chi Minh to killed veterans of all nations participating to protesting hippies. Never is a conclusion reached.

Channel 316 is reality TV as foul and moronic as any in The Land of the Living. There is one topic: multiple marriage and divorce. Nobody who is less than a three-time loser qualifies. Serial brides and grooms remarry. The camera follows them everywhere including the bedroom throughout weeks or sometimes days of marital bliss. The program then foots the bill for a trip to Vegas and a quickie divorce.

Channel 667 is solid documentaries. Guess the topics? Yeah, the French Indochina War and our conflict. They are narrated by unseen voices that range from close facsimiles of David Frost to Eric Sevareid to Edward R. Murrow to Oprah. The war stories alternate with sensational biographies of famous serial brides and grooms. You know who I'm talking about. Liz and Mickey and Zsa Zsa. Lesser knowns too.

The boy-girl has nothing to do with Vietnam. If I were paranoid, I might take this insipid fare personally, me and my matrimonial disasters.

Nonetheless, it's a struggle shutting off the tube. At one elevator music stretch, "You Light Up My Life" played for a week, permeating the walls of my home. The headaches I had that ticketed me here are gone, but an hour of The Great Beyond Television Network makes me wonder why I don't have one.

I go for long walks. Winding narrow streets bristle with deserted cul-de-sacs, carbon copies of mine. Every quarter mile or so there is the same dreary strip mall. I'm through wondering how they do this or anything else.

Dry cleaners. Nail salon. Teriyaki. A payday loan outfit that loans money that does not exist to non-people who are on no payrolls. *Phở* cafes. A hairdresser with no customers (note: my hair never grows. Or it's trimmed at night by the same beings who stock my fridge and larder). A tax preparation place. Since we have no income, it logically follows that we don't pay taxes. It's staffed by a middle-aged woman with hair pulled into a gray bun and horn-rimmed glasses held by a chain. She just sits there.

Again, I have seen no vehicles in The Great Beyond, but the strip mall lot is stained with dripped oil from the beaters that never park here. Empty pop cans and candy bar wrappers are scattered. I try to police them up, to make myself useful. They're holograms.

Those aforementioned rumors? Why am I unable to participate in the chitchat? Because the people who operate and frequent the shops, who exchange gossip regarding multi-levels of The Great Beyond, are nonexistent. You can walk right through them, as if you're in the middle of the field in Madden Football. So fiendishly lifelike are *these* holograms that at first sight I'm deceived. I shake a hand and squeeze air.

I am the only visitor. Ever. A non-customer, if you will.

I am in the midst of sadistic and well-planned chaos.

I trudge home from the mall, so alone.

That is about to change, but the craziness of 1965 Saigon is not.

Captain Dean Papersmith came into the 803rd and summoned us to his office. We reported with snappy salutes. Something was different I couldn't quite put my finger on.

"Are you men cigarette smokers?" he asked, knowing the answer if he'd had one ounce of observational skill.

Smoking was the one bad habit Ziggy and I had somehow declined to take up.

"Uh, no sir," I said.

"That's splendid, troopers. Smoking isn't good for you. It cuts down on your wind and stains your fingers and teeth. Let's saddle up. We have important work to do."

Now it registered what was different. There were dark perspiration spots at the captain's armpits. His air conditioner was gone.

"Sir," Ziggy said, pointing at the naked window. There was nothing on the sill except the deep gouges we'd made wishing the unit into the tight opening. "How come, sir?"

"As you were, Private Zbitgysz. We are embarking on a special assignment. Keep your mind on business and come along."

We trailed him out of the 803rd like faithful puppies.

I sneaked a peek into Colonel Jake Lanyard's office. Captain Papersmith's air conditioner was in the colonel's window, humming a sweet tune and dispensing chilly air. I knew why Colonel Lanyard had called Captain Papersmith into his office yesterday. He'd pulled rank on the captain and re-requisitioned the air conditioner. We were all afraid of Colonel Lanyard, but Captain Papersmith was terrified of him.

All the better for me, as it distracted the captain from the missing Dragon Lady Polaroid. Which had spent the night under my pillow and in my heart.

We hopped into the colonel's Jeep, which was still the captain's Jeep. He told me to drive. Ziggy rode shotgun. The captain sat in the rear, ramrod stiff, as if he were Patton advancing into Germany. He directed us to his bachelor officers' quarters.

"Those air conditioners that arrived yesterday at the annex, sir? Couldn't they spare one for the detachment adjutant and company commander?"

"This isn't *Twenty Questions*, soldier. Pay attention to your driving. Left at the corner. That door. There."

Yes sir, no sir, yes sir, no sir, fuck you, sir. We triple-parked and he went in to his BOQ. You couldn't blame people for not telling us things, but I couldn't help but be offended. Phantom air conditioners and the captain asking us if we smoked. Gimme a break. Nobody was concerned about our health in general and our lungs in particular.

An astronaut the spitting image of Pat Boone starred on the cover of Ziggy's magazine. He was negotiating a path in a forest of giant asparagus. The asparagi had eyeballs, but Pat didn't seem to notice. Twin suns beat down on him, reminding me how toasty it was in Saigon, even in the morning.

I walked to a Howard Johnson. That's what GIs called the food and drink carts that were all over town. I bought a sandwich and a *Biere Larue*. I didn't know what went into the sandwich, didn't want to know, but it tasted edible. Same with the *Larue*. Brewed nearby, *Larue* looked like watered-down piss, but it'd been cooled in a bucket of water. I chugalugged, cutting the sharp edges of yesterday's Johnny Red.

Ziggy was so intent on his sci-fi reading and so anxious about Mariner 4's Mars approach that we hadn't commented on the Annex's new air conditioners. I asked what he thought the Fighting 803rd Annex actually was.

Eyes on his magazine, he said, "Joey, our outfit and the Annex, it's gotta be high muckety-muck shit they're doing on account of we're hiding in plain sight where the Cong and everyone else thinks the 803rd is a zero or it'd have a big fat title and be at Tan Son Nhat or Washington, D.C. and be guarded by like a division of Marines, but since it ain't, you think it's so diddly-shit nothing, it's invisible, which is the highest security in the world for what them oddballs are doing over there, whatever it is they're doing."

Ziggy could throw you a wicked curveball. From being more silent than any strong silent type, he'd go logorrheic. His cockeyed insights had a stunning clarity. My hunches agreed with that assessment, but no way could I put them into words so inarticulately logical. I thought of Ziggy as an idiot savant with an IQ of either fifty or three hundred, depending on what side of the bed he got up on. Most of the time he was scarily smart. These days, you'd call him dyslectic and autistic and introverted and disturbed and brilliant, any and all of the above.

His outrageous opinions careened out of nowhere. The other day he'd blathered on about the 1964 Olympics in Tokyo. He said the Games were like Pearl Harbor, except they were jamming a foot in the door instead of firing a torpedo into a hull. He said that they'd be flooding our market. Before we knew it, we'd all be driving Jap cars, watching their TVs, playing their record players, and snapping pictures with their cameras.

Crazy. Looney Tunes, I'd thought. Not a chance. A popular saying of the day was that Japanese cars were made out of American beer cans.

Yeah, uh-huh, crazy, I think now, as my mortal remains decompose in a Japanese-made coffin.

"So what's with the air conditioners, Zig?"

Turning a page, he shrugged and grunted. End of analysis.

Captain Papersmith swaggered outside in jungle fatigues and an Aussie bush hat. We didn't recognize him till he climbed into the Jeep. We couldn't look at him or we'd crack up. Next stop was the U.S. Navy Commissary.

The captain handed us each $6.25. We knew what to do. Each GI in Vietnam was entitled to five cartons of American cigarettes per month at a commissary or PX. They sold for $1.25 per. They went for $5 on the black market and wound up on the street in individual packs for somewhat more, which was why they were rationed. American smokes were like gold. Ruby Queens, the domestic brand, tasted like asphalt and stunk like a car fire.

Ziggy, the captain, and I bought our allotted five cartons of Salems. I decided to hold onto a carton for Charlie, Ziggy's and my Vietnamese buddy. The captain bought all the Tide detergent we could carry (Tide and Salems were the nylons and chocolate bars of the Vietnam War). He also bought Royal Crown whiskey, frozen chicken parts, canned peaches, toilet paper, Louisiana hot sauce, and Tampax.

He steered us toward Cholon, Saigon's Chinese district. Ziggy winked, letting me know he knew what was going on in case I didn't. *The Dragon Lady!* My brainstorm had borne fruit faster than I dreamed. My heart pumped supersonically. I was woozy, barely able to stay in my lane, not that it much mattered in Saigon traffic.

We parked on an alleyway of a street. The captain ducked under a low doorway, making several trips in with his contraband. The neighborhood people, whether squatting or strolling by or hanging up laundry or emptying buckets, if they gave us a glance, it went right through us. We were a million miles from Tu Do Street and we were unwelcome.

We were as inscrutable to them as they were to us. We were The Unfathomable Occident. "East is east, and west is west, and never the twain shall meet" ran in both directions.

We figured the captain would be taking his own sweet time, to hell with us sitting out here, broiling under a relentless sun, smelling the consequences of an inadequate sewage system. I'd like to've brought a book on the French Indochina War I was reading, so I got caught up on doing nothing by thinking of the Dragon Lady and her cartoon counterpart. My flesh-and-blood Dragon Lady was down that alley, accommodating Captain Papersmith's needs.

I took out her photo again and sighed.

I didn't care if Papersmith was paying her with cash and PX goods, she was mine. I was jealous beyond words.

She was no longer a comic strip and a photo. She was baby-smooth skin and the slightest of overbites and long silken hair. I pictured her beneath the captain, stifling a yawn and doing her nails as he inexpertly rutted.

A lovely Vietnamese woman in a black and white *áo-dài* emerged from where Captain Papersmith had entered, shaking a small rug. Her cheekbones were high, her hair glossy and long. The set of her mouth indicated displeasure.

It was *her*.

I must've levitated, for I found myself standing on the driver's seat without awareness of bolting up. She looked up from her chore. She had been waiting her entire life for her true love. She was waiting for me.

I saw what the Polaroid only hinted at. My Dragon Lady was exotic because she wasn't exotic at all. She was as wholesome as wholesome could be. She was a little older than me, not old but intriguing, alluring, mature-woman old. There was something in her eyes, a blend of lust and wariness. Those eyes did not deviate from mine.

As if playing a knuckleheaded character out of a Frankie Avalon-Annette Funicello beach party movie, I blew her a kiss. Expressing no emotion, she squinted at me, then went inside.

"Ziggy," I said hoarsely as I sat. "My Dragon Lady. I blew it by blowing a kiss. I was a witless dipshit dork right out of *Beach Blanket Bingo*. Oh man, I fucked up royally!"

Ziggy hadn't seen her. He jabbed a finger at the cover of his new pulp, a picture worth at least a thousand words. The She-Devil of Alpha Centauri had tights, a whip, a sneer and three breasts.

"The captain's gal," said Ziggy. "I betcha this here gal's finer."

Ziggy and his love of the moment, his tri-titted Amazon from outer space. He was putting more and more distance between himself and reality.

I looked at him. A parking strip of eyebrows shaded small dark eyes that seemed to narrow as he concentrated intensely on his sci-fi. A glance at the overall package, and you might gauge the Zigster as a retard. Big fucking mistake.

"Dragon Lady from another planet. It's gonna be tough to get a date with her, man," I said. "My woman is earthly. Didn't you see her, Zig? How could you've missed her? The captain's gal, my Dragon Lady, who maybe isn't the captain's gal. I mean, what's he doing while she's shaking that rug?"

Our leader lurched outside, blinking in the sunlight and hitching up his trousers. He had one jungle boot on and the other dangling from his mouth by a lace. That guerrilla fighter hat was on sideways, Napoleon-like.

A woman chased out behind him, cackling and pinching his bare, skinny ass. She was a plain Vietnamese in black pajamas, well over thirty-five, far older than my Dragon Lady. The cackler was nothing to write home about, thin and shapeless, a Vietnamese Plain Jane, although a mild improvement to the captain's horse-faced, slide rule heiress. Definitely not exotic. Not my Dragon Lady. Not even close.

Neighbors made sure to avert their eyes. Not because of Captain Papersmith, I sensed, but rather the cackler. Was she the neighborhood honcho?

"Captain, sir," I said when he'd stumbled into the Jeep and we were underway. "The lady in the premises doing housework, who is she, sir?"

"My friend Mai," he said with a belch and a hiccup. "Mai can be a prude. Plays hard to get. She arouses me, then pawns me off on her sister, who thinks that's amusing. It was really Quyen's idea. She bosses Mai and the whole neighborhood around."

Mai.

I'd heard her name for the first time.

He hiccupped again. "The sister, Quinn. That bitch has a man's name, which figures. Everybody jumps when she says *boo*."

"I believe that's Q-u-y-e-n, sir, not Q-u-i-n-n."

55

"Stop splitting hairs, soldier. Have you ever been in love, Joe? Achingly, intensely in love?"

"Oh, yes, sir."

"And have you ever been treated this shamefully, after bearing generous gifts and all?"

"Uh, maybe Mai *is* hard to get. Maybe it isn't an act, sir."

"Good Christ Almighty, Private!" he slurred. "Is this your first day in-country? Vietnamese whores don't play hard to get. White women play get to hard. I mean hard to get. White women have convenient headaches. My wife and her headaches. Mildred has a migraine that automatically strikes when the sun goes down. I thought you were a man of the world, Joe."

I didn't reply. I was too elated to speak. Mai had rejected Captain Papersmith's sexual advances. The good captain had a case of lover's nuts and was forced to settle for a second choice, Quyen the Cackler and Neighborhood Boss.

He didn't say anything the rest of the way and was curled in the fetal position on the back seat and snoring when we reached his BOQ. As we poured him into the lobby, each holding him by an armpit, a fantasy developed. Mai had seen me through the window before crossing her legs for the captain. She had orchestrated the switcheroo, not Quyen.

She had pledged her devotion to me, her true love.

Chapter Six

The 803rd Liaison Detachment had no barracks, so Ziggy and I were billeted in a fleabag hotel three blocks from our duty station. The room was furnished with two bunks, a sink, and a dresser. The crapper was down the hall. Rats on the prowl were as big and ugly as poodles. Water that dribbled out of our sink was an interesting shade of ochre.

We were slacking on our beds, sucking on Mr. Singh's Johnny Red, me reading a letter and devouring my purloined Polaroid photograph of preeminent pulchritude (pardon my Agnewesque alliteration.).

The photo now had a name. Mai.

Mai, my Dragon Lady.

I watched a gecko on the ceiling right above me. You could stare at them for hours and they wouldn't budge. But look away for a few seconds, then look back-- they'll've moved two feet.

My one letter was my weekly average since my sort-of-fiancée had married my best civilian friend, Doug. Little did we know that if Judy had clung to me, she would've been the first of *six* wives, my first innocent marital victim. At her husband's behest, contact was severed, despite it being friend-to-friend correspondence. No sweat. She'd done the smart thing.

The letter was from my mother.

Dear Joe:

Your brother has applied for three fellowships while he does his research and writes his dissertation. Boeing has been recruiting, no, hounding him to write his own ticket when he receives his aerodynamics PhD and moves on to postdoctoral work on Lord knows what. So so many choices! I'll let you know. Your stepfather and I remain on speaking terms. Barely. There is business to conclude when a family parts and we are accomplishing this amicably. To his credit, he arranges that his paramour be indisposed when we confer. Please be cautious. Vietnam is becoming more prominent in the news. I don't care for what I see, read and hear.

Your concerned mother

It was a routine letter. We never were an intimate family. Our communication could have been notes from an insurance agent to a client. However, that colon after "Dear Joe" was a dagger through my heart. We'd been distantly polite for the longest time, but the affectionless salutations were always punctuated with commas. The colon meant movement. It meant increased coolness. It was businesslike, verging on iciness. The Pentagon would term it escalation.

There was an underlayment of crabbiness in the letter too, no doubt a result of the betrayal and separation. Frankly, I wish it'd happened long ago. Aside from her unhappiness, my only regret was that she was the dumpee, not the dumper.

On the plus side, the letter included last Sunday's comics. Terry Lee was in topnotch form, yet another confrontation with the Dragon Lady brewing. It must have saddened Mother that I, at age twenty-four, had as my only passion a woman spun off from the funnies. Only Ziggy knew of my Dragon Lady obsession. Mother would have a cow.

In contrast, my brother Jack, a tender twenty-two, was a light shining as intergalactically bright as a plot line in a Ziggy magazine. Unfortunately, Jack was a helluva good guy. He made it impossible for me to hate him.

And don't get me wrong, I'm not whining. Mother hadn't reminded me lately that my IQ score was only fifteen points below my brother's, who was the second smartest person I'd ever known. A bewildering waste of potential, she'd often said.

From where I am nowadays in The Great Beyond, with nothing earthly but memories, I'm glad she could enjoy Jack and her adoration of him while she could. Poor Mother. Not long after this glowing letter, Jack began to change. He fell head over heels for a hippie girl who knew all the tricks in and out of bed.

He went totally gaga and bohemian, no halfway measures for him. Jack had no further desire to spend his life in a wind tunnel. He smoked a variety of vegetation, burned his draft card, told the Establishment in many a way to go shit in its hat. Right when he had a Nobel in his sights.

Well, a Nobel was a stretch on Mother's part, but you get the idea. Her disappointment with him was like a piano falling out of a sixth floor window on her. In comparison, I was a dull, lingering toothache. Jack eventually shaped up and went on to teach grad students at MIT.

My kitchen in my The Great Beyond pad and the rations that needed no cooking? I finally get the gag. The inspiration for that jab by my keepers, the sadistic bastards, was my moderately successful career as a chef, a culinary career that was a long segue from army cook to civilian fry cook to dinner cook to sous chef to executive chef. My kitchens were cramped and crowded, and as hot as where everyone predicted I'd be now. When you were slammed out front, the job was a carefully frantic choreography to keep up with the orders while avoiding an accident with a hot spill or a stove burner.

Those celebrity chefs on the food channels and their cutesy stunts? For the most part, that is one-hundred-percent USDA-prime bullshit. Those spacious kitchens and support staff behind the camera do not exist in the real world. To me, those people are in the category of dancing bears and leprechauns.

Yep, Mother's little boys have done her proud.

My stepdaddy was a different story.

My mother taught algebra and differential equations. He taught freshman composition and creative writing at the same Seattle-area junior college. A frustrated, unpublished author, Stepfather wrote worse Hemingway than entries in the Bad Hemingway Contests that came along later.

Stepfather was contemptuous of JC academic standards, bitter that no four-year school had been at all impressed by his barrage of application letters. Not so contemptuous, it seemed, of the sophomore honor student for whom he left my mother to shack up with. I'd never seen her, so I couldn't comment on my pseudointellectual stepdaddy's attraction other than it was unlikely due to her intellect and superior grades.

Regardless how I felt about him, I did feel semi-badly when he succumbed young to a coronary in 1970. In spite of his professional bitterness (a factor in his demise?), he had led a useful life. I know I felt worse than Mother.

My mother reported that Stepfather's "tramp's" name was Wendi and that Wendi dotted the "i" with a bubble. According to her, Wendi was broad about the beam, wore horn-rimmed glasses, and had a permanent wave right out of a *Which Twin Has The Toni?* advertisement.

I considered offering to put a move on Wendi when I got home, a son getting in a shot for his mama with a one-night stand, a slap in the wrongdoer's face. But that was too crude, even for me.

Or so I thought at the time.

Oh, if I could reach Mother now! Our extra-worldly gagmeisters have provided telephone directories and she is listed. My father, late of Inchon, is too. However, no names I recalled from Vietnam were, a growing puzzlement to me. Virtually everybody else is listed. Amelia Earhart, Judge Crater, Jimmy Hoffa, anybody and everybody. We have telephones, all cellular. You can call any number, anywhere, and never ever get anything but a busy signal.

I shouldn't whine about my home life, not after meeting Ziggy. He'd had it much, much worse. A native of Detroit, a Hamtramck Polack, he, too, had scarcely known his dad. The old man appeared on the doorstep every Christmas Eve, to hit his mom up for a loan and a quickie, unwilling to take no for an answer to either. Ziggy's three brothers had different pops they never knew. If Zig kept in touch with any kin except his mom, it was news to me.

Naturally, Ziggy's face was buried in a sci-fi magazine.

"Zig, wanna go to mama-san's for a short time?"

The inflection in his grunt translated to no.

"Yeah, me neither. I guess I'm not in the mood for poontang myself, but thought I'd ask."

I was relieved. I had a fanciful sense that I'd be unfaithful to my Dragon Lady.

"Joey, I don't mind if you wanna take the pitcher of that gal of yours to the latrine and pull your pud."

"Thanks, Zig. I already have, twice."

He laughed, thinking I was kidding.

Mama-san's might be a nice diversion if just for a social call, to say hello, drink a beer or two, and pinch some ass before we barhopped. To her and her girls, we were friends as well as customers, even the young ladies who were probably Vietcong agents.

We couldn't walk into Mama-san's now without being asked by one or more girls when South Vietnam was going to become the fifty-first state. That rumor was now on everyone's lips, and the majority view was that it couldn't come soon enough.

Mama-san's was an easy three-minute walk, down an alley across from a bicycle repair shop, in an unmarked building with a blanket hanging in the doorway. Mama-san wore black pajamas and a black-toothed grin from chewing betel nut for the past century. She charged the standard two-hundred piasters (approximately $1.60) for a short time. You were literally in and out.

Mama-san ran a quality cathouse. She maintained an orderly row of curtained cribs, and she changed sheets kind of frequently. Her girls were cute and they got weekly penicillin shots. Since we were regulars and mama-san liked us, we could take our shoes and pants all the way off without worrying that somebody'd rifle through our pockets. That was as close to romance as it got.

Thanks to Mama-san and her dedicated staff, Ziggy lost his cherry straddled by a ninety-pound wisp of a trollop who'd ridden him expertly, a rodeo champ on a bull. For him to be on top was unthinkable. I suspected that Ziggy's ideal woman was a winged, bat-eared Martian siren, but Mama-san had none of them to offer at any price.

Mama-san's was where we'd made friends with our Vietnamese buddy, Charlie. His relationship to Mama-san and his Vietnamese name were unknown. Charlie was a "cowboy," a young Saigonese male who raced around town at night on a Honda motor scooter with his buddies instead of serving his country in the South Vietnamese Army--officially the Army of Vietnam (ARVN)--fighting or pretending to fight a fearless, fanatical, and terrifying enemy.

Charlie and Ziggy and I were of a consensus that confronting monolithic communism and propping up the domino were noble callings. We simply didn't want the goddamn thing falling on our sorry asses.

Cowboys liked to buzz by a GI on a sidewalk and snatch the Seiko right off his wrist or to roll one for his wallet and kick in his ribs for the fun of it, but Charlie had not a mean bone nor the gumption for pure cowboy behavior. If he'd ever bent to peer pressure, his heart surely was not in it.

We hit it off immediately. Charlie spoke good English and spoke his mind with a sense of humor. When we first went out for beers, we learned that we smelled like butter to him, and he learned that he smelled like fish to us. He claimed he didn't live on fish heads and rice as we'd believed most Vietnamese did. In fact, he'd developed a taste for hamburgers, hold the onions.

We all looked alike to him, even Ziggy.

"Me?" Ziggy asked. "I look the same as Joey and Westmoreland and every other round eye?"

"You look same same Joe, same same Westy, same same LBJ, same same Elvis, same same Beatles," Charlie told Ziggy, looking him up and down. "Only you have more of you."

I didn't blame Charlie for dodging the South Vietnamese draft. ARVN soldiers were treated like week-old dog shit. Their commanders skimmed their pay, the piaster equivalent of fourteen Yankee dollars per month. What Charlie did when he wasn't out goofing around with us, I hadn't the foggiest. Charlie didn't try to hustle us, and where criminal activity was concerned, well, you know the old saying about those who live in glass barracks.

"Hey, Zig, wanna go by just to see if Charlie's there, see what he's up to?"

Same grunt, different verse.

I asked, "The captain and his special assignments, what else do you think we're gonna have to steal for him?"

"Dunno."

"Enough air conditioners to drop Indochina's temperature ten degrees going into the Annex is nuts, but this is the army, right?"

"Uh-huh."

"What are they building in there that has to be so cool?"

"Dunno."

"Price is no object, you know. Whatever it is they're doing, they're at the front of the requisitioning line."

"Uh-huh."

"They have their reasons even if they don't have reasons. Remember what they told us in Basic? There's the right way, the wrong way, and the army way."

"Joey, I ever tell you? The Martians, they're already out there amongst us."

A startling change of subject and a new wrinkle.

"Uh, where?"

"They're out there all over. I betcha we pass them on the street every day."

"We do?"

"They'll show themselves when Mariner 4 snaps its snapshots. They'll make their move. They got to."

"They do?"

"Don't you know shit, Joey? Their cities and bases, they'll be exposed. Once we have bigger missiles, they'll be sitting ducks."

To deflect the looniness, I asked, "Your Mariner 4's still on course?"

"A million miles out, steady as she goes," Ziggy said.

"Until that spaceship, nothing has ever seen Mars up close? Correct?"

"Damn straight."

"Tell me again how much it weighs and when it was launched, Zig."

Ziggy took a long swig and handed me the Scotch. "Its dry weight is five-hundred-seventy-four pounds, sixty of it instrumentation. On 28 November 1964, it lifted off from Cape Canaveral on an Atlas D booster."

He ticked off the gadgetry on sausage fingers. "TV camera, solar plasma probe, ionization chamber, trapped radiation detector, helium vector magnetometer, cosmic ray telescope, cosmic dust detector. Omnidirectional antenna, four solar panels, nitrogen gas jets for attitude control. You got your pressure vanes and gyroscopes too."

"And lookie at this." He dug into the heap of pulp magazines and newspapers at the foot of his bunk and fished out a paper. "This article in here says Mars got no life on it. The guy claims to be a scientist, but he don't know jack shit. He wants to get his name in the paper is all, the stupid motherfucker."

It was not prudent to argue with Ziggy on this subject. I said, "Yeah, some people are born dense."

"Joey, all you gotta do is look at them encyclopedia pitchers and the ones in that 1955 *National Geographic* I got down in my stuff somewheres. The fertile red soil. You could grow anything in that dirt. Canals and polar caps, they're as plain as day. Tell me there ain't no life on Mars."

"Not me, Zig."

"Percival Lowell, the astronomer, way back in 1895, he saw the canals and deserts and oases from his telescope."

Apocrypha or not apocrypha, that was the question Mariner 4 sought to answer. "No argument."

"How come they're saying Martians ain't there *and* here?"

"Can't tell you," I said, although I didn't think that even Ziggy's most imaginative astronomers saw gondoliers and high priests and zombies.

To steer the conversation elsewhere, I asked, "Hey, Zig, 4578 times 865?"

"Cut it out, Joey."

"C'mon, Zig."

"Up yours, Joey. Up your butt."
"C'mon, Zig. C'mon."
"Up your nose with a rubber hose."
"C'mon. 4578 times 866."
"You said 865," he corrected.

I'd tried talking him into using his gift to benefit mankind, namely us in barroom bets. He'd have none of it. I wasn't goading him to be cruel. I was fascinated, waiting for him to be stuck or wrong just one time.

"How much?"
"3,959,970."
"946 plus 454 divided by 8 times 25."
"4375."
"State capitals. Oregon."
"Salem."
"West Virginia."
"Charleston."
"South Dakota."
"Pierre."
"The elements. Atomic weight of bismuth."
"208.9804."
"Zirconium."
"91.22."
"World Series champ, 1947. In how many games."
"Yankees in four."
"Are you sure it was four?" I teased.

Ziggy ignored me. He wasn't done on Mars. "In a matter of days, Mariner 4 will snap pitchers. Then they'll find out."

"Sure will."
"Joey, ever see *War of the Worlds*?"
"Yeah. Scary flick. Those Martian machines zapping you with a death ray and a tin smile."
"I'd be pissed if I was a Martian."

"How come pissed, Zig?"

"Their attitude's probly we oughta be minding our own beeswax. Can't blame 'em."

I completed my calculation on paper, verifying the 3,959,970.

"No. No you certainly can't blame them."

He reburied himself in his magazine and said, "Don't blame me for the shitstorm when it comes."

"No. No I won't."

Ziggy had told me about the reformatory he'd been in. There'd been a disturbance. A hack had caved in the side of Ziggy's skull with a Louisville Slugger. Ziggy boasted that he'd bounced off cell bars and dropped to a knee, but hadn't gone down for the count. They'd put a metal plate in his noggin. Maybe or maybe not exaggerating, he said it was the size of a playing card. I would not rule him out as a walking extraterrestrial antenna, making radio contact with those Martians of his.

Our gecko was parked on the other side of the ceiling.

I reached for a book. The Tan Son Nhat library carried a fine selection, and they were accumulating in our cubbyhole, piling against and under my bed as if a berm, most overdue. Some had acquired a patina of dust.

They were an eclectic mix of esoteric subjects. None was on a waiting list. But let me be five minutes tardy with best-sellers like *Kiss Me Deadly* or *Peyton Place,* and the library Gestapo would be on me like a bad smell.

I'd been on a history jag lately, unable to get my fill. My current page-turner was on the French Indochina War (1946-1954), when the Vietnamese commies were called the Vietminh.

Once upon a time, back in 1954, the French got sick and tired of the Vietminh's hit-and-run tactics. The war was going on and on, ever since the end of World War Two, a drain on France's manpower and budget. The Frogs were fidgety on the home front, anxious for results, so they laid a trap.

They set up a sprawling base at the floor of a valley out in the boonies by the Laos border, at a village named Dien Bien Phu. The valley was surrounded by forested hills. Taking the low ground was a warfare no-no, but there was no way the Vietminh could hump artillery up to the tops of those hills. The plan had been to lure the Vietminh out to engage in a conventional battle, to fight like men, a fair fight instead of sneaking in and out of the jungle like sissies. They'd slaughter the little guys.

I paged to the photograph plates. The Vietminh were building trails up the hills. They'd disassembled the heaviest guns and hauled them up piece by piece, foot by foot. A hundred men might tug a single cannon barrel along by ropes. They were like ants. They were patient and well camouflaged and team-oriented.

They attacked the French when they were ready to.

I was at the part in the book where the Vietminh were marching French troops from Dien Bien Phu to a prison camp. I read a few more pages, had a pull of Johnny Red, and stretched out. I couldn't sleep. I got up and told Ziggy I was going out. He was too absorbed in his reading to even grunt.

Saigon streets were even more chaotic at night. City policemen dressed in white. We knew them as White Mice. They stood on intersection kiosks, signaling and whistling, risking their hides directing traffic. Nobody paid them the slightest attention. Cyclos, motorcyclos, scooters, military and civilian vehicles, pedestrians and the ubiquitous cream-and-blue Renault taxis went as they would, from Point A to Point B.

Le Loi Boulevard, the Street of Flowers, perpendicular to Tu Do, had the goods I sought. I walked into a Monet garden and a perfumery rolled into one. I picked this and that individual flower, making a rainbow of petals. I stopped when funds ran perilously low and rode a taxi to Mai and her sister's.

The farther I walked in from the main drag, the darker and quieter it was. For all I knew I'd be walking into the weekly meeting of the local Vietcong Benevolent Society. The night throughout the land did belong to the Reds.

Nobody bothered me in the pitch blackness. A butter stinker in this neighborhood at this hour, with only blossoms to defend himself, had to be off his rocker. Demented people in any culture were dangerous to handle and were given a wide berth.

Quyen, the big sister, answered the door. "You, huh?"

"Sorry to barge in on you at this hour, ma'am. Do you speak English?"

She shook her head so quickly that I knew she did.

I played the game. "For Mai. *Biết?*"

I was ashamed to admit that *biết*, Vietnamese for "understand," was one of the few non-profane Vietnamese words I'd troubled myself to learn.

"I *biết*. You with captain war hero today, huh?"

"I do. I am. I mean I was."

Quyen smiled and extended her thumb and forefinger two inches apart. "Captain, him like this."

A wonderful anecdote told in passable English. I had to smile.

"What you want?"

I'd frozen in a moronic grin, my tongue tied in knots. Even if I could stammer out the words, I could think of nothing further to say. Jesus H. Fucking Christ, where was I? In the seventh grade at the Friday afternoon sock hop in the gym? Too bashful to tap a girl on the shoulder and ask for a dance?

I thrust the flowers in Quyen's hands, idiotically repeating, "For Mai. *Biết?*"

She did not accept them. She stepped back, and I thought she was going to slam the door in my face. Then she called inside. I didn't understand a word, but they held the tone of a command.

Mai came out and took the flowers.

"For you, Mai."

Without a word, she blew me a kiss and quietly shut the door.

Chapter Seven

I got back to the room, all atwitter, too wound up to sleep. To grab a wink I tried to get my mind off Mai by counting, not sheep gamboling over a fence, but those Vietminh ants in their black pajamas and coolie hats. I finally dozed into half slumber, half recollection. The ants had led me not to the French garrison at Dien Bien Phu, but to Seattle's Armed Forces Processing Center on the 9th day of 1964.

Doug Hooper and I were taking our draft physicals together. And why not? We'd been best buddies since the middle of the fifth grade, when his family had moved in across from us in West Seattle, in a modest neighborhood of crackerbox ramblers and competitive lawns. They were Navy people and Doug had attended four different schools, but his dad was retiring soon and they stayed put. Upon graduating from high school, we went our separate ways, me to professional studentdom, Doug to Boeing, working swing shift at the Renton plant, bucking rivets on the 727 wing line.

As previously stated, the Selective Service System was losing patience with me and my academic meandering, a career in itself. They cynically presumed that six-plus years with umpteen majors and sophomore status did not constitute scholarly achievement. They likewise cynically presumed I'd stuck in school only to hang on to my student deferment. To avoid Uncle Sam in those tense times, either you went to college or you knocked up your girlfriend and did the right thing by her.

I think Judy was willing to go along with the knocked-up part, but I wasn't ready to do the right thing. That entailed buying a ring, saying "I do," picking out furniture, settling down, et cetera. I knew Judy was losing patience with me, too. I couldn't blame her. The role of sort-of fiancée left her in romantic limbo.

Doug wasn't serious about anybody at the moment, although I suspected he had a secret crush on Judy. He was no keener than I about going into the army, but when he told me what he was gonna do, I didn't believe him. Doug could be as full of shit as a Christmas goose and you never knew when.

It was nearly as cold inside the processing station as out. They marched us from here to there with our shirts off, poking and probing and measuring and ordering us to fill a bottle whether we had to take a leak or not. I might've known from that goofy grin plastered on Doug's face that he wasn't kidding. Nobody else had so much as cracked a smile. We had no reason to.

Then they lined us in a row, fifteen at a time. The medic told us to drop our drawers, bend over, and spread our cheeks. The doctor came along, looking for whatever he was looking for. I could see out of the corner of my eye that he was not young. He had acne scarring at his collar and a wispy pompadour. He didn't seem any happier to be here than we were. I felt halfway sorry for the poor bastard. This had to be the Siberia of medicine. Somewhere in his past was a clamp sewn inside a patient.

Doug was next to me. Redheaded and freckled, he was the spitting image of Howdy Doody. That is, if you twisted Howdy's mouth into an evil smirk and threw in a giggle or three. I shushed him, but he continued snickering.

The doctor came to a dead halt behind Doug and his pink silk panties. They were awfully baggy. He'd swiped them from his mom, who was a big lady. He hadn't dropped them all the way down. He was holding them at knee level to make sure they weren't missed. Doug would do almost anything on a dare, but he'd dreamt this up on his own.

The doctor said, "Nice try, son. Ever read *Catch-22*?"

I had. I loved *Catch-22*. I guessed what was coming, but Doug didn't. He wasn't a recreational reader.

He answered, "Who?"

The doctor explained, "*Catch-22* is a famous novel. Its primary protagonist, Captain Yossarian, was a bombardier in World War II Europe, an extremely hazardous vocation. He attempted to get out of combat duty by claiming he was crazy. Captain Yossarian fell victim to a catch in the regulations known as Catch-22. Catch-22 said that if you tried to get out of combat duty by claiming you were crazy, it proved that you were perfectly sane. Are you getting my point, young man?"

Doug was getting his point. He muttered "shit" and allowed his mom's pink silk panties to fall to his ankles.

"You have balls to pull this stunt," the doctor said as he moved along, examining whatever he was examining. "Your country needs you."

We waited out front till they called us to the counter one by one and said yea or nay. By then everybody'd heard about Doug. The enlistees were disgusted and gave us plenty of room. The draft bait hung close, acting as if Doug was John Wayne who'd taken out a Nazi pillbox.

All anyone could talk about was what they hoped was wrong with them. No one was anxious for syphilis or cancer, mind you, but we were yearning for nearsightedness or farsightedness, trick knees, high or low blood pressure, flat feet, slipped disks, neuritis, neuralgia, post nasal drip, the heartbreak of psoriasis. We were praying for a backassward Lourdes, where 4-F was the miracle. I had no illusions. If you could fog a mirror, you were probably in.

I told them of a friend of a friend of mine who'd been rejected last year because of a dropped testicle. Three guys asked at once how far it had to drop. I didn't know. There were limits how far you'd tolerate your testicle dropping, army or no army.

Doug and I passed with flying colors. We went to a tavern down the street. I didn't know what you called the opposite of celebrating, but that's what we were doing. Doug didn't even bother calling in sick at the Lazy B, even though he was supposed to clock in at 3:30. Other future GIs tagged along with us and we ordered pitchers.

"Maybe I should've—what's my mom call it?—accessorized," Doug said. "You know, nylons and earrings and perfume and lipstick, too, if it wasn't too slutty."

That brought down the house. He was dead serious, and they thought he was being funny. We toasted him. We drank to his pink silk panties and his accessorizing. Doug's money was no good at this table.

I went to a pay phone to call Judy. She wanted to know as soon as I knew. My coin jammed in the slot. It was either a Canadian nickel or an omen. I'd been debating whether breaking up now would be easier than getting Dear John'd later.

I returned to the table and it wasn't long before the suds were doing our talking.

Some of the guys were considering enlisting. It'd cost three or four years instead of a draftee's two, but at least you had options in duty and assignment.

Doug said, "What's the difference? It's all shit, just a different color."

"This recruiting sergeant told me that the North Koreans are tunneling under the DMZ," a beanpole with a crew cut said.

In 1964, Vietnam was a sidebar. We were sweating South Korea. Rumor had it that if you were drafted, you were automatically assigned to the infantry and shipped there, where you'd freeze your ass off sleeping in tents as the first line of defense against the commies, who were itching to come across and slit your throat and stuff your balls in your mouth, not necessarily in that order.

"My buddy's older brother was in the Korean War," said a guy, who wouldn't quit bellyaching that his feet were a whole bunch flatter than they said they were. "He got overrun twice by the Red Chinese. The Chinks, they went on over his foxhole, blowing their bugles, hopped up on opium."

"If Goldwater's elected President, he'll H-bomb Red China so it won't make no difference."

"Cuba," was spoken through a belch. "We'll be invading."

"Nope. Don't have to. My dad says Castro's days are numbered. The CIA's gonna slip a stogie loaded with TNT into his cigar box."

"This friend of mine has a cousin whose best friend chopped off his trigger finger on purpose."

The table quieted down.

"The army made him into a southpaw marksman."

We booed him, and this general line of conversation went on and on, growing goofier and goofier. We liberally and loudly used "fuck" in all eight parts of speech, so the banter was colorful if not always intelligible.

Doug had stopped contributing. He was staring into his glass, brooding, normal behavior for him after seven or eleven beers.

Suddenly he looked up. "Goddammit, it ain't fair! We gotta go in while college boys have these fucking deferments. We work for a living and pay our fucking taxes and don't spend our fucking lives in college. No offense, Joe. I'm talking rich frat rats."

"None taken," I said, mildly offended.

"How come we gotta go and they don't?"

We looked at one other and nodded. Doug was making perfect sense. We hoisted our glasses and said goddamn right it wasn't fair.

Doug shook his head. "Now we gotta go and protect them against communism. The motherfuckers, they graduate and get management trainee jobs that pay upwards of four hundred dollars a month and marry the best-looking girls. We're out there digging foxholes. Know the money we'll be making? A buck private draws seventy-eight clams a month."

"We oughta fucking go and fucking tell those fucking draft-dodgers what we fucking think of their fucking candy asses," somebody yelled.

That was a mistake. A big mistake. It qualified as a dare. I'd witnessed Doug's dares. Somehow he'd lived through them. Jumping off bridges into cold water, lighting firecrackers in unusual places, and such.

It got Doug to thinking, like he'd been thinking when he swiped his mother's pink silk panties. From the way he fidgeted, I knew he still had them on.

"On to the University District," he responded. "We'll tell 'em a thing or two! You guys with me?"

Of course we were with him. This was no time to be a pussy. These were the days when everyone smoked (me the only weirdo in the group who didn't) and nobody got too excited if you drank a brew in your car. We stocked up on weeds and six-packs of cold Olympia stubbies, piled into Doug's '51 Chevy Bel Air, and off we went.

He'd had that red-and-white Bel Air hardtop since he was a junior in high school bagging groceries at the A&P. He'd customized it in small ways--like spinner hubcaps and a necker knob. He Simonized it monthly. He'd never bitten on a dare involving that Chevy, playing chicken or anything. A big reason Doug didn't want to go into the service was that he couldn't bring his beloved five-one with him.

This was pre-skyscraper, pre-freeway Seattle, though construction on some interstates had begun. The burbs were still separate towns, not part of an amorphous sprawl. Seattle's tallest structure was the Space Needle, an eyesore (in my opinion) erected for the 1962 World's Fair. On top of the Needle was a flying saucer of a restaurant the Jetsons would feel at home in. Seattle had no major-league professional teams. The Rainiers of the AAA Pacific Coast League was as close as it got, and they were overshadowed by Seattle University basketball and University of Washington football.

It was to the UW we went. We cruised Greek Row. Many of the fraternities and sororities looked like old gingerbread mansions. I hadn't been inside one and never would be, but they couldn't've been too swell with fifty or more guys or gals jammed in, or so my sour grapes informed me.

Doug said we had to find the ideal frat-rat house, the ritziest, with the most brick and ivy.

"Those pussies, we'll rattle their cages," he said. "Their mommies and daddies got the dough to keep them in school forever."

He found precisely what he was looking for, three stories of shutters and porches and tradition. Doug nosed the Bel Air over the curb onto the sidewalk and climbed out none too steadily. A squirrel on the lawn ran up a tree that looked older than the house.

We were with him, kind of, standing to his rear, shivering. An icy drizzle had begun, soaking through our clothes. I had to wonder what the hell we were doing there. The weather was sobering everyone up except Doug, who lobbed his empty Oly. It smashed on the front door of the fraternity.

"Hey, you fucking lily-livered, draft-dodging, turdbird, dick-licking, fucking faggot cocksucker pansies!" he hollered, cigarette dangling from a corner of his mouth.

There was no response. Doug went to the trunk and pulled out a gun. I'd seen it before. It was his dad's Colt .45 pistol that he'd forgotten to turn in to the Navy when he'd retired. I didn't know the dumb shit snuck it out and carried it around in his car.

"What the hell are you doing?" I asked.

Doug whipped his best Howdy Doody grin on me. "Gonna put a little fear in them is all."

"You're going too far, man," I told him. "Put it away before they call the cops."

He pointed the gun in the air and cocked the hammer. "Quit worrying. It's not loaded. I'll show 'em cold steel, make 'em shit their knickers. We'll haul ass before they get our license number."

"Doug, how do *they* know it isn't loaded? Could be one of them is in there, us in his sights. His gun *is* loaded."

Doug was mulling that over when the .45 went off, sounding like a cannon.

"Holy fuck!" he cried, looking at the smoking barrel. "I've seen the old man clean it a million times."

We did have their attention inside the frat house. If you thought we'd be greeted by pipe-smoking, four-eyed weenies in cardigan sweaters, you are sadly mistaken. A dozen ROTC uniforms marched out. The cadet in the lead had a neck wider than his head.

"What's your problem, turkey?" he demanded. "What are you doing with that weapon?"

Doug turned, gun at his side, and gave me a what-the-hell-are-we-doing-here look. I shrugged. I sure didn't know.

Doug was listing a bit to starboard. "You're the fucking problem, Rot-see shithead."

The cadet held out a large paw. "Fork over that weapon, Dilbert."

Doug told a short tale that concerned the cadet's mother and a German shepherd. Maybe his reply should've been less disgusting, but I guess he realized his face was gonna be busted anyway, so he decided to try to save some. The cadet decked Doug with one punch and yanked the pistol out of his hand on his way down.

He asked if I had a problem too. Well, you know me and how my fists engage before my brain does. But our new friends had vamoosed, nowhere to be seen. It was Doug and I by our lonesome, the former on the ground. I was just sober enough to dislike the odds, to do the smart thing. I said *no thank you sir*. The cadet told me to get my stupid drunken friend the hell out of here.

"I'm unloading this weapon before somebody gets hurt," he added.

He was handling the pistol as if he knew what he was doing, but it went off again.

The cadet fell on his back, feet flailing in the air, howling like a banshee. He'd shot himself in a calf, a flesh wound by the looks of it, as there wasn't much bleeding. His pals helped him stagger into the frat house. I heard one say that they weren't due for .45 training until spring quarter.

I would've been more sympathetic if I'd known what I know now of that cadet in The Great Beyond. He did recover from the injury, and his military career was not blemished by the incident. Nothing ever came of the shooting. Because of what it could have done to their illustrious scholarly and military careers, the cadets closed ranks and patched up their leader on their own, mum's the word.

I learned his name was Ron Gibbs. Two years later, First Lieutenant Ronald Gibbs was leading his men on patrol in the Delta, near Can Tho. He triggered a mine on a jungle pathway.

This was not the generic kind of land mine that got Father at Inchon. It was an especially nasty gizmo named a Bouncing Betty. Designed by the Nazis, Bouncing Betties spring up to waist level and detonate at the victim's midsection and family jewels. It definitely qualified as a weapon of terror. It had to be an excruciating way to go.

Doug was sitting in a mud puddle, slimy water seeping into his mother's pink silk panties. He spit blood and an incisor and said, "This wasn't the way it was meant to go."

"Gimme your hand, dummy."

I poured Doug into his Chevy and somehow got us home. First thing in the morning, we volunteered at our friendly, local neighborhood draft board for the next call-up. The army would be a good place to hide. It was better than waiting for the inevitable, not to mention the cops.

Our "Greetings from the President of the United States of America" letters came within a week. By early February we were at Fort Ord for basic training. Marching and shining our boots and pulling KP and being screamed at. The more intense their pressure on me to conform, the fewer my inhibitions to do so.

After Basic, as you know, the army kept me at Ord and trained me to be their macabre version of a chef. Doug went to Fort Rucker, Alabama to aircraft mechanic school, where he received orders to Vietnam. Doug and I lost touch. Nothing happened, we simply drifted apart. In the last letter he ever wrote me, he said nine out of ten Rucker trainees had orders to Vietnam and that every map of the country had been torn out of every atlas in the post library. He'd had no idea where he was going.

I'd heard that Doug got into a disagreement with the Vietcong. While he was on night guard duty at his Bien Hoa airbase, they tried to blow up the place. They did so to a degree, but Doug went after them, expending his clips, making them pay, killing three of them. He went home with a Silver Star and a Purple Heart.

In Basic, I'd taken the cowardly route of ignoring Judy. After ten unanswered letters, she reciprocated. My immaturity was one of the luckier events in her life. While on leave from Vietnam, Judy and Doug eloped in Coeur d'Alene, Idaho. Doug re-upped and became a lifer.

Judy became an army wife and Doug retired after twenty years as a master sergeant.

A month following my MRI, Sally and I attended my high school class reunion. Thanks to Sally's TLC and my medication, I was still in pretty decent shape, able to stay on my feet and converse normally, in good enough condition to say I was in the pink and get away with it.

Doug and Judy were there, too. She looked okay, matronly and pleasant, but I couldn't conjure the Judy I'd known from that Judy.

I'd know Doug anywhere. He was a little heavier, and what remained of that carrot top was silver. He still had his goofy Howdy Doody smirk.

I believe he would have taken me up on a dare, but I couldn't think of one.

Chapter Eight

I am awakened one morning in The Great Beyond by noise that sounds close, noise like a door slamming, noise that drowns out the soft piano tinkling of "Tiny Bubbles," courtesy of those responsible for our multi-ultra-quadraphonic elevator music. A door slams again. This cannot be.

I rush to the living room and peek through drapes. A dark-complected young man is sitting on the front steps of the home to my left. He has shaggy black hair and Bambi eyes. He's Middle Eastern, from somewhere in that part of The Land of the Living. His chin is cupped in his hands. He is not a happy camper.

Another cruel joke on me, I think. It's one thing to people a strip mall with humanoid holograms, but to install one as a next door neighbor--. It isn't much classier than whoopee cushions and exploding cigars.

I take the bait, though. I dress, walk outside and up to him. He looks up at me in surprise. I extend a hand. He extends his. In frustration, I squeeze air hard, expecting fingernails in my palm.

But it's not air, it's flesh and bone.

"Ow!" he cries, pulling his small, soft hand back.

I damn near jump out of my shoes. "Who the hell are you?"

"Who are you and where am I?"

"I'm Joe. The second part of the question is a bunch more complicated."

He introduces himself. I catch only parts, syllables like "smi" and "eth'.

"Okay, Smitty." I say.

"Smitty?" he says, gaining his feet.

Smitty is five-foot-five tops. "Smitty'sa fine, upstanding name."

"If you say so."

He's still a sourpuss, so I say, "It's not perfect, but it's okay here in The Great Beyond. It could be a hell of a lot worse, pardon the pun. Nobody's mistreated me. Not physically."

"Tell me then, Joe, where are my virgins?"

I'd lay money he was one himself. "Well, Smitty, that's a tough one to get your hands on, as is sex in general hereabouts."

"But I was promised seventy virgins," he wails.

Seventy. Holy shit! Smitty's in The Great Beyond thanks to a dynamite undershirt he detonated. I yearned and yearned for human companionship and this is what I get. Wherever you are, dead or alive, kind reader, be careful what you wish for.

"Where did you blow yourself to smithereens, Smitty?"

He replies as blithely as if I'd asked him for directions to the public library. "In a market."

"What market?"

"A crowded one."

My neck is burning. "I think your bosses fibbed to you, Smitty."

"No, cannot be! They promise seventy virgins if I do it."

I'd like to stomp the homicidal little son of a bitch into a grease spot, but I force a smile and say, "Really and truly, they made that promise with their fingers crossed. And trust me, virgins are overrated. When I was your age and younger, I dated some. I'll tell you, they were projects. When I dropped them off and we had our good-night kiss, after all that sweating and heavy breathing and ear-licking and kissing and lies at the drive-in movie or lover's lane, they were still virgins, their panty girdles in place. Man, those things, they were like a suit of armor. No fun at all."

He doesn't reply.

"You were bullshitted by cowards who didn't have the balls to do it themselves, pal."

I had blasphemed. Smitty gives me a hateful glare before I head back home.

Which makes my day.

Forty-five-plus years earlier, in 1965 Saigon, I awakened one morning by noise, too, to an earthquake, not a biggie like Prince William Sound, Alaska's 9.2 last year, but no minor tremor either. It was a ground-rumbling, lampshade-quivering sensation that I, a Seattleite, knew too well.

I flew out of bed and flung open the shutters. It wasn't tectonic plates shifting. It was tanks in the streets, a line of them rumbling along ours. We had us yet another coup, the latest chapter of *Götterdämmerung*, South Vietnam style. The generals were playing musical chairs for the second or third or fourth time this year, one kleptocracy replacing another.

Nervous ARVN troops flanked and trailed the tanks, carrying rifles and carbines, patrolling for nothing in particular. The ones who appeared the most scared were the scariest. They were young and didn't know who they were working for today. There were few civilians or civilian vehicles out and about.

My first instinct was to crawl under something, like we'd done in grade school air raid drills in the 1950s. A siren would sound, as if it was the real warning for Uncle Joe Stalin lobbing in ICBMs. We'd quickly hunch under our desks. I never understood. If it was the real deal, where they'd drawn an X on the principal's office for the target, we'd be vaporized while curled on the floor, rather than seated, struggling with long division.

Ziggy and I dressed, to do our duty. On the way to the 803rd, we whistled and forced smiles. We did not look anybody in the face.

There'd been rumors of a coup, but there were constant rumors of coups, so as far as I was concerned, the coup rumors didn't qualify as rumors. A coup was not a surprise. Only the timing was.

What of Mai, my Dragon Lady? Had she watered my flowers and gently arranged them in a vase? Had she been in bed with an ARVN officer when I had come calling? In retrospect, her expression had been dreamy. I conceded that she surely knew senior brass, knew them carnally. A woman of her beauty and presumed charms, she wouldn't settle for a paramour below the rank of colonel. My Dragon Lady in the funny papers was always in the thick of the intrigue, her sexuality easily read between the lines.

What side of the coup were her partners on? Was she privy to the coup planning? Was the lover I'd concocted an important player on today's winning team, Mai escorting him in his triumph, she the next Madame Nhu? If not, would they be dragged out of bed and taken for a ride, her along as a collaborator?

I paused and breathed deeply. I had to cease this madness before I upchucked the breakfast I hadn't eaten.

Captain Papersmith wasn't in, not a huge stunner. He must have blundered out of the sack with a head-splitter, then crawled back under the covers. There'd be no special assignments for us today.

Company clerk PFC A. Bierce was in, at his typewriter.

"Colonel Lanyard wants to see you ASAP, Joe," he said.

"Just me?"

"Just you."

"Whoever calls us on the carpet usually asks for both of us."

I looked at Ziggy, who shrugged.

Bierce typed on. "I am only following orders."

"Let me ask you a question, Herr Eichmann. Captain Papersmith said we were to assist you on your clerical duties as he sees fit, as you work like a dog, quote-unquote. What'll that entail?"

"Don't worry about it. I'm caught up."

"Another question, PFC A. Bierce."

He nodded and continued working.

"Is your first name Ambrose?"

The hunt-and-peck stopped.

He changed the subject. "That tattoo on your arm, are you from Montana?"

"No. How about yourself?"

"Nogales, Arizona."

I'd suspected that he was versed on many topics, fine art included. "Believe it or not, Bierce, it was supposed to be a Mondrian. Long story."

"Color fields. Ho-hum. I prefer the surrealists."

"Dalí?"

"René Magritte is my favorite. That apple floating in midair, you can pluck it off the canvas and eat it."

Before we drifted too far afield, I said, "I took a course on American humorists and satirists. Ambrose Bierce was prominent. He was a misanthrope. He was a sick puppy and he was hilarious. Kept me rolling on the floor.

"I especially enjoyed *The Devil's Dictionary*. His definitions had me in stitches. His short story, *Oil of Dog*, too, where the protagonist perfected a concoction with his wife's aborted fetuses, it was the sickest thing I have ever read. I loved it.

"I love his quotes, too. The one about war is a classic. War—a byproduct of the arts of peace."

Bierce glared at me and said bitterly, "You know, Joe, the one reason I welcomed the draft is that I knew that nobody in this man's army had ever heard of Ambrose Bierce."

"I'm an exception to a lot of rules. I've had more college majors than Carter has pills. Like Ziggy, I possess a ton of trivial and absolutely useless information. My name is a bad family joke. Yours too?"

"I'm Ambrose Bierce's illegitimate grandson."

"You're jerking my chain, Bierce. I remember his bio. His children preceded him in death, and his own demise was a mystery. He went to Mexico when one of their civil wars was going on, 1910 or 1920, that era, and joined up with Pancho Villa."

"It was late 1913 and no mystery to me. I'll leave it at that."

"May I ask you yet another question, Ambrose?"

He sighed. "Why not? I have all day for you, Joe. But please lose the 'Ambrose,' especially in public."

"No sweat. Can do. If you'll tell me what're you working on, working like a dog. All that paper seems to go nowhere in the Fighting 803rd's vast routing system."

"Confidentially?"

I nodded.

"My novel."

Okay, maybe Ambrose was who he said he was. A writer. Like grandfather, like grandson. "Tell me about it?"

"I'm unpublished. It's bad luck for an author to divulge his story line. That's common knowledge in the industry."

"C'mon, Bierce, a brief summary, a synopsis."

"In utmost top-secret confidence?"

"Top secret crypto." I crossed my heart. "And hope to die."

"It's called *Jesus of Capri*. Jesus lived during the reign of the Roman Emperor Tiberius, from 14 AD to 37 AD, you know. Tiberius spent most of his days as a recluse on the island of Capri. Tiberius heard of a rabble-rouser in one of their colonies, some sort of reformer whose following was growing. In my historical adjustment, Jesus isn't nailed to timbers. Tiberius had Jesus hauled to Capri to see what made him tick and to quell whatever he was stirring up. Neither converted the other to their brand of politics, but something else clicked. They became lovers."

"I think it's a helluva'n idea, Ambrose. Very slick and original and sacrilegious. But the faithful are not gonna appreciate their Savior packing fudge."

He resumed typing. "Bible thumpers don't buy nonreligious books, Joe. They don't read literary fiction. Some say that the Bible's the world's greatest sci-fi novel."

"Sci-fi. I'll have to run that by Ziggy."

"The colonel, Joe."

"You can be court-martialed for blasphemy, Bierce." He shook his head in disbelief.

"Really. You can be court-martialed for everything in this man's army. The resurrection after the crucifixion and so forth? How're you handling the supernatural bit?"

"I'm not there yet. I'm plotting as I go. You'd better get on in to the colonel, Private Joe. Pronto."

From my vantage point in The Great Beyond, I can tell you that jungle drums by bored merchants in my wretched, unpatronized strip mall say that Jesus and his Twelve Disciples are with us and they stay as isolated as Tiberius was, but not by choice. There are rumors they were hatching a coup d'état. There are rumors of heavy security.

I have to scratch my head. If Jesus could walk on water, do the fishes and loaves thing, and perform various and sundry miracles as I was taught in Sunday school (a failed experiment by my Mother to make me a better person), how hard would it be to break out of some detention camp? Are we talking urban legend here?

Ambrose Bierce the Youngest is not in my extraworldly telephone directory. He remains flesh and blood, a ripe old age amongst the mortals. Like everyone, he will eventually check out there and check in here. I'm looking forward to sitting down with him over a cold one and chitchatting. If this isolation and/or censorship I'm enduring will ever end.

"We'll have to sit down over a cold one and chat, Bierce."

"I'd like that," he said unconvincingly.

"Hey, a final question, Ambrose. You're a company clerk. You're in the know and you guys essentially run the army. South Vietnam as our fifty-first state, is there anything to it? The rumor's hanging in there like a hemorrhoid. What've you heard?"

He replied with a Cheshire cat grin that gave me the shivers, it was so out of character for the wooden-faced Bierce.

"What the hell's that mean, man?"

He jabbed a finger toward the hall. "The colonel, Joe. Your ass and a lawnmower."

I could take a hint. I knocked, entered, and reported to the colonel, coming smartly to attention, heels locked, salute affixed to my forehead.

Jut-jawed, gray-eyed Colonel Jake Lanyard was a recruiting poster. Imagine Clint Eastwood playing John Wayne in a movie. Lean and muscular, the colonel had more hair on his arms than I had on my entire body. Lanyard's West Point ring was big enough to work as brass knuckles. His boots and insignia were blinding, and you could cut a mess hall steak with the creases in his fatigues. He was the 803rd Liaison Detachment's one true soldier, as much an alien in this goofy outfit as Ziggy's Martians.

The colonel didn't initially acknowledge me, and his air conditioner was doing zilch but make a hellacious racket. The GE was gone, replaced by a hand-me-down hunk of junk.

The colonel had my personnel jacket on his desk. I was amazed that he had room for it. There were stacks of papers covering two-thirds of it, all with TOP SECRET CRYPTO cover sheets. They were as neat as could be, too, every stack parallel to or at right angles to the others. They could be pieces in a Pentagon war game. As nosy as I was, I'd never dare snoop when he was out. I pictured a

Bouncing Betty popping up if I lifted a cover sheet. I noticed that his walls were bare.

Colonel Lanyard seldom left his desk unless to go to the latrine or to General Whipple's office or to wherever he went on his overnight trips. I almost piped up and asked if he'd heard about the coup, but I knew he hadn't. Here at the 803rd, the officers were too busy keeping current on events to know what was going on.

He held my jacket up and let it drop, making a face as if he'd stepped in something.

"You and your friend, how did you two duds ever get into this man's army?"

"Judge Bergstrom made Private Zbitgysz enlist, sir. It was that or the pokey. As for myself, I was driven by an intense hatred of communist tyranny and all it stands for. I had to do my share."

"You are a draftee, not an enlistee, trooper."

"Yes, sir, but the result's the same."

The colonel ignored my guano and said, "Soldier, you do realize that American fighting units are being deployed in-country. Victor Charles is on the run, his tail between his yellow legs. We are playing a crucial part in fulfilling that mission. The 803rd Liaison Detachment is a can-do outfit."

I didn't get what he was getting at. "Sir, yes sir."

"There are advocates of bombing North Vietnam back into the Stone Age."

Colonel Lanyard, too? I desperately wanted to kiss his ass, but I held my tongue. It'd be unwise to guess and offer an opinion that differed from his.

"Not I."

"Nor I, sir."

"Foot soldiers win and lose wars, Private, and we're turning the situation around with the buildup. It's phasing into a mopping-up operation for us and our South Vietnamese allies."

The ARVN staged a coup to celebrate their mopping up of Victor Charles and the boys from Hanoi?

"Yes sir."

"Private Joe, are you and Private Zbitgysz bored with the Saigon gravy train?"

A question as loaded as the aforementioned Bouncing Betty.

"No sir," I said. "Sir, we are not, sir."

"Are you bored with your soft duty?"

"No sir."

He opened my file. "I see Captain Papersmith's notes. He's having your MOSs changed to clerk typist."

"Yes sir."

"How's your typing speed?"

"Improving every single day, sir."

He looked at me suspiciously. "If you're restless, I can reclassify your MOS to eleven-bravo-ten. Eleven-bravo is Light Weapons Infantrymen. I can send you into the bush to seek out and kill guerrillas. Unless they seek out and kill you first."

"No sir. Yes sir."

Air-conditioning or not, it wasn't a degree colder in here than outside. I was sweating like a racehorse. The colonel was dry as a bone. I'd never seen the colonel perspire. The war would end in ten minutes flat if they put Colonel Lanyard in charge. Team him with Terry Lee, and Ho Chi Minh would be on his knees begging for mercy.

"We have an ample number of the enemy to kill. There is no shortage."

"Yes sir."

"There are plenty to go around, for genuine soldiers and clerk-typists alike. I can cut the orders, put you and Zbitgysz on a chopper, and have you in the Delta in thirty minutes."

"Yes sir."

"Captain Papersmith informs me that you men occasionally demonstrate resourcefulness. Correct?"

"If I do say so myself, sir, Private Zbitgysz and I are outstanding on special assignments."

"You may have some can-do in you after all."

I didn't like where this was headed, but I had to keep giving can-do answers or my ass *was* grass.

"Yes. Sir. Whatever it is you need, we can can-do for you, sir."

"I ordered you in here alone because you have soldierly potential, Private Joe. Despite appearances, I'm confident you do. Soldierly bearing and military performance are not beyond your capability."

That was news to me. I was more insulted than flattered. "Thank you, sir. I appreciate your confidence in me. I am truly trying to be a good soldier, sir."

The colonel shuffled paper stacks and cocked a thumb at the air conditioner. "I requisitioned a replacement unit. Put out a tracer and see how the request is moving through channels. I expect the mission accomplished by the end of the day."

"Sir, the end of the —"

"That is all."

I controlled my mouth and didn't ask how come he didn't just go across the street to the Annex and take his pick. I whipped my smartest salute on him. The colonel returned it with his eyes on his paperwork so they wouldn't have to be on mine. That the colonel was also corrupt affirmed my faith in the human race. It was heartwarming.

I tiptoed to General Whipple's office-terrarium. His door was cracked. He was in, and so was the GE, in his window, humming a sweet tune. Even in the hallway you could feel a pleasant autumn breeze.

The general didn't see me. He was busy watering his plants that lined the shelves and hung from the ceiling in baskets, as dense as a nursery, growing denser by the day, nearly impenetrable. Saigon's atmosphere was a natural humidifier, and that delighted him. He was watering his vegetation from an olive-drab watering can that had a silver brigadier general's star painted on each side. He'd been given it as a going-away present by his botanical research colleagues before he shipped out.

Smiling and watering, that's all I'd ever seen the general do. Former Supply Sergeant Rubicon once told us that the general was the smartest man he ever knew and that he'd gone to college for upwards of ten years and then taught in colleges until he was summoned from his National Guard unit to active duty. I guess that's why he was in charge of writing reports when he wasn't busy smiling and watering his plants.

On the rare occasion that General Whipple addressed his men, he was given to plant-animal comparison, frequently reaching into metaphor and aphorisms. He believed that troops and plants craved a natural photosynthesis. While our need for oxygen and carbon dioxide were the opposite, plant and man both required water and sun. We required nourishment and energy to thrive and to be productive organisms.

General Whipple spent sixty hours a week in his office, minimum. By order of General Westmoreland, everyone at MACV Headquarters worked at least sixty hours a week, even if it meant creating busywork to maintain sanity.

The top brass thought sixty hours per week was a sound military tactic. Seeing the midnight oil in the offices, Vietcong infiltrators would be so impressed by our resolve, they'd conclude it was fruitless to resist.

By order of General Whipple, we worked sixty hours, too. Theoretically. Ziggy and I tended to be a tad slippery in that area. Our working hours were inversely proportional to our amount of supervision. Our new special assignment duties made malingering less a challenge than a sacred responsibility.

General Whipple didn't look like a general. He was slender and bespectacled. He looked like a dad in a TV series. You know, those shows where the kids screw up, not doing their homework, a serious offense along those lines, and the dad sits them down at the end and gives them a mild-mannered lecture and the kids promise to straighten up, and sure enough, they do.

General Whipple made me wonder how I'd've turned out if I'd had my dad who was killed at Inchon or had General Whipple for a stepdad rather than my dildo of a stepdad, who wasn't there even when he was there.

When I walked out to the orderly room, Ziggy was paging through a little red book with gold lettering and a gold star on the cover. He was moving his lips.

"What've you got, Zig?"

"Don't know exactly. 'All reactionaries are paper tigers.' What's that mean, Joey?"

He handed me the book. It was *Quotations from Chairman Mao Tse-tung*, his infamous Little Red Book, with which Chairman Mao brainwashed a billion Chinese Reds. I pushed Ziggy into a corner, away from prying eyes and ears. It was like winching an Olds 98 out of a ditch, but my adrenaline was pumping.

"Zig, are you out of your gourd?" I sputtered in his ear. "The colonel sees this, he'll have us shot. No, wait, he'll do it himself. Where the hell'd you get it?"

"The oddballs were getting off the bus, going in the Annex. It fell out of one of their pockets."

On the inside flap, Ralph Buffet, one of the idiot-genius warrant officers, had written his name. Proof of ownership, proof of misdemeanor treason. Those oddballs and their zero common sense.

I hurried outside to dump it into a sewer grate.

Then I had one of my self-destructive inspirations.

I stuffed it in a pocket instead.

Chapter Nine

Military traffic was thinning. A smattering of taxis and cyclos tentatively ventured out. South Vietnamese Air Force (VNAF) airplanes were circling and swooping like dragonflies. They were propeller planes, obsolete hand-me-downs from some past war of ours. There were itchy trigger fingers by air and by land, and who knows what was happening on the Saigon River.

Might be the VNAF was supporting the coup. Or supporting the generals who used to be in charge. Or staging a coup of their own. Or the coup had simply fizzled out, political attention spans in this country being what they were.

For my Dragon Lady's sake more than mine, I wished the last. Marauding troops would take one look at her and judge her politically incorrect, an unlovely phrase from the future. Summary punishment would be gang rape.

Captain Papersmith remained out. We took the colonel's Jeep, the one the captain hadn't gotten around to giving him. Where we were going, we didn't know. Brand-new GE air conditioners on the back of USAF flatbeds stuck in traffic did not grow on trees.

"Lanyard will rip us new poopers if we don't come up with a unit. Suppose we do, it'll cost an arm and a leg," I thought aloud. "Where the hell do we get the money?"

Ziggy patted the side of the Jeep. "We're riding in it, Joey."

Was my giant compatriot a genius or what? I U-turned in the direction of Bombay Tailors. This vehicle wasn't contributing much to the war effort anyhow. The antique warplanes continued their circling and swooping. Rockets and bombs hung on their bellies. As I drove, Ziggy watched for objects falling out of the white-hot blue sky.

I'd had my fill of fireworks of any definition before I shipped out. My worst trouble had been in the Fort Ord AIT barracks one morning, when the barracks NCO, an illiterate three-striper named Spangler, had flicked on the lights to awaken us, one of the few duties he'd been competent to perform. When I hadn't sprung out of my bunk, he'd marched directly to me and blown a whistle in my ear. There had already been bad blood between Sergeant Spangler and me, blood brought to a boil as he'd been drunk and I'd been hung over.

I'd come out of the prone position faster than either of us anticipated. Versions varied as to who'd thrown the first punch. It was on record that I threw the last. The sergeant had gone down with a gushing eye, a broken nose, and teeth on the floor.

That I'd only been reduced in rank and reprimanded was due to extenuating circumstances. Even my barracks mates who'd slept through it all volunteered to testify that I was provoked and attacked. Spangler had been unanimously despised, and, fortuitously for me, he had been busted not two hours earlier for drunken driving by police in nearby Salinas.

My idle threat to hire a civilian lawyer had been the clincheroo. My CO and the post JAG (Judge Advocate General's office--armyese for legal advisory services) had wanted nothing to do with outside talent. There was a pervasive fear in the military hierarchy of the superiority of anything civilian. They had swept me under the rug. I'd graduated from cook's school without honors or further incident.

Ziggy and I arrived at Bombay Tailors and presented our dilemma to Mr. Singh. He beamed his thousand-watt smile on us and said, "Gentlemen, I have a solution. It has providentially come to my attention that your own United States Navy Exchange has received a shipment of household air conditioners."

"How do you always know all?" I asked.

Singh's smile brightened to two thousand watts. He made no comment.

"Okay, Mr. Singh, how much will you give us for the Jeep?"

"You Americans and your impatience for immediate action, Mr. Joe. That is why you rule the world. One hundred American dollars."

"Ouch," I said. "You oughta run a used car lot in California, Singh."

"Gentlemen, there are complications. This vehicle is not accompanied by a title of ownership. This poses additional administrative costs."

Additional administrative costs: a euphemism for forgery.

"Well," was all I managed.

"What is your expression? The air conditioners, they shall sell faster than cakes that are heated?"

"What's your deal, Singh?"

He rubbed thumb against forefingers. "There is a waiting list for those air conditioners that can be circumvented for a supplemental consideration of one hundred dollars."

"Impossible, man. Highway robbery."

Mr. Singh literally kicked a tire.

"This cream puff has low miles and the USARV Motor Pool rebuilt the engine last week," I said sincerely.

Mr. Singh squatted and looked underneath, then made the same sourpuss face he'd worn had when we'd brought him the Spam.

"There are fluids seeping and dripping."

"Normal part of the break-in process on a rebuilt mill," I said.

We haggled, and he wound up paying us less than I wanted and more than I thought we were going to get. He paid us in piasters, which the PX wouldn't accept. So we had to change them back to him for greenbacks at a discounted rate, $90.25 net to us. Basically, Singh screwed us twice. He did give us a name of a "helpful" PX employee.

I'd been a business major for a quarter, a marketing major for two. In retrospect from The Great Beyond, I should have used the G.I. Bill upon my army discharge, gone back to college and actually graduated, then on to grad school like Baby Brother. But, yeah, I know, hindsight.

My real world experience in Saigon was invaluable. A potential master's thesis title: Microeconomic Exploitation of First World Individuals by Subcontinent Individual in Macroeconomic Third World Environment. It would've been a breeze; the research was already done.

Mr. Singh asked, "When is it we shall become the fifty-first province in your great nation? The stories of such an impending occurrence are rampant."

"Any day now," I said.

"I shall then be an American citizen?"

"You and Patrick Henry and Sonny Liston, Mr. Singh, same same."

I think of Mr. Singh now as I page through The Great Beyond's useless telephone directory. Is he with us? Who can say? There are a zillion Singhs listed. Half the surnames in India are Singh and half the cabbies in the U.S.A. are likewise.

My directory is half an inch thick but it lists *everybody*. Though it should be ten miles high, I can thumb though all those Singhs while it stays a slender volume. How? You'll have to ask our ringmasters to explain their hocus-pocus.

Ziggy grabbed an English-language *Saigon Post* from a newsstand, where we were on the lookout for a still-scarce taxi.

"What's new on the coup?" I asked. "Didn't their ace reporters know about it yesterday?"

Ziggy snorted, a noise like a sewage backup. "Who gives a diddly-shit about this rinky-dink coupe-de-tot when they'll go and do it again next week?"

A valid point. I finally spotted a taxi, practically threw myself in front of it, and we piled in.

"Here's another fuckin' genius," Ziggy said, reading on. "He claims Mars is cold and it got thin air. Yeah, maybe. He says Mars don't have no water and nitrogen neither."

When Ziggy got excited, his voice carried. In this little blue-and-cream Renault taxi, it had nowhere to carry. I expected glass to shatter. The cabby couldn't keep his eyes out of his mirror.

"Easy, Zig. This guy in the article's a scientist?"

"He's the village idiot is what he is. Listen. He claims it's according to this spectrographic analysis they done. Ain't that a crock of shit?"

"If you say so, Zig."

"Mariner 4 ain't even there. He oughta hold his horses for the pitchers before he opens his trap. The Martians here now, they'll rise up. He's gotta be high up on their shit list. His ass'll be the first one they fry."

"Uh-huh," I mumbled, hoping he'd change the subject.

Unfortunately, he did.

"There are not a few people who are irresponsible in their work, preferring the light to the heavy."

Ziggy had spoken, but it was not his voice. One of his Martians? I looked at him.

He grinned and dug Mao's Little Red Book from a back pocket. I'd gotten cold feet and had given it to Ziggy to carry until we put our plan in motion.

"This stuff in here, Joey, it ain't too bad, like that quotation I quoted."

"You're amazing, man. You're a speed-reader who absorbs like a sponge," I said, yet again awed.

"It is man's social being that determines his thinking. Once the correct ideas characteristic of the advanced class are—"

"Zig, please put it away before we're arrested," I said, plugging my ears until he did stop.

At the PX, we saw the gentleman Singh had told us to see, a Vietnamese backroom employee named Vo, who refused eye contact or conversation. We paid him the $90.25, which, remarkably, was his exact price. Into the taxi beside the driver, we loaded our purchase, a brand-spanking-new GE air conditioner, and had him head to Tan Son Nhat so we could poach a replacement Jeep.

I waited in the taxi at the gate, soothing the cabby's nerves with piasters. Ziggy was back in ten minutes at the wheel of said Jeep. It was a rat, but we had no time to be picky, and Captain Papersmith wouldn't know the diff. It had an engine knock, ripped seat covers, and a shimmy. We released the relieved cabby, then went to the Esso to have new markings sprayed on.

Back at the 803rd Liaison Detachment by 11:30, I felt like we'd put in a full day. We removed the rattletrap from the colonel's window and stuck it in the new a.c. It was so powerful that the lights flickered when we switched it on.

Colonel Lanyard sat at his desk doing his work, completely ignoring us. I guess if we weren't there, none of what was going on was going on. Despite pretending we didn't exist, he angled the TOP SECRET CRYPTO cover sheet of the pile he was working on so we couldn't see what was beneath.

His packed duffel bag was in a corner. When he was gone on one of his trips (all classified, naturally), the 803rd's testosterone level plummeted.

A bus pulled up to take the oddballs to "noon chow." We went outside, my screwball plan to say we had a telegram for Warrant Officer Ralph Buffet. That usually meant that somebody on the home front was dead or dying. We'd be able to cut Buffet from the herd without anybody questioning us too severely. It was a cruel thing to do, but, hey, we were in a war.

Then I saw Mai. She stood alone at the next corner, unmoving. Enchantingly demure in her *áo-dài*, she was the most delicate of statues, delicate as translucent Renaissance marble.

Captain Papersmith wasn't with her, and I knew she wasn't here to see him.

I knew because she was looking at me, holding a single white lily.

Chapter Ten

Eyes locked on Mai, whose eyes were locked on mine, I told Ziggy to play out the phony telegram hustle. I told him to look sad and to snag Ralph Buffet however he had to. If anybody raised an objection, call them heartless bastards who couldn't possibly have loved ones of their own on the home front or they'd understand.

Like a Ziggy sci-fi character, I teleported or levitated or dream-walked to my Dragon Lady. Face to face in full daylight, she was even more breathtaking. She was simultaneously as fragile as that lily and as tough as titanium.

"Why you give me flower?" she asked, expressionless.

I was gaga, on the ragged edge of drooling and swooning and peeing my knickers. I tried to dredge up a semblance of cool, of savior faire. In a pathetic stab at a mix of David Niven and Rock Hudson, but probably coming off as Larry, Moe and Curly, I said, "Flowers are the only gift that comes close to matching your beauty."

With no visible reaction to my treacle, she said, "I am Mai. I saw you when you bring Dean to house. I saw you looking at me. Who are you?"

"Joe. I'm Joe. Joe."

Puzzled, she said, "Joe, American GI soldier give me Crisco and Pall Mall and Anacin. American give me dollar and piaster. American give me dental floss and Schlitz beer. They give me Ritz cracker, Louisiana hot sauce, Clorox, Campbell Chicken Noodle and Cream of Tomato. They give me transistor radio and Canon camera and Akai tape recorder. They give me anything the PX and commissary have I tell them to give me. Did you buy flower for me at PX?"

"No. On Le Loi. Street of Flowers."

"Why you do?"

"It's lovely. You're lovely."

That was the unvarnished truth coming from a guy whose long suit was not candor with women. Not so many months later, barely discharged from the service, after a three-day, brawling bender, battered and filthy, brimming with self-loathing, I underwent a crude precursor of the vasectomy when few people had heard of the procedure. I likened it to being gelded in a barn. I empathized with any woman who endured a backroom abortionist and his coat hanger.

I had not wanted the responsibility of bringing a creature such as myself into the world. The physician had accepted my logic and the remainder of my mustering-out pay.

During normal child-bearing age, I'd been married to Lea, Charlotte and Janelle, One through Three respectively. They had not questioned the purported causes of my sterility, despite how absurd. My reasons had ranged from Agent Orange to Vietcong torture to Pentagon radiation experiments to a parachute opening improperly. That I hadn't always kept my tall tales straight was irrelevant. They weren't as naïve as they were relieved.

My elasticity with facts when I wanted something made truth-telling a vivid memory.

Mai paused. I knew she was attempting to absorb what I'd said. It was so abstract. It did not mesh with her knowledge of interaction between Vietnamese women and American GIs. The latter paid to fuck the former, renting their bodies in the short-term (as in "short time" or "boom boom," both slang for a quickie) or in the long-term, paying directly with piasters or indirectly with gifts, a charade of love, or a "relationship" in exchange for cash and/or goods.

"No man ever give me beautiful flower. I can not eat or drink or sell flower. Why you give me flower?" she pressed, disoriented and suspicious.

"Uh, romance," I said. "The flowers say I care for you."

"You no know me, Joe."

"I do know you, I know you better than you think," I said, then shutting up before I stupidly blabbed my cartoon Dragon Lady hang-up.

"I no know romance. What does romance mean?"

"Romance is an English word, an American word. It means emotion and love of a guy to a girl and a girl to a guy, something along those lines. You know, like boy-girl in the movies."

"Romance?" she asked, looking at the lily, still suspicious. "Is this romance?"

Romance. Yeah, the perfect word. *Romance* conjured Hollywood and its love affairs that, outside of the movies, usually went up in smoke. Debbie Reynolds and Eddie Fisher. Tony Curtis and Janet Leigh. Liz Taylor and whomever.

With Judy and I, in retrospect, it had not been romance beyond empty words and groping and heavy breathing and dry-humping and, at long last, "going all the way" at the drive-in theater. Judy and I went all the way while *The Longest Day* had played. It had taken me nearly to the end, when beachheads were secured, to score.

Until that occurred, every drive-in movie with her had been the longest day. The romance of entry inside her pantyhose meant entry into the kingdom of commitment and marriage and living happily ever after. Romance was conformity, meeting the expectations of others.

"Romance," I said, bobbing my head as if addled, deciding what the hell. I dug the Dragon Lady cartoon panel out of my wallet so clumsily the rubber came too, landing at my feet. The rubber was a "gold dollar," so named for its gold foil wrapper. It was not inconspicuous.

"Shit." I did a goofy fandango to get a shoe over it, stomping on it as if an insect, though much too late.

In reaction to my awkwardness, Mai covered what I knew was a gorgeous smile. I handed her Terry Lee's nemesis. "You, her. Her, you. Romance was her who is you. Romance *is* you. *Biết*?"

Her nose twitched, as if whiffing raw sewage. She wadded and dropped it. "Ugly old lady. You say me ugly old lady, Joe?"

Well, the cartoon version did pale in comparison. "No. Oh no. No way."

"Joe, you know Dean Papersmith, huh?"

Dean and his two inches of manhood. "Sure do."

"Dean say he lead men into jungle fighting communists."

I managed a nod and a straight face. "Absolutely. A special assignment if there ever was one."

"Dean says he marry me and take me to America. He have no love with wife Mildred. No romance as you say. He say he divorce her, marry me. I do not think he have romance for me. If he marry me, romance, if there is, will be all gone. People marry, *fini* romance. Here."

She gave me the lily. "You buy flower for me, I buy for you."

Before I fainted and/or said something else dumb, Ziggy came to us, jerking along a pear-shaped guy with a cowlick and smudged glasses. I presumed that Ziggy's disobedient mutt was Warrant Officer Ralph Buffet.

"His buddies, they gave me a ration of shit, Joey. I told them I was with the Red Cross."

"Nice work, Zig," I said as Mai looked Ziggy up and down, as if he was one of his own Martians.

"Is it my Aunt Peg?" Ralph Buffet whined. "Is it? She has diabetes. She's had a leg amputated."

I waited till the oddballs' bus turned the corner, then flashed Buffet his little red book. "Aunt Peg is in finer shape than you are, pal. We're not Red Cross. We're with a hush-hush agency that's CID and CIA, with the FBI sprinkled in. We don't have much patience with fifth columnists."

Buffet's whining rose an octave and fifty decibels. "I can explain."

Mai watched me, hopefully impressed.

A cyclo deposited an unsteady Captain Dean Papersmith at the 803rd. Mai's back was to him. The eyeballs of Dean, groom of Mildred, looked as if they needed tourniquets. Had he seen us? I didn't think so, but if he hadn't he might unless we scrammed.

Multitasking was a buzzword of decades hence. Buzzword was also a buzzword of the future. Regardless, I was multitasking within spitting distance of far too many people. We had to scram before Papersmith saw us.

"Hey," I said. "My stomach's growling. Who's ready for lunch?"

♦

The Continental Palace Hotel was a downtown Saigon institution. Open air, ceiling fans, white-jacketed waiters older than Ho Chi Minh. They claim the atmosphere hadn't changed since the 1920s. A zillion deals had been cut on the Conti *terrasse*, lies told in twenty languages. This joint was a blast. It was a zoo. You ate and drank while you gawked at the two-legged wildlife.

I thought it was as safe as a popular American hangout could be. VC sappers were flinging satchels of *plastique* into Saigon bars at an increasing rate. My theory on them avoiding the Conti was the open walls on three sides. A satchel charge wasn't powerful enough to blow out the pillars that held up the four stories of hotel above us and without walls to hold in the explosion. The concussion wouldn't kill enough folks to be worth the risk. Besides, half the antique waiters were probably Vietcong sympathizers and spies, listening in and taking notes.

We ordered Nha Trang shrimp and sautéed chicken and stir-fried vegetables and a heaping bowl of sticky rice. Eating family-style was my idea, to eliminate tension, especially my own. To wash down the food, I ordered *Biere 33* all around. It was the premier Vietnamese suds. Known as "ba-mi-ba," a mild corruption of *ba-muoi-ba*, the Vietnamese number 33.

They say it's brewed with formaldehyde. I was a believer. Drink a dozen or so, and you'll wake up in the morning feeling like you were dead and embalmed, and wishing you were.

Mai demurely asked for a cup of tea.

"So, Comrade Buffet," I asked. "How long have you been a fellow traveler? Or are you a card-carrying Red feeding the enemy classified info? Which is a quick ticket to a firing squad."

The chopsticks that he hadn't mastered fell out of his hand. "You have me all wrong. My brother found it at a Toronto bookstore. All manner of subversive literature is available in Canada. Titles like *U.S. Imperialism Will Be Defeated* and *Revolutionary Armed Struggle of the Indo-Chinese Peoples Will Certainly Triumph*. He sent it to me as a gag. A lark. I've been reading it. I'm curious how those people think. That's all."

"You, who is working on a top secret project vital to our nation's defense. A likely story. What's going on in there?"

"I can't tell you. As you said, it's top secret."

I nodded to Ziggy, who quoted from *Quotations from Mao Tse Tung*, "People of the world, unite and defeat the U.S. aggressors and all their running dogs."

"Ouch," I said. "Some lark."

A nervous Mai touched her lips with a manicured and lacquered fingernail.

"I want a lawyer," Ralph Buffet said, absently digging at earwax.

"A military or civilian lawyer? Which are your druthers? Neither one can save your sorry ass. You can have Clarence Darrow for all the good it'll do you, Comrade Buffet."

"Please don't call me that. How do I know you guys are who say you are? You look familiar. Haven't I seen you across the street?"

"'The army in the Liberated Areas must support the government and cherish the people,'" Ziggy recited.

"What did he say?"

I said, "I'm asking the questions. Whip some ID on me, soldier."

He did not comply. He stared at me. I stared at him. It was Dodge City, Marshal Matt Dillon (me), in front of Miss Kitty's Long Branch, faced off with the villain. I won the bluff. Buffet finally slapped leather, drawing his wallet.

Ralph Buffet was Chief Warrant Officer CWO-2 Ralph J. Buffet. Warrant officers were in a twilight zone between commissioned officers and enlisted personnel. Warrants had many privileges of commissioned officers, but technically a twenty-five-year man, a CWO-4, the highest warrant grade, was outranked by a fuzzy-cheeked second lieutenant. In practice, that was not the case. If the second louie knew what was good for him, he wouldn't try to pull rank.

"Are you gentlemen at the Annex all warrant officers?"

"If you know so much, you tell me."

"Talk to us about the Annex."

"You know I can't."

"Okay, stop right now. It you're not gonna cooperate, we have no choice but to remand you to the proper authorities. I guarantee you won't be playing your little games for long. They have their methods. Major Zbitgysz, take our prisoner into custody, him and his Marxist smut."

Buffet looked at Ziggy and gulped.

"Quote another incriminating passage, Major."

Ziggy sounded like a truck speeding on gravel. "'We must see to it that our cadres and all our people constantly bear in mind that ours is a big socialist country but an economically backward and poor one, and that is a very great contradiction.'

"Joey, this guy who wrote this book, he's one inscrutable Chinaman."

"All right, all right. Whoever you are, what do you really want?" Buffet insisted, the whine partially out of his voice.

Mai delicately patted her mouth with a napkin.

She got up and said, "Must leave. Must go."

"Excuse me, gents."

I followed my Dragon Lady out to the street. Five taxis miraculously materialized, desiring her and her fare.

"Mai, I'm sorry. I didn't mean to make a racket and to ignore you. Honest. It's just that we grabbed this traitor and can't let him go."

"Am not angry at you, Joe. You captured a horrible communist. You must do your work. Is time I go."

"When can I see you? Just, you know, you and me."

Mai took from her purse a slip of folded rice paper. "Day after tomorrow night, Joe?"

"Yes," I said, opening a taxi door for her. "Not tonight?"

"No can do."

"Day after tomorrow it is."

"You come late, Joe. At night."

"Until then," I said, hoping I came off as Cary Grant, but figuring I was again closer to Larry or Moe or Curly.

Back at our table, I read: *421 Hai Ba Trung Street.* I reread it, thinking how odd. This wasn't the Cholon home of Cackling Quyen. It was walking distance from the Fighting 803rd.

Ziggy had cleaned his plate and was working on CWO Buffet's. "He don't have an appetite, Joey."

"I don't have much patience left either."

I knew our con game was petering out. "Answer one question, Buffet. The little red book is yours and we're out of your life. What the hell goes on in the Annex?"

"We've been through this. That's classified top secret crypto."

I held up *Quotations*. "The brass gets wind of this, Buffet, they'll resurrect Tailgunner Joe McCarthy to ream you a new pooper."

"Why are you so anxious to know?"

"Curiosity," I said. "That's all."

"Tell me who you really are."

Ziggy said, "'After receiving political education, the Red Army soldiers have all become class-conscious and have learned—'"

"Please tell me who you are."

I tossed the book to him. He almost ripped a pants pocket stuffing it in.

"I'll give you clues to our secret identity, Buffet. Our primary MOS is Scrounger. Our secondary MOS is Fuckup."

Buffet snapped his fingers. "I have seen you. I've heard of you too. You work for Captain Papersmith."

"Guilty as charged. We still have a deal?"

Buffet didn't reply.

"Hey," I said. "We forked over the book in good faith."

"Curiosity is your only motive?"

"Scout's honor."

CWO Buffet sighed. "I can't tell. I can't."

"If you can't tell, then show. Your choice."

"Please."

"C'mon. Just a peek. We won't stay long."

CWO Buffet sighed louder. "Very briefly. Day after tomorrow, at nightfall."

"I'm tired of being put off a day," I said, exasperated.

"It can't be helped. I need time to invent an excuse to be away from the rest of the team."

Chapter Eleven

I do not dream in The Great Beyond.
Does anybody else?
Let me know when you get here. No hurry.
In The Land of the Living, shrinks say that if one cannot dream, one will go mad. Something to do with the release of whatever it is that must be released from the unconscious mind. Dreams are similar to a pressure-relief valve on a boiler. At a prescribed PSI, the valve pops and releases steam. If the valve doesn't pop, the boiler goes *ka-boom*.

Where I am now, there is no *ka-boom,* not inside my head, or elsewhere, not that I've heard. I won't go bugshit from not dreaming. I'm confident that I won't. My higher-ups have more creative ways to tailor a straitjacket for me.

I wonder if Smitty dreams. He's in The Great Beyond because of a *ka-boom* he himself triggered, the stupid murderous deluded little shit.

Can you keep a secret? It's only been a few days since he appeared and I already miss him. I am *so* lonely I'd miss Adolf Hitler.

I'm pitying myself and wondering about Smitty in slumberland when I hear a knock. I double-time it to the front door. Of course it's Smitty.

"Joe, we hate each other."

Dragon Lady

A statement, not a question. I say nothing.

"I am asking for your help. There is nobody else."

"Nobody else" is a heartless understatement. Smitty looks different. He was thin the other day, but now he's downright gaunt.

I ask, "What can I do for you? Would you like to come inside?"

He jabs a finger upward. "Does that music ever go away?"

I'd never before heard "Louie Louie" done on a harp. It ain't half bad.

"Afraid not."

"Come to my house, Joe."

Not until I have a little fun. I quote an unlovely query that was whipped on me any number of times during my cup of coffee at Sunday school. "Smitty, have you accepted the Lord Jesus Christ as your personal savior?"

He ignores my sacrilege. "Joe, to my house."

"Say please."

It obviously hurts, but he says, "Please."

As I trail him next door, it's dawning on me that his English is as good as mine. Was it before or have we been fitted with communication devices? Yet another unanswerable question.

I go in to furnishings identical to mine. The style is Early Discount Furniture Store. Lots of spindly legs and fake wood finishes. The sofa and easy chairs are unadorned and covered by upholstery made of materials not found in nature. Colors are non-colors--gray, tan, beige.

Smitty angrily flings open his pantry. "Look what they give me to eat."

Neatly stacked on floor-to-ceiling shelves is Spam, bags of pork rinds, canned hams, and pork and beans.

"This is worse," he says, gesturing to his fridge.

I look at a freezer compartment filled with pork loin and chops.

In the refrigerator compartment is bacon, sausage, sliced ham, and cartons of eggs.

"I am Muslim. To eat pork is forbidden. I have been living on eggs," he says, flapping his arms. "Soon all I can say is cluck-cluck-cluck."

The demented little douche bag has a sense of humor.

I say, "Terrorist cannot live by omelet alone."

Either he doesn't get it or he is so starved he doesn't care. "What can I do, Joe?"

I crook a finger. "Come on to my place. I think we can work something out."

We do, swapping much of my chow for much of his. I don't have sufficient variety to do the complex dishes for which I was noted as an executive chef, notably my creative sauces and soups, but now I can *cook*. A small victory for my stomach and my masters' sense of humor.

Smitty cannot get enough frozen mac and cheese.

◆

I did dream in the Land of the Living. But can you dream when you cannot sleep? I could and did on that 1965 night, Mai with me on every toss and turn.

Day after tomorrow night. 421 Hai Ba Trung Street.

That night was a cakewalk compared to some years hence, in my post-Vietnam, post-U.S. Army, worst Horse's Ass Phase, when I was a walking disaster. My ability to sleep and/or dream was the least of my problems. I was drinking far too much and my second ex-wife had had a bellyful. Blaming Vietnam for my outrageousness had become the most cacophonous of broken records.

This was when Richard Milhous Nixon and Henry Kissinger were withdrawing us from Vietnam a barrel of blood at a time, railroad tanker cars of it while they negotiated the shape of the fucking table with the boys from Hanoi.

This was when Vietnam was also Nam. This was when I heard too many guys who hadn't been there namedropping "Nam." This was when I'd challenge them, asking what right did they have to refer to Vietnam as "Nam." It was when I had the notion that only Vietnam vets were entitled to "Nam," even Joseph Josiah Joe Goldbrick IV.

Realistically and honestly, I was not entitled to "Nam" either, but they were a helluva lot less entitled than I was. So I had believed--after swizzle sticks from my Johnny Red and water numbered in the double digits.

I'd swivel on my barstool and ask for justification of the "Nam." If the reply was an apology, no sweat. But given the slightest provocation, him standing his ground, or worse, a smirk, or worst of all, an expression of pity, I'd un-ass him from his stool with a wild, drunken punch, and the donnybrook was on.

Back in Vietnam, as my alarm clock rang and rang, I slowly crawled out of bed. I didn't recollect when I last climbed out of the sack so early voluntarily. Last time I was up at this wretched hour was in Basic Training when they switched on the barracks lights and blew whistles, à la Sergeant Spangler.

Our Vietnamese pal Charlie had invited us to a public execution, a firing squad, at which the guest of dishonor, a wealthy Chinese rice wholesaler and speculator from Cholon, was to be staked in front of sandbags and dispatched to his ancestors. He'd been convicted of withholding the Vietnamese staple to reduce supply and raise demand, and, concomitantly, price, the grist of Econ 101.

Charlie told me to be out front of our hotel and don't be late. When they say dawn, he said, they mean dawn, a rare punctuality in this land.

After the execution, I'd have a normally abnormal day's duty at the Fighting 803rd, then a going-away party for an old buddy tonight. Tomorrow, a peek-a-boo into the Annex, then to Mai's.

Two big big big big big days.

The mufflerless jalopy on the other bunk was a snoring Ziggy. Although he'd never been to an execution either, he said to let him know when they started holding them at a decent hour, like high noon. He'd bring a box lunch.

Just as well. No way would both of us fit on the back of Charlie's Honda motorbike. He was waiting outside, silently chastising me for being late. My tardiness was due to my scrounging for a water glass that'd serve as a vase. I'd keep Mai's white lily in it until it turned into shriveled black goop.

Charlie and I slalomed through semi-dark streets, avoiding pedestrians and vehicles I couldn't see till we blurred on by so closely I could smell fish sauce and tobacco layered upon the smells of humanity and the smells of inhumanity. Bugs pinged against the Honda and us. I could not ascertain if Charlie's transportation had functioning brakes.

I yelled, "This guy they're shooting, how long was his trial?"

"Trial?"

"No trial?"

"Maybe trial, maybe no trial."

"How do they know he's guilty? How'd they convict him?"

"Rich Chinaman," he yelled in explanation.

Charlie's casual racism didn't offend me. He had nothing on us. Soldiers from northern states stationed in our South in the early- and mid-1960s spoke incredulously of bus stations with segregated bathrooms for His, Hers and Colored, of White and Colored drinking fountains. Of cross burnings illuminating the night sky, a white-trash jamboree, as American to the good ol' locals as apple pie.

I was reminded of Henri Michaux, an entertainingly-goofy Belgium writer. His *A Barbarian in Asia* routinely referred to Chinese as Chinamen. In one sentence, he wrote that Chinamen should be thought of as animals. In another, he suggested that the Chinaman could've invented the fork, but that the instruments required no skill or manipulation (as opposed to chopsticks), and was thus distasteful to him. Talk about contradictory feelings.

The busy noises of a new day were in the air. Americans claimed that the "gooks" were lazy because of their afternoon siestas and their passive ways, but here they were, up at first light, raring to go. Ziggy and I were likewise partial to siestas when we could sneak one in, as performing our duty at the 803rd Liaison Detachment when it was 100 degrees and 100 percent humidity, as it was every day, tended to enervate, whether we were doing anything useful or not.

"Always the Chinese," I yelled. "Always the same offenses."

"Chinaman make *bookoo* money on rice. Hoard rice. Price go up. Sell. Vietnamee no can buy. No eat."

If they shot everybody in this town who made a piaster under the table or on the war, they'd have to hold the executions in Arabia, where there was enough sand for the sandbags. Vietnamese Chinese had the rice trade sewed up, and Singh and the East Indians were the shopkeepers.

Both ethnic minorities were the engines of Southeast Asia's economy. Leaders who crowed like roosters as they gave the Chinese and the Indians the bum's rush in the name of nationalism soon had no economies. They were easy scapegoats, the Chinese in particular. Vietnamese Vietnamese liked Chinese Vietnamese as much as Vietnamese Buddhists liked Vietnamese Catholics. And vice versa.

I asked, "The latest coup, what's going on there?"

Charlie rattled off names, who was in, who was out. Thieu, Khanh, Minh, Chieu, Ky, Co, Thi. Some registered to me as major players in the ongoing soap opera. All were generals.

"Old general in National Palace," Charlie said, making a sweeping motion with a hand I wished he'd keep on the handlebars. "Fly out on Air France Caravelle jet. Go visit money in Swiss bank account."

"The new guys, any improvement?"

"Same same."

I wondered what the Dien Bien Phu ants thought of the Saigon political circus, the musical chairs. As much as I feared and loathed them, I severely doubted if North Vietnamese generals had Swiss bank accounts.

The execution was to be in a plaza between Cholon and downtown Saigon at an intersection of three wide streets. We made the scene as the sun was coming up.

The crowd was jam-packed, jabbering, shoulder to shoulder. We dismounted and Charlie walked his bike through. If he'd put the kickstand down and left it, he'd be Hondaless in two minutes flat.

We were fifty yards out when we heard a volley of shots. Charlie cussed in his own language, using fully half of my Vietnamese vocabulary.

I'd been asking myself since accepting his invitation if I was being polite or if it was bloodlust. And was my fussing to find a flower vase subconscious procrastination? That I was relieved we missed the killing provided the truthful answer.

"No sweat, Charlie. We'll catch the next one."

"We go up and look, Joe," he said, inching forward.

"In case they didn't collect all the body parts?"

"Soul not go when you killed as bad man."

"There's something to see?"

"No. Feel. In the air. For soul. Feel if it go."

"You believe that, Charlie?"

"Maybe believe. Maybe no believe."

This was the closest we'd come to talking religion. I wasn't sure if Charlie was Catholic or Buddhist or a member of my Atheist faith.

We pushed ahead, fighting a reverse tide. Spectators were listless and drowsy, yawning, breakfast on their minds. The fun was over, as if the gun ending a football game had sounded.

What remained were sandbags against a cement wall. There were holes in them, some traced with fresh blood. The guest of honor and the timbers they'd tied him to were leaving in the rear of an ARVN deuce-and-a-half truck. I saw a wooden post and the bottoms of his sandals. If Charlie felt a post mortem slipstream, he didn't say so.

We rode across the Thi Nghe Canal Bridge to the Dakao neighborhood and had French pastries and coffee at a sidewalk café that was Charlie's favorite. He'd introduced Ziggy and me to it, and we liked it, too. The place was far from Charlie's home and his hangouts. Having American buddies wouldn't set well with his cowboy pals.

When I bit into a rich pastry, I thought of the French. Most had skedaddled to France following the Indochina War, but there were signs of them, and not exclusively in the seedy swank of Tu Do. You'd hear their music on phonographs and jukeboxes. You saw their gingerbread on buildings. You'd hear French pop up in the vernacular, like Charlie's *bookoo* for *beaucoup*. I didn't know Charlie's parents, but I'd bet that if they'd gone far in school, they spoke fine French.

The French who stayed behind kept their noses a mile in the air, so superior were they to the natives and us American interlopers. To prove my point, I'd say hello to any I passed in the street. Bone-sewer Mon-sewer, bone-sewer Madame.

They didn't once disappoint me by reciprocating. La-di-fucking-da.

Charlie immediately began chain-smoking into the carton of Salems I gave him, the carton I'd held out after our black market foray with Captain Papersmith. It'd been a while since he'd enjoyed healthier, tastier American cigarettes. He thanked me up one side and down the other. He hadn't asked me for them—he hadn't asked us for squat, unlike a lot of locals who cozied up to GIs—so it must've been Christmas to him. Charlie's regular brand was Ruby Queens, so I regarded the Salems as an elixir. I didn't want his lungs turning into black goo by age forty.

I bought an English-language *Saigon Post* at a corner newsstand. The coup was front page. The new government was wonderful, the ousted government was inefficient and corrupt, blah blah blah. U.S. bigwigs were quoted as "hopefully optimistic and impressed by the new regime's resolve to eliminate corruption, to establish stability and to defeat communism."

Charlie was reading a Vietnamese paper that was all Greek to me. Napoleon stuffed in his mouth, smoke exiting his nostrils, he batted my newspaper with his coffee spoon. "Washington DC bosses, they say our new general good?"

"They love them today. They loved the old generals when they took over from the old old generals who they loved when they took over from the old old old generals."

Charlie laughed. Someday, I'd have to ask him what his real name was. But I never did. He was just plain Charlie to us. We'd ride him on that, asking him if he was a *Charlie*. He's say, and it made sense, "How can I be a Vietcong with that name? Am I stupid?"

Charlie was not stupid. He was around my age of twenty-four, short and thin as most Vietnamese were. He didn't have a GI haircut, nor was it Beatles long. Charlie's hair didn't attract attention, a wise move on his part. Far as I could tell, the ARVN Draft Board operated solely on wheels, no paperwork needed. The first thing they screened for was curly locks. If you were careless or vain about your coiffure, troops piled out of their trucks and asked for ID.

If your documents weren't in order or you didn't have a wallet plumped with piasters to buy invisibility, you'd get a free ride in the truck to Quang Trung Training Center. As the song went, you're in the army now. I'd witnessed desperate knock down-drag outs on the sidewalk involving guys reluctant to serve their country.

There was a piece in the *Post* on two more battalions of U.S. Marines landing at DaNang. I showed Charlie.

"Okay, good," he said through a smoke ring. "Kill VeeCee."

Charlie and I rarely spoke of the war, except how we were each in our own way avoiding participation in situations such as patrols and punji sticks and live bullets.

I asked, "What's your opinion, man? We gonna win?"

"Win."

"How come win?"

"VeeCee and Ho Chi Minh come Saigon, *fini* napoleon, *fini* Honda." He paused to run a finger across his throat. "No let that happen. Fight VeeCee to death. House to house, alley to alley. For democracy and pastry. *Fini* Charlie."

I laughed. "Familiar with Dien Bien Phu?"

He shook his head. "Dien Bien Phu no same same. Dien Bien Phu no nothing to what me and you speak."

"How do you figure?"

"Dien Bien Phu was Frenchie frog war, not American. USA have more plane, more tank, more chopper, more cannon, more rifle, more *bookoo* money than France."

"Will money win the war?"

"For sure," Charlie said. "French lose Dien Bien Phu and Hanoi. No lose Saigon. Vietminh no come Saigon. France go to peace talk, keep Vietminh out of Saigon. America stronger and richer. America keep Vietcong out of Saigon."

His Honda was on its kickstand at the curb and we were eating goodies. In Saigon. Therefore we were winning the war. If he lived in Hanoi, there would be no Honda, no goodies, because the French had lost their war. His illogic was logical.

"Know what else, Joe?"

I shook my head.

"South Vietnam to be American state. Number fifty-one state is number one. VeeCee no attack America. No can do." He tapped his temple. "VeeCee bad, but VeeCee no crazy."

Charlie knew that statehood for South Vietnam was in the works. Everybody knew. But if the rumor was legit, shouldn't it be in the *Post* I was reading? Six years earlier, in 1959, Alaska and Hawaii had been admitted as the 49th and 50th states. They'd already been territories, but still had to jump through hoops.

I'd been fiddling with a bottle of *nuoc mam* fish sauce on our table. It was as ubiquitous in their eateries as catsup was in ours. Charlie had told me that a Vietnamese could not live without *nuoc mam*.

I finally managed, "Charlie, what if an American GI loves a Vietnamese girl?"

He dropped his spoon on his saucer. "You?"

"No," I lied.

"Who?"

"Nobody. Anybody. Could the girl love the GI too?"

He looked at me and my flushed face, instantly seeing through my tissue-thin hypothetical boy-girl. "No can do."

"Why no can do?"

"Boy and girl no same same. Two different planet of friend Ziggy? *Bookoo* book he read on American spaceship to Mars. Vietnam girl, American boy—Mars and Earth. This nobody-anybody, if smart he forget love. Love taxi girl, love mama-san girl. Love her for two hundred Ps. When time to go home America, go home. Love American girl."

Charlie returned to his newspaper. He'd taken offense. I had encroached. I had exceeded limits. Friendship and sex, yea. Genuine intimacy, nay. Kipling's East-is-East ballad slapped my face yet again.

It was probably a product of my blushing chagrin, but I thought I'd caught a glimpse of my Lee Harvey Oswald facsimile, Chief Warrant Officer R. Tracy. He was on the next corner and then he wasn't.

I checked my watch. "Gotta go. I'm late to work. War is hell, man."

Charlie looked up from his paper. "War is hell if you in it."

On my feet, I asked, "What's on your busy schedule today?"

He lit a cigarette from the one he was smoking. "Stay out of hell."

Chapter Twelve

Despite having an East Indian doorman decked out like a rajah in a Khyber Pass flick, the Hotel Caravelle kept its doors wide open, its air conditioning on full throttle. To walk in front of the Caravelle on a concrete sidewalk radiating visible heat waves was to walk into a glacier.

Its top-floor bar boasted Saigon's hottest floorshow. Every night was the Fourth of July. At the horizon, artillery boomed and flares flashed and tracers streaked. Ziggy and Larry Sibelius and I sat quietly through three *Biere 33s* each and a serious barrage.

Make that six beers for Larry. He was matching us two-to-one, putting us to shame. I didn't recall him being such a sauce hound.

"You're pounding them down hard, short timer," I told him. "Not that I'm criticizing."

Larry Sibelius was a buddy from the Tan Son Nhat hootch where we'd briefly billeted. I hated Larry's guts. I hated him because he was shorter than short. Tomorrow, he was heading back to the World, to the Land of the Big PX. A Pan Am Boeing 707 was lifting off Tan Son Nhat at 11:15 in the morning. There was a seat on it with his name, rank and service number. I hated him doubly because at his final stop, Travis Air Force Base in

California, Larry Sibelius was receiving his army discharge.

Of course I didn't hate Larry at all. I just told him I did as we toasted him. Of course I didn't covet a discharge and a trip home either. Not any longer. I held that to myself, lest anybody overhear and have me hauled off to a loony bin.

Larry was a draftee, a medic at the USARV dispensary here. In my humble opinion, he was the finest chancre mechanic in the United States Army. Come down with a dose of the clap and go to Larry, he'd slip you a bottle of tetracycline, a self-cure that kept the infection off your records. There'd be no punishment if you had a prig for a company commander. There'd be no order to report to a chaplain for a lecture.

To further demonstrate what a terrific fellow Larry Sibelius was...a GI from a small compound in the Central Highlands near where Larry had been stationed earlier in his tour had been bitten by a stray dog. The compound's doctor had wanted to go by the book and give him the rabies series—twenty-some shots right through the stomach lining. Ouch. Double ouch.

Larry's friends had caught the pooch and had it choppered down to Tan Son Nhat, where it tested negative for rabies, so the GI didn't have to go through needle hell.

Larry Sibelius was a war hero up there, too. Charlie had mortared their compound one night. The attack had killed eight and wounded fifty. It had gotten a lot of press, and stateside readers began learning the word "escalation." Larry had been awarded a Bronze Star for heroism and a Purple Heart for minor injuries. Ask him to elaborate and he'd clam up. The subject was taboo.

Larry hoisted his beer bottle. "I'm too short to take your unconstructive criticism, Joe. Remember what I said I wanted to be when I grow up? Well, that was then, this is now. I'm devoting my life to a career that you gents were instrumental in inspiring me to, a career as a professional goof-off and pseudointellectual. I'm gonna be a beatnik. I'm gonna grow a goatee, recite poetry I don't like or understand, bathe when I feel like it, drink espresso and funny-colored liqueurs, and bang lady poets."

In 1965, most Vietnam duty was a cakewalk compared to what it would be a precious few years later. But twelve months in-country had changed Larry as it did everyone. When he'd arrived, his lifelong goal had been to go to med school and become a family physician. He had a BS in chemistry, the smarts, and the drive.

I chugalugged my bottle and raised the empty. "To Larry Sibelius, beatnik. To his ambition. To the American dream."

I was drinking faster, catching up to our esteemed guest. Mai had intruded, drifting in and out of my thoughts.

421 Hai Ba Trung. Tomorrow night.

"I'm pounding them down? Joe, easy, man, or you'll be on your lips and we'll carry you from bar to bar," Larry warned.

"Not me," I said. "I'm perfectly capable of crawling on my own."

"Joey's drowning his sorrows," Ziggy said, looking up from his magazine. On the cover, Sonny and Cher *doppelgängers* were in spacesuits with fishbowl helmets, strolling a moonscape that resembled green cheese. "Joey didn't get to see 'em shoot some Chinaman."

I told Larry of my morning tardiness.

Sympathetically, he patted my back. "Cheer up, man. There'll be other public executions. Corruption ain't going away."

I said that really wasn't it. Tongue loosened by the suds, I spilled my guts about my Dragon Lady.

Larry Sibelius listened intently and said, "How long've you been in Vietnam, Joe?"

"Eight months, four to go. You know damn well, Lar', and I know goddamn well where this's heading."

"How long since you been in the same room with a nice girl?" Larry asked.

Insinuation that Mai was not a nice girl came within an eyelash of getting the table tipped over on him. But I accepted and appreciated his context and his concern for me. Compared to Charlie's racism, Larry's was benevolent.

"That's got nothing to do with it," I said defensively.

"Zig, talk sense into this boy."

Ziggy had as many dead soldiers lined up on the table as me, but there wasn't enough ethyl alcohol in the city of Saigon to move him beyond a mild buzz. After twelve beers, he might belch, emitting visible shock waves.

"Joe, she ain't no girl. She's Vietnamese."

Larry said, "Well, if she is the Dragon Lady you've obsessed over to wretched excess, congratulations. I read *Terry and the Pirates,* too. Everybody who has comes here with the notion of finding his very own Dragon Lady. The exotic East, you know."

He tapped his temple. "As long as you separate creation from flesh and blood, you'll be all right."

He paused, waiting for my assurance. I didn't respond.

"You're not alone, Joe. Let's put it that way. The outcome may not be as important as the hunt. I envy you. You're persevering, you're maintaining your standards. Best of luck, whichever way it turns out. The flower-exchanging business is neat. You may have something going, but if your girl is like Terry Lee's, you've got a handful. I gotta worry about you boys in general when I'm not here to keep you off the straight and narrow?"

We clinked beer bottles and conversation petered out.

Skinny and intense, Larry Sibelius had thin hair that presaged cue-ball baldness by age thirty. If he had a family, dysfunctional or otherwise, I didn't know the details. Nor was he forthcoming about a stateside love life. Was he estranged? Had he been Dear John'd?

He was oddly sober, too, fidgety, picking at the label on his bottle. I asked, "What's wrong?"

He took a swig and said. "What I've missed in the Mysterious East is what's wrong. You and your Dragon Lady reminded me. Brought it to the surface. I'll never return to this country. Years from now I'll kick myself for not savoring the experience to the fullest."

"You missed getting killed. Barely."

"Besides that. I'm talking exotic and not only dragon ladies. No offense, Joe."

"None taken. Give us a hint?"

He gazed at the fiery horizon. "How much you think Madame Nhu would charge for a short time? How much for all night?"

I said, "I've asked myself that very question. More than you and I will ever earn in a lifetime. More than the Gross National Product of Vermont. Plus you'd have to fly to Rome, where she is with her daughter, conveniently abroad when Diem and Nhu were popped. Have you seen that little girl of hers? She's a doll."

Larry smacked his lips in agreement.

"They're irrelevant, too. They're not likely coming back to Vietnam, sure as hell not to have a ménage à trois with Larry Sibelius."

"Yeah," Ziggy offered. "You ain't got a Chinaman's chance with them."

"What else?" Larry coaxed with his hands. "The inscrutable Orient. A symbol thereof? C'mon, guys."

"What you dole out tetracycline and penicillin for?"

"Opium dens. Haven't you seen those pictures? These emaciated duffers flopped on bunks. Cribs, they call them. They're smoking pipes, a million miles off in the enchanted kingdom. Man, I haven't even smoked a reefer. How am I gonna be a respectable beatnik if I pass up this chance?"

"You can fake it."

"Karl Marx said religion is the opiate of the masses. Millions throughout the world use opium. If you ask me, opium is the opiate of the masses."

"Marx and Engels. *Das Kapital*," I said. "Workers exploited by capitalists so badly they can't afford to buy opium."

Larry said, "An Englishman in the last century wrote that when he took opium, it was music like perfume. He lived a hundred years in a single night."

Eyes locked on the travails of Sonny and Cher, Ziggy said, "In China, the struggle to consolidate the socialist system, the struggle to decide whether socialism or capitalism will prevail, will still take a long historical period."

Larry looked at me.

"Long story," I said. "What the hell does music like perfume mean?"

"Damned if I know, but it sounds cool, doesn't it?"

"What happened to the Englishman?"

"I think he died in the gutter, dreaming deranged dreams of crocodile kisses that gave him cancer."

"Swell."

"He's not the point. The experience is."

Ziggy and I hadn't gotten Larry a going-away present. We'd planned to surprise him with a massage and all the trimmings. So why not paid admission to an opium den? By God, like Doug Hooper and us lemmings hassling the frat rats after our induction physicals, I wasn't chickening out. I wasn't gonna be a pussy. I said to drink up and signaled our waiter for the check.

I'd thought finding an opium den would be a challenge, but the first cabby we asked said, no sweat, GI, he knew a good opium den. Number one. Best in town.

I wasn't too drunk not to cop a feel of the 25-caliber peashooter in my pocket. Saigon had no shortage of dangerous neighborhoods, and I doubted if your average opium den was on the same tree-shaded stretch of walled villas where MACV brass and foreign ambassadors resided.

The taxi halted on an unlit street.

I said, "Do we wanna do this? Sincerely wanna do this?"

No reply.

"Boys, this is not a rhetorical question."

The taxi driver broke the silence. "Uncle me. Two times week, go to den, smoke three pipe. Do for forty year."

"How long ago did he die?" I asked.

"No die. Healthy," he said.

"That's encouraging," I said without conviction.

The cabby drooped an index finger. "Uncle me, no can go boom-boom."

Okay, what the hell. There were worse things than winding up as an impotent dope fiend. But outside the taxi, Larry stood, not budging.

"Sorry, guys. I'll have to pass. I know I'm sobering up and chickening out and it was my bright idea. I'm afraid they may make us piss in a cup at Travis."

"No problem," I said, figuring that we had an out too. "It's not worth stockade time when you oughta be home and learning to be a civilian beatnik."

Larry took a deep breath. "I need to unload, gentlemen. I have to tell this to somebody or it'll explode inside me. My Bronze Star is bullshit."

"How so?"

"The VC who mortared us were damn accurate. It was the middle of the night and all personnel were asleep and unarmed except those on guard duty. The guard hootch was next to ours, where off-shift guards snoozed. They missed them, but killed three in ours, wounding the rest of us.

"I got off lucky. A few nicks, a little shrapnel. With the other ambulatories, we were airlifted to the hospital at Nha Trang for surgery either there or on to Clark Air Force Base. The second day I was at Nha Trang, a four-star general and a high Saigon diplomat and a big-shot civilian presidential advisor from D.C. came through our ward. You know who they are. They've all been on the cover of *Time*, even the arrogant, four-eyed asshole advisor.

"This general was warm and fuzzy. I think he genuinely cared about us. He shook our hands and said they got the VC who did this to us. They chased them down and made mincemeat out of them. True or not, we felt better.

"The diplomat was at his rear. He struck me as a good guy, too. He was warm too and shook our hands.

"Four-Eyes was another story altogether. He was sweating like crazy. He shook no hands. We had a great view of dense green hills inland a few klicks. There were booming noises in and to the immediate rear that had him nearly shitting his britches. The cocksucker couldn't get out of the ward too fast. That almost made their visit worth it. Almost.

"Four-Star asked us who'd been at the attack. All of us had. Four-Star proceeded to whip Purple Hearts and Bronze Stars on us. The Purple Hearts, fine. You're awarded one if you get a hangnail or if it's posthumous, no distinction. Bronze Stars are supposed to be for heroism, not being at the wrong place at the wrong time, snoring in the sack. My buddies who were blown apart, they were not alive to receive Bronze Stars and their Purple Hearts were given to their mothers and wives.

"Just our ward got the Bronze Stars. The trio had limited time before they moved on. It was public relations bullshit. If Bronze Stars are for heroism, why did we deserve them if we didn't at least have the balls to tell Four-Star we didn't deserve them? I have pondered my cowardice every day and have dreamt my cowardice every night.

"I've worn the decoration on my uniform. As you know, medals have currency in this man's army. NCOs and officers don't harass you. The medals made life easier for me. If I had stateside duty left, I'd pin the motherfucker on my forehead.

"I didn't want to smoke an opium pipe so I'll have a beatnik war story. I wanted to know if opium will make what I told you go away, if only for a few hours. If a pipe or two will make my dead hootch mates leave me alone. For any amount of time. Booze does not do the trick. Sleeping pills I steal from the dispensary do not do the trick. Opium is my last shot, my music like perfume."

Stone-cold sober now, Larry was sobbing, tears streaming. He was ramrod stiff, fists white-knuckled at his sides. Ziggy and I didn't say or do anything. Years in the future, men could hug men. Not in 1965, not unless you were queer and/or were behind closed doors.

I hoped the unburdening was a relief to Larry, though. Poor bastard, his skull was jam-packed with demons. We exchanged addresses and vowed to stay in touch, and Larry got back in the taxi.

We didn't stay in touch. That was typical of buddies in the service reentering the World and living hundreds and thousands of miles apart.

I've been searching for him in my The Great Beyond phone directory. He is not listed. Good. No hurry, Larry. If he is indeed leading a long and unconventional life, I hope it's been a good one. I do hope he is still ready, willing, and able to bang lady poets. Larry was far too hard on himself that long-ago night. He's had decades to shake those demons. I am cautiously hopeful that he has.

I led Ziggy to our music-like-perfumery and rapped on the door like they did at speakeasies on *The Untouchables.* It opened promptly. A man of a certain age greeted us with a nod and in we went. It was dark and ratty, smaller than I thought it'd be. Built-in cribs lined a narrow hallway, similar to mama-san's arrangement. They were uncurtained, possibly for the fire hazard, possibly because in the state of euphoria we were purchasing, privacy was of no consequence. Three or four of the cribs were occupied by bony Vietnamese geezers in undershirts, eyes at half-mast, lost in space. I didn't see much smoke, but could smell it hanging sweetly in the moist, stale air.

Everybody was too wasted to notice that we weren't your basic opium den clientele. We paid our money, a measly three hundred piasters each. A little kid who might've been the grandson of one of the old boys in the cribs prepared our pipes.

The pipes were bamboo, two feet long, with ivory bowls stained brown. The youngster kneaded a thumbnail-sized wad of chocolate-brown opium gum and pressed it into the bowl. He inverted the bowl over a lamp until the gum bubbled, then handed it to Ziggy. He repeated the process for me with assembly-line efficiency.

We took ours standing up, leaning against a wall.

The drug hit home fast, but not with the punch I'd expected. I did become light on my feet and feel carefree. I was no expert, but I theorized that the beer beforehand may've semi-neutralized the opium.

Ziggy had a coughing fit that would have woken up a normal household.

We finished our pipes, declined a second, and went out into fresh air. I was feeling a bit too drowsy for comfort in this unfamiliar neighborhood, but we found a taxi and got out of there safely.

In our room, the opium remained with me. The room spun in the opposite direction as the ceiling fan. I saw countless, imaginary geckos on the ceiling. I must have slept, for all night long I dreamt of Martians. They floated along the sky on pinkish-red clouds as if riding on the tops of blimps. My Dragon Lady was curiously absent.

In the morning, I told Ziggy about my Martians.

He asked me to describe them.

I couldn't. All that stuck with me were the pinkish-red clouds.

The Zigster said he hadn't dreamt about a solitary thing.

Chapter Thirteen

Smitty is going to become a pest. I am conflicted on how I feel about this, me and my melodramatic loneliness. The day after the food swap, he's at my door, already filled out a little from (presumably) gorging himself on the mac and cheese.

"Joe, please help me. I am required to pray on my knees to Mecca five times a day."

"So?"

"I do not know which direction Mecca is."

Who the hell am I, his ayatollah?

Nevertheless, I can't resist the challenge. I go out into the yard and look upward at our non-weather. It's noontime, so the sun should be high in the sky. Except that we don't have a sun. We have blue skies during the day, sometimes with a scattering of puffy clouds. At nighttime, the sky gradually darkens, as if controlled by a rheostat. It never is completely dark; there is an illusion of twilight. In the early morning, the process begins again. Outside temperature is always room temperature. Never in my tenure has there been a drop of precip.

I squint into a sky the color of blue topaz. I breathe deeply, breathing in no smells of humanity or inhumanity. I smell nothing. I find myself missing 1965 Saigon's nasal goulash.

I say, "That's a tough one, Smitty. Without a sun, we can't even compute north, south, east, or west. Then even if we do, where's Mecca from us, since we don't really know where we are?"

Smitty spreads his hands in despair.

Listen, I really and truly believe that the average Muslim, the vast majority of them, are good people. They're as appalled by the Smittys of The Land of the Living and The Great Beyond as I am. Those fanatics who made Smitty what he was and is are reprehensible to the extreme, but that's no excuse for the kid strapping on a cordite T-shirt, his mind on unsullied wall-to-wall pussy.

"Tell you what, let's establish where we *hope* Mecca is."

"I do not understand."

"I'll arbitrarily aim in a random direction. So long as you pray in that direction each and every time, it'll be a de facto Mecca that nobody can quibble with. Okay?"

"I think so," he says, puzzled, but too eager for a solution to debate my logic.

I extend my arms, press palms together, and point toward the strip mall's teriyaki shop.

"Okay?"

He beams. "Yes, thank you, Joe."

I go inside, wondering if their hologram teriyaki is made with chicken, beef or pork.

◆

We did have weather in 1965 Saigon, plenty of it.

Next morning, while Ziggy and I breakfasted on sweet rolls and coffee at a café near the 803rd, the sky blackened as if a bucket had been placed over the sun. A spectacular lightning display accompanied horizontal rain. Streams and puddles formed on the street. Whitecaps formed on the puddles.

Just as quickly, it was over. The sky cleared and pavement steamed, smelling like laundry. Saigon weather could change as rapidly as weather does these days on television news when the talking haircuts speed up satellite images for effect.

Despite humping a hefty poundage of mail and paper and punch cards to the Annex door, the day dragged. Hands on the 803rd's wall clock moved as if cast of lead. The only saving grace was that Colonel Lanyard and General Whipple were away, and that Captain Papersmith had no special assignments for us.

Behaving like a child whose parents had left him home alone, the captain disappeared for long absences, returning with alcohol on his breath. When in, he spent as much time in the colonel's office as his own. You'd have to be deaf not to hear drawers slamming. I believed I knew what he was doing in there. He had finally noticed that the Polaroid was missing from his all-American-family picture frame.

But why the colonel's office? Did he think Lanyard appropriated the photo as a fetish? I could not visualize the colonel playing with himself unless there was an army regulation (AR-658B, subheading 47) on Authorized Masturbation Procedure.

Any and all possibilities were irrelevant. The Polaroid had a permanent home in my shirt pocket, bonded to my bosom.

Ziggy took advantage of slack periods by curling up on the supply room desk, a woolly mammoth in hibernation. I considered writing a letter home, but had a nasty dose of writer's block. I had much too much on my mind.

I took advantage of my free time by badgering PFC Ambrose Bierce into joining me for lunch. I said I'd buy. My unenthusiastic guest and I went to a nearby *phở* café. I'd eaten there often. It was good and cost practically zilch.

Phở was a noodle soup. While we watched, the cook dipped a strainer of cooked rice noodles into a vat of boiling water to heat, yanked it out, and with a snap of the wrist, sprayed off excess water. Then he emptied the steaming noodles into a bowl and added broth, mystery meat and vegetables.

We foreigners regarded *phở* preparation as a theatrical meal, a minor floorshow. In my later career as a chef, as dishes became more and more complex and silly (i.e. food shows on TV), I increasingly admired *phở's* unpretentious simplicity.

The company clerk impatiently spiraled noodles around chopsticks. "I have a morning report to finish."

The army's morning reports are probably generated nowadays on wireless laptops, but back then it was on a painstakingly typewritten form completed by company clerks, few errors or strikeovers permitted. The morning report was the daily Sermon on the Mount, detailing any change in the organization's status—promotions, transfers in and out, discharges, AWOL. I was convinced that a crackerjack and corrupt company clerk could make an individual administratively vanish. I wondered what PFC Bierce's price was to do so. Hypothetically, mind you.

"Relax, Bierce. Papersmith isn't here to sign it anyway."

"Get to it, will you, Joe?"

"Get to what?" I asked innocently.

"Why we're here. To grill me on my claim that I'm Ambrose Bierce's illegitimate grandson."

I snapped my fingers. "Hey, since you mentioned it."

"The draft freed me of grad students wanting to use my background as a thesis topic. Now you come out of nowhere. In the army, of all places. "

"I'm buying lunch, Bierce. Be nice."

"I am not Ambrose the Trey," he began. "My father was Gwinnett Bierce, after Ambrose's middle name. Ambrose was thought to have had three kids. Gwinnett was the fourth. Ambrose was traveling with the Villistas during the Revolution, a freelance reporter seeking lively stories. There is no dispute about that. He became a favorite of Pancho Villa.

"The standard version of their falling-out, Villa having him taken for a stroll amongst the cacti, was because Ambrose was disillusioned with Villa's role in the Revolution. Ambrose shot off his mouth once too often, saying that Villa and his followers were no better than bandits.

"The truth behind the friction is that Ambrose knocked up my grandmother, one of Pancho's favorite girls. She had to escape or she'd share her lover's fate and be left in the desert for the vultures. She fled across the border to Nogales, where my father was born."

"Bierce was over seventy. Not the worst way to check out," I said.

"He made his living as a wise-ass and died as one," PFC Bierce said, nodding reverently. "There are worse epitaphs. Satisfied?"

"Yep. So how's *Jesus of Capri* coming?"

"A little further along than yesterday. Yesterday a little further along than the day before," he replied vaguely.

"I had an idea, an inspiration I'll whip on you for no charge."

"I'm listening."

"To spice up the plot, how about a triangle on the Isle of Capri?"

He looked at me.

"A swarthy Carthaginian slave and a ménage à trois."

Bierce made a face and returned to his lunch. "That's smut, Joe. Pornography. It is anything but literary."

A fat, walleyed French girl in a tennis outfit walked by us, presumably en route to the *Cercle Sportif,* the snooty French club that was open selectively to Americans of higher ranks. I'd seen her occasionally. After months in-country, many GIs came to idealize that rare species, the round-eyed woman. This one was blonde and freckled, which qualified her for deification. But I was immune. I had Mai, my Dragon Lady.

I watched the European goddess lumber by, she and her cottage-cheese thighs. I doubted if she played tennis in Saigon's heat. Nor would Lee Harvey Oswaldesque R. Tracy, whom I saw her pass two blocks hence. Chief Warrant Officer Tracy saw me seeing him and scooted, blending into the camo of crowded Saigon sidewalks.

"Bierce, that shit-eating grin of yours when I speculated on the fifty-first state rumor. What's the deal?"

He sighed and dropped his chopsticks into his bowl. "You know my other secrets, Joe, so why not this one? I started the rumor."

I answered with a skeptical smile.

"Prior to stepping off the plane at Tan Son Nhat, I started by telling all the stews. They were highly dubious, but the concept appealed to them compellingly. They'll tell it to all the officers they date while on layover."

"Assuming your nose shouldn't be growing, how come?"

"To end this abortion of a war. What state are you from, Joe?"

"Washington."

"What's Washington's capital?"

"Olympia. Ziggy knows them all."

"If Victor Charles tossed a satchel charge into an Olympia, Washington bar and killed a dozen state employees having a few after work, wouldn't our righteous wrath be upon him and everybody up the line of his chain of command, all the way to the top?"

"True. Go on."

"Same in Saigon, if it were capital of the American State of South Vietnam. An attack in Saigon is an assault on mom and apple pie. No difference. Toss a bomb into a public market, it'd be like hitting the Safeway in Elm City, USA.

"The Vietnamese have been beating off foreign invaders for two thousand years. If we make the South part of *our* country, we're no longer invaders, the North Vietnamese are. Curtis Le May and his Strategic Air Command would have carte blanche to drop his eggs if they misbehaved."

"I don't question your rationale, Bierce. I do question your ability to spread the rumor as fast as it's spreading."

"It's a hopeful rumor isn't it? If it's legit, most of us go home."

"Granted."

"Did you take a lot of math in school?"

I said, "I majored in it for one disastrous quarter."

"Did you cover exponents?"

"I don't remember what we covered."

"In the most basic definition, an exponent is a number raised to a power." He scribbled on a napkin: 2^2, 2^3, 2^n. "Two squared, two cubed, two to the fourth power. And the fifth. Two, four, sixteen, thirty-two, sixty-four, one hundred twenty-eight, two hundred fifty-six, five hundred twelve. That's where the word 'exponential' comes from. Get the picture?"

Him and Ziggy, a pair of polymaths who sure did know their math.

I said, "Every person you tell tells two people, and awayyy we go."

"Right. If you're asked if you could have one million dollars or a penny doubled every day for a month, most people will grab the obvious, the one million. In fact, if you choose the doubling penny, you'll have over ten million dollars in a month.

"Same principle. I pass the rumor on to everyone I can. It doesn't hurt that the bulk intensely wishes it to be true. To get the hell out of here ASAP and in one piece. They eagerly pass it along. If nothing else, it's a pleasant fantasy. Then it grows into something more. The ubiquitousness gives it currency."

"I'd like to volunteer Ziggy and myself to assist in this patriotic and mathematical endeavor."

"Welcome aboard," PFC Bierce said, shaking my hand. "This conversation never happened, you know."

"Top Secret Crypto is my middle name. The State of South Vietnam should have a state flower, though. If it's been picked already, it'll add texture to the rumor."

"Good idea, Joe. What flower?"

"Easy," I said. "The opium poppy."

PFC Bierce smiled. "State bird?"

"Whirlybird, the gunship species."

By the time we got to the state plant (shit-smeared punji stick), we were cracking up, pounding the table and howling, laughing so loudly that we were attracting an audience.

◆

Precisely at sundown, CWO Ralph Buffet appeared at the Annex, a colony of ants in his pants. Buffet wore dark glasses and palpable fear. The shades made him look like the world's clumsiest cat burglar.

"This has to be quick. You do promise to keep it under your hat?"

"Scout's honor."

"I can get the firing squad," he whined, unlocking the door.

I tried to cheer him up. "There are worse ways to go. Ambrose Bierce got it at age seventy-one for dipping his wick in the wrong place."

Buffet muttered unintelligibly, hurried inside, latched the door behind us, and flicked on the lights.

"Holy shit," I said, gawking.

Every single day in Vietnam I bumped up against the purely weird. But this little field trip took the cake. Walls and ceiling had been torn out to make one big bare room the size of a small gym. Mixed with the mildew was the aroma of a lumberyard. The only finished wall had cockeyed shelving, floor to ceiling. It held stuff we'd carried here to them: paper, punch cards and mail.

Air conditioners were bolted below sections of torn-out flooring and ducted to blow upward. Others were mounted on bare walls. They weren't plugged in and no holes were cut into outside walls. Cranked up full bore, I'd bet those babies could ice down Hawaii so thoroughly that you'd mistake it for Alaska. Strewn wiring evoked images of an explosion in a spaghetti factory.

"You know how many piasters and Yanqui dollars we could make selling those a.c. units on the street, Buffet?" I said.

"Don't waste your breath on me with one of your crooked schemes. Computers run extremely hot, Joe. We're not professional carpenters and we all have blisters from the work. The wood and the bigger computer components were brought in at night. The heaviest portion of the construction is done, and, as you see, the cooling is installed."

Computers? My 1965 knowledge of computers consisted of knowing girls who'd studied to be keypunch operators at business schools. They'd tended not to lay down for you without at least a hint of serious intentions.

"Like those big IBM machines the giant corporations have?" I asked.

"Ours is far more advanced," Ralph Buffet said proudly.

He swept an arm to a row of upright wooden boxes with their front sides removed. "These cabinets are to be moved into position soon. General Whipple feels that we're at a security-sensitive stage and should have 803rd people exclusively do the work, so you guys may be brought in for grunt labor."

"Uh-huh, right. They'll take us after they take Uncle Ho."

"We'll see." He led us to a row of tables and big funny-looking typewriters.

"Keypunch?" I asked.

"Correct. We've done substantial preliminary work on the blank cards. We'll be set to go when the hardware's memory is where it should be. We'll need much more stationery brought in."

"Swell," I said. "Are we your first party-crashers?"

"You are and that's not as odd as it seems. In spite of how the war is heating up, the 803rd works nine to five. This is smart. Up the street at USMACV HQ, Westmoreland has the troops riding their desks sixty hours a week, whether there's work to do or not.

"VC infiltrators observing midnight oil are aware that MACV typing is on schedule. We nobodies, not involved in that, not involved in anything particularly important, are innocuous, not worth any effort. We're invisible to the enemy."

I let him take the credit for Ziggy's insight. "No security is the best security?"

"Plus we're ignored by MACV. We're out of the table of organization, out of the chain of command. We aren't impeded by bureaucracy. We'll have the freshest data from troops in the countryside, straight from them to us. We can turn on a dime."

"'The masses have boundless creative power,'" Ziggy said.

"Excuse me?"

"Your boy, Chairman Mao."

"You'll never let me go, will you?"

"No comment," I said.

Ziggy and I inspected the upright crates. CWO Buffet hovered. "Please be careful. The thousands of vacuum tubes in the components are as fragile as eggs."

The gizmos inside the wooden crates were metal boxes larger than mess hall walk-in coolers. They had rows of buttons and lights and unrecognizable

153

doohickeys and those tape reels the mad scientists have spinning in sci-fi movies. The most advanced gadget across the street was a hand-pull adding machine.

Ziggy squinted at something with a bunch of square pushbuttons on it and said, "This story I read, *Killer Electro-Sirens of Mars' Moons,* they was dead ringers for this here."

"We can play cupid, Zig, this baby and them. Set up a blind date. Unless it'd be incest."

Ziggy presented a middle digit the size of a bratwurst. "Go do it to yourself, Joey."

CWO Buffet said, "The computer runs CAN-DO, our program."

"As in TV *program*?"

"No. Each of these tape drives has enormous memory capacity. Each holds 256K of core memory. That's 65,536 words, a small novel's worth if you require text. Can you believe that?"

Jesus of Capri and other novels on one of those thingamabob tape drives? That'll be the day.

"Nope, I can't believe. Can do can do what?"

"Computer Analytical Numerical Data Operations," he said. "In caps with a hyphen."

"CAN-DO," I said, feigning a swoon. "Pentagon poetry is so damn lyrical. What *can* CAN-DO do?"

"We have every confidence CAN-DO can and will significantly shorten the war."

"How?"

Buffet shrugged. "I really don't know. None of us know. The specifics are classified at the highest level. Our access to incoming mail is compartmentalized and we've been repeatedly warned of dire consequences if we even think about comparing notes. We won't be told until we implement CAN-DO. The general and colonel may know, but they've given us no indication that they do. They do screen the mail here before we input one word or digit."

"Shorten the war, my ass. It can't shoot nobody," Ziggy advised.

"CAN-DO can do everything but. CAN-DO does the computation drudgery that men perform. It does it considerably faster and does it flawlessly, as well as analyzing and collating data.

"The ship with the remaining tape drives has docked on the Saigon River. They'll be here momentarily. The computer console, the keypunch terminal, and the magnetic drums, too. The drums hold an incredible six megabytes of random access memory!"

"Super duper," I said to be polite. The only mega bite I knew of then was Ziggy in a mess hall.

Today, we all know that six megabytes is less than zilch. Today you can buy a five-buck flash drive the size and shape of a stick of gum that'll hold a thousand times as much. But who'd've guessed that was possible in that prehistoric computer era?

"We'll be in business! Computers have two major elements. Hardware and software. The hardware is the Cerebrum 2111X, which we'll soon assemble. The *software* program is CAN-DO."

"Hard and soft," I said. "We got some kind of kinky innuendo going on here?"

"The guys who invented all this, were they pounding their puds?" Ziggy said.

Without replying to us, Buffet expanded, his computer jabber delving into vacuum-equipped feed arms, card readers, 36-bit integers, main processor logic, and floating point arithmetic. It went beyond all-Greek. It was ancient Greek.

I said, "I'm still not getting it, Buffet. Why a super-powerful and super-secret computing machine right here, deep in the heart of Saigon? We've got the climate of a sauna and you'd have better security than the ARVN and local fuzz if you hired playground monitors."

"Speed. As I'd stated, the capability of turning on a dime. Reaction time is virtually instantaneous. Instead of mailing the punch cards to the Pentagon and queuing up for time on one of their machines, we can do it on the spot. A lightning-speed modem will transmit our data to the Pentagon at 2400 baud."

"Okay, sure, I see," I said, although I didn't. I don't think my smart parents and smarter brother would see either. This was Buck Rogers stuff beyond even Ziggy. He knew sci-fi computers inside and out, yeah, but CAN-DO was out of his league.

Once, the Zigster had told me that someday computers will be no larger than a kitchen stove and we'll all have one at home that can balance our checkbooks. It seemed ridiculous in 1965. Insane.

"You've heard the saying that the right hand doesn't know what the left hand is doing."

"Sure," I said, "I learned it in Basic Training."

"Well, electronic data processing picks up everybody's bits and pieces. CAN-DO arrays the information in a usable format." He paused in awe. "CAN-DO is the most sophisticated program in the world. It'll be running in the most advanced hardware in the world. The Cerebrum 2111X isn't remotely close to being available to business, industry, and universities."

"A chance to work on the most-advanced CAN-DO, is that why you joined the army?"

"Yes. I was recruited for this specific project by the Department of Defense."

I had one problem with this specific project. If CAN-DO did arithmetic faster than a hundred or a thousand or ten thousand smart people, why the hell didn't the army draft a hundred or a thousand or ten thousand more troops with slide rules who were good at math? GIs worked cheap, didn't cost squat to maintain, and didn't belong to a union. Nor did we/they use the huge amounts of juice the Cerebrum 2111X will when fired up. There was no use arguing common sense with a true believer like Buffet, so I didn't.

Ziggy chimed in with Buffet. "Mariner 4's flight ain't possible without computers. The spaceship got one on board. Otherwise it'd get lost in outer space."

"So it'd have to pull over at an asteroid and ask directions at a gas station, Zig?"

"Lick my dick, Joey. Mariner 4's central processor and sequencer operate stored time sequence commands via a 38.4 kilohertz synchronization frequency as a time reference. Data's stored on a tape recorder with a capacity of 5.24 million bits for subsequent transmission. A command subsystem that simultaneously processed twenty-nine direct command words or three quantitative—"

Ralph Buffet gaped at him, an oddball to the oddest oddball.

I sensed what was coming. They'd be yakking indefinitely. I thanked CWO Buffet and said I had to scoot. He didn't hear me. Ziggy either. He wasn't finished with Mariner 4's innards.

When he was done and I was slipping out the door, Buffet told Ziggy he liked science fiction too, rattling off magazines and books he'd read, and various intergalactic heroes.

An oddball digging sci-fi.

Knock me over with a feather.
Outside, I saw a light on in the colonel's office.
I scrammed.

Chapter Fourteen

At the restroom of our sumptuous quarters, after letting the water run until it was transparent, I had a washcloth bath. I hoped that made me olfactorily (a word?) presentable. I'd clung to Mai's white lily, having transferred it to an empty Johnny Red bottle on our dresser. I theorized that the Scotch residue might provide nutrition and act as a preservative. It was hopelessly shriveled and bowed, but I added water nonetheless.

Wasting no time, I departed for 421 Hai Ba Trung, canceling any benefit of makeshift bathing. Compared to the Hai Ba Trung tag, our Main Street and Grand Avenue and Sunset Boulevard names were prosaic.

Hai Ba Trung celebrated the Three Sisters Trung. In 40 AD, they led a revolt that sent Chinese conquerors boogying. Then they proclaimed themselves the queens of an independent Vietnam. Three years later, China counterattacked in overwhelming force. Figuring death before dishonor, the Trung sisters plunged into the Saigon River.

I was on the lookout for a hostess gift, anything but flowers, which would be trite and repetitive. At this post-dinner hour, nothing decent was available except food and drink, and the wares of hustlers hissing at me from doorways. I had to chance it that I, Joseph Josiah Joe IV, was sufficient reward.

The address was a three-story apartment house of patchwork design with a rear courtyard, eight to ten units altogether. It was the sort of place that attracted a combination of middle-class Vietnamese and short-term Americans. My Dragon Lady hadn't given me her apartment number and I hadn't thought to ask. As I was beginning to suspect that she'd been jerking my chain, she peeked between third-floor curtains and crooked a finger.

I zoomed up the stairs without touching them. She opened her door and my legs damn near went out from under me. Mai was wearing gold hoop earrings and a metallic red dress. The dress had a tall collar. It was floor length and slit at the sides. She was the cartoon panel from my wallet she'd torn up, with a jasmine fragrance to boot.

I stammered an apology for my tardiness.

"It is fine, Joe. I just cut up pork."

Had we discussed this as a supper date? I nodded approvingly, confused.

Her tone was semi-obsequious, spoken with a hint of a curtsy. This was neither the flesh-and-blood Dragon Lady I knew nor the exotic she-devil I'd fantasized.

"I really really like your dress, Mai. Really."

"Thank you, Joe," she said demurely.

Mai took my hand and gave me a tour of her pad. The main room held a bed, a nightstand, a wardrobe, and a small dining table. A ceiling fan slowly paddled slabs of warm, moist air. An adjoining bath contained a shower and bidet. The latter had me wondering yet again about French hygiene habits. The kitchen was narrow and efficiently laid out, a sink, small fridge and gas range side-by-side. An open porch held an enclosed toilet. It was the European style, featuring an upper tank and a pull chain.

A small bookcase atop her bedside nightstand caught my eye. Some titles were in Vietnamese, some in French, some in English. They were college texts. The English titles: Engineering Drawing, Principles of Trigonometry, Intermediate Surveying, Solid Geometry.

"Impressive," I said. "Yours?"

She hesitated. "My father's."

"He was an engineer?"

"It was long time ago, Joe."

"Where's your family from?"

"The north."

"Dien Bien Phu?"

"Why you say that?" she asked, startled.

"No reason."

"Father dead long time," she said.

"I'm sorry I'll never meet him. I know some math. A little. I know exponents."

"Are you hungry? I am," she said, abruptly ending the subject.

Mai was making a stir-fry, and I insisted on assisting her in chopping vegetables. To a Vietnamese male, kitchen duty was probably emasculating, totally unthinkable. No matter. We were side-by-side, shoulders grazing. The business of food preparation kept conversation banal.

I was all thumbs, fortunate that I didn't lose one. Some greens I recognized, some not. Mai seemed not to mind that I hacked them into uneven sizes and shapes.

In the early 2000s, in one of the last restaurants at which I was executive chef, and one of the most successful, I introduced The Dragon Lady, a highly popular dinner entrée. The meat and vegetables I remembered from this memorable evening were sliced expertly by my staff, then sautéed rapidly in sesame oil and a high-octane mix of peppers and herbs.

Mai cooked them with the pork in a wok. She served the luscious mix, a steaming rainbow, over a bed of rice. It'd dawned on me far too late to bring a bottle of wine. It wasn't a normal accompaniment to Vietnamese cuisine, but a nice Western touch that Mai had anticipated, as she went to a cupboard for a bottle of a California white with a 1963 date and a PX price stamp.

"I buy dress today," she said, as I popped the cork. "You like?"

"Oh, yeah. I like it very, very much," I said, understating.

"Cartoon lady in your wallet, I want to be pretty as her."

Be cool, be cool. This is not the Friday afternoon sock hop. I am not in the seventh grade. Think romance. Think suave. Think Cary Grant.

"She should be half as pretty as you," I said as we clinked glasses.

A sip by her, a gulp by me. We ate a quiet dinner and killed the wine, mostly my doing. I got up to take the dishes to the sink. Instead, I bent behind her. I kissed her ear and cheek and lips, first gently, then less gently.

She rose and turned into my arms. My hands slid to perfect buttocks as I kissed her lips, her neck, her cheeks. She pushed me back.

"Joe, we leave dish. I go bathroom. You go bed."

Just like that. I didn't have to be asked twice. Mai switched off all lights but the kitchen's. It cast intriguing shadows. She brought out another red garment from the wardrobe, this one flimsy and gauzy, and went into the bathroom with it.

I didn't know if I was disappointed that she was so compliant or whether I was elated. Fast and easy were relative terms, I rationalized as I peeled off my clothes in record time and got under the bedding, a sheet and a lightweight blanket.

This was a war zone, after all. Locals lived in an inflationary economy inflamed by us aliens and our money and our appetites. The wishes of our hosts, these strange little yellow people, be damned. A lady did what a lady had to do. But this lady was feeding me and breeding me, and she hadn't asked for a single piaster.

As Mai ran the water, I lay on my side, up on an elbow, facing the bathroom. Speculation on what she was doing in there had me on the ragged edge of shooting my wad.

I tried to concentrate on the technical books, contemplating vectors and theorems and exponents. If that didn't control my hair-trigger glands when she returned, I'd conjure myself falling out of an airplane, driving a car over a cliff, chatting with my stepdad, any distraction to settle me down, to spare me sticky mortification.

Complex geometric angles and parachuting sans a chute were not doing the trick. I could focus only on that closed bathroom and what she might be doing in there. I forced my gaze to the wardrobe, an ordinary assemblage of shellacked wood. I noticed that Mai had left a door ajar. There was a blouse hanging in it that was too long for my Dragon Lady.

I slipped out of bed and investigated. The blouse wasn't a blouse. Nor was it red and filmy and gauzy. It was a familiar shade of green, baby-shit green, better known as olive drab. It had the consistency of cardboard. It was a set of United States Army fatigues, shirt over pants on wire hangers. On one collar was a silver colonel's eagle, on the other the crossed muskets of the infantry. The name strip above a pocket: LANYARD.

The colonel had requisitioned more from Captain Papersmith than an air conditioner. This is where he'd been earlier tonight. No wonder Papersmith had been tearing Lanyard's office apart for the Polaroid. He knew perfectly well where the colonel went on his overnight business trips.

I hadn't an inkling what Mai was wearing or not wearing when she came out of the can. I was in bed, in shock, staring at the ceiling fan, thinking that sloppy seconds was the last thing in the world I wanted. She got in beside me and snuggled against rigor mortis.

"Joe, what wrong?"

She knew good and goddamn well what was wrong or she'd have exercised discretion and shut the closet tightly. "Who's paying the rent here, Mai?"

She reached for me and repeated, "Joe, what wrong?"

Thanks to that wardrobe and its contents, my equipment was as limp as her lily. "Erectile dysfunction" and the myriad therapists who treated it were in the distant future, along with the miracle stiffener pills advertised on NFL games. But whatever you wanna call it, it was a literal anticlimax to what should have been the most glorious evening in my twenty-four years.

"Mai, Who. Is. Paying. The. Fucking. Rent?"

My Dragon Lady got my message and got into my face, eyeball to eyeball.

"You are first man I know, Joe?" she counterpunched. "I wait all my life to starve to death waiting for you?"

She had a valid point, I again rationalized. It was my own fault for putting her on a pedestal that extended into the stratosphere. She did have to eat. She could be a housemaid for Americans or a shop clerk and make a lousy $50 US per month, or do what she was doing for big paydays. That she was a "bad" girl should have heightened my desire, not extinguished it. But I was too immature to stop pouting.

Behind the scenes, Terry Lee's Dragon Lady was no cherry. I had come to that realization when I'd learned what a cherry was. So what was my problem?

Mai straddled me and fumbled. Same pathetic result. She fellated me expertly and futilely, another wobble in her pedestal. I should've responded instantly to her advanced skills, but I contracted further.

She sighed angrily and sat up, cross-legged, immodestly displaying all. "Okay Joe, I know Dean. I know Jakie. I know many men. You think me virgin who wait for you forever, Joe? You and Dean and Jakie same same. All American same same, American think you fuck me, you own me."

The "fuck" jolted me, another ludicrous and confused reaction to my idealized Dragon Lady's behavior. I had to admit that fear was also a major factor in sending my family jewels scrambling for cover. If Colonel "Jakie" Lanyard walked in, the unpleasant surprise would be mine. I continued my pout.

"Okay, Joe. You be baby-san. I thought you like me."

"I do like you. I like you a whole big bunch," I said. "Tell me, Mai, where do I fit in? My army rank is way, way below colonel and captain and everybody. I'm twelve grades below nobody."

Mai was all seriousness, she and her exposed womanhood. She was as unsexy as it got. "Joe, you listen to me. Dean talk big shot. He talk computer. He say he boss of computer. Dean afraid to come here. He know Jakie come here. Jakie pay rent. Dean go to sister me, Quyen, where you see me, I see you."

"Yeah, Quyen. What's she all about?"

She glared. "No talk Quyen."

"Why not?"

"Jakie no talk. Even when I spank him like he like. Jakie no talk 803rd and what they do. But he sometime talk in his sleep. No understand. He grind teeth. He scare me when he sleep."

No comment on Quyen and, aha, the top-secret computer thingamabob at the Annex. It's what the officers and I were to her. Papersmith and his blabbermouth, what'd he told her?

"Dean doesn't know as much as he has you thinking he does," I said.

"Dean, he drink and drink. He pass out. He speak Mildred in sleep. Sometimes wake up in cold sweat."

Who could blame him? "You really spank Jakie?"

"Spank hard as I can. He like."

I had blackmail leverage over the colonel if I were foolish enough to give it a whirl. The sick puppy had a .45 on his hip and ached to use it. He'd put an end to my extortion attempt with a lead slug.

"Why are you so curious what the Fighting 803rd does?"

"What you do in Annex, Joe? Tell me."

I shrugged. "I don't do anything in the Annex. Ask Dean. Ask Jakie."

"Dean start to talk. Then he stop and say nothing."

"I know nothing, Mai. That is the honest truth."

"What you know, Joe? You say you no big shot. Maybe you lie. Talk to me on computer and 803rd."

"Mai, why do you want to know about some computer? I know of no computer."

"Tell me. Show you love me."

"Huh?"

"Is trust, Joe."

Is bullshit, I thought.

"You trust me, tell all about you if you love me. Can have no romance if no trust."

"That's romance?"

"Romance is have no secret, Joe. You no trust me, how can I trust you. No trust, no romance."

So Mai had added spy to her Dragon Lady résumé. Terry Lee's Dragon Lady's politics were slick and expedient, but I didn't recollect hardcore espionage in her curriculum vitae.

That demure servility jazz when I'd arrived tonight was right out of Miss Coquette's Finishing School. A setup. It'd lull me into pillow talk after my femme fatale and I had screwed each other's brains out. This evening was down the crapper, an unmitigated disaster. I climbed out of bed and started dressing.

"Jakie speak statehood, Joe. He say statehood make South Vietnam part of America. Fifty-first state will be America. He say statehood *fini* war. Dean speak statehood. People on street speak statehood for Vietnam. You know statehood, Joe? Is computer for statehood?"

When I enlisted in PFC Bierce's Army of Misinformation, the budding novelist hadn't specified that our rumor-mongering had to be confined to Americans.

"Statehood for sure, Mai. In fact, a state gemstone has already been picked for the State of South Vietnam."

"Gemstone? Jewel?"

"Uh-huh. All American states have state gems and flowers and trees and various stuff. South Vietnam's is gonna be the star sapphire."

"When?"

Statehood, my ass, I thought. Her tactic was to pry open my mouth talking statehood guano, then segue to the computer.

"Statehood's coming soon. Mai.

"When?"

"Soon. C'mon, once more, Mai, why are you so curious what the 803rd does?"

She replied by unzipping me and groping between my legs. No improvement.

"Cerebrum 2111X. What computer look like, Joe? What it for? Statehood?"

"What computer? What statehood?"

"Joe, you go. We have next date when you not so upset, okay?"

"The 803rd is strictly a liaison detachment. We do liaison. All we do is liaison. Detachedly. Scout's honor."

"Scout? Who is scout?"

"Long story."

"What liaison mean? I never know."

"Liaison is communication. Between groups, different army outfits. And whatnot."

"Communicate what?"

"You want the truth, Mai?"

"Yes. Truth."

I knelt to tie my shoelaces. "Liaison is usually gossip. You know, like old ladies at the market."

"Communication on fifty-first state?"

"Oh yeah. Definitely."

"You say liaison is communication. Communication on what else? You like me, Joe, you trust me. You talk to me."

I sprang up. "Talk to me about where you're from, Mai. Romance is no secrets, right? No trust, no romance. So talk to me about your textbooks. Talk to me about who was before Dean and Jakie and me. Talk to me about your older sis, Quyen, okay?"

"No."

"Why not?"

"No!"

"Talk to me about—"

"You talk first, Joe. I ask you first to talk."

Piss on it. I skulked out. No goodbye kiss was offered or given, nor even a bon voyage.

When I reached the ground floor, it'd completely sunk in. My Mai, my Dragon Lady, wasn't merely a high-class whore. She was without an iota of a doubt a *Commie spy*. A Mata Hari, an Ethel Rosenberg. My Dragon Lady was *the* Dragon Lady in spades.

Cerebrum 2111X. What computer look like, Joe? What it for? Statehood?

Hell's bells, she'd known of the computer machine in the Annex long before I had. What was she trying to squeeze out of me?

On the sidewalk, my erectile dysfunction was history. I sprouted a boner that wouldn't quit and limped home.

Chapter Fifteen

I have a permanent case of erectile dysfunction in The Great Beyond. Whether it's been programmed into me by my masters or it's just me, it's a good thing. What am I gonna do with a boner? Unless Smitty's promised seventy-virgin-strong harem appears and he's willing to share, the desired outlet is an impossibility.

I'm thinking about this one morning as I lie in bed, looking at the ceiling and listening to "Bridge Over Troubled Water."

And smelling cigarette smoke.

I'm dressing while I go to the living room window and open the drapes. Sitting on the porch of the house to my right is a plain and dowdy woman in early middle-age. She is of average height and weight, and appears shapeless in a flowered dress. Her hair is unkempt brown, streaked with gray. She stares off into some middle distance as she blows a smoke ring.

I tuck my shirt in, slip into shoes, and go outside. I'm too anxious to see who and what she is to tend to personal hygiene. I don't think she'll mind.

"Who the hell are you and where the hell am I?" she looks at me and asks in a husky voice.

"I'm Joe and where we are is a good question. I call it The Great Beyond."

She takes a big drag, exhales, and after a pause, says, "The great beyond. Yeah, that makes sense. I'm Madge."

"Your cigarette, where did that come from?"

"I guess it come here with me. They don't let you smoke, but they do let you after your last meal."

"Last meal?"

"Tater Tots and corn dogs. My favorites." Madge touches a bruise on the vein between her forearm and bicep. "They say lethal injection ain't bad if they do it right, and they did. Beats the holy hell outta your other choice, the chair. They say smoke curls outta your ears while you're still alive."

"Why?"

"Why what?" she says, flicking her smoke onto to her lawn after she lights another one from it.

I can't be sure she's real. "May I touch you?"

She treats me to a smile and a rotting picket fence of yellow teeth. "I gotta take off my panties?"

I feel myself redden. No erection is forthcoming.

"I don't mean that way."

"Maybe later on you can touch me where you wanna touch me, but I don't know you good enough yet."

I touch her arm and feel flesh.

"What did you do, Madge?"

Expressionless, she looks at me. "I went and poisoned three husbands for the insurance. They only caught me on the last one."

"Oh."

"His name was Earl and he deserved it, insurance or no insurance. He used to slap me around."

"Uh-huh."

"What's that music we're hearing?"

I say, "Elevator music without the elevator."

"Don't they do nothing decent like shitkicker?"

"Not that I've heard."

"Who lives on the other side of you?"

"A young man named Smitty. He is--was a suicide bomber."

"Like them over there in those A-rab countries?"

"You got it."

Her face is a question mark. "Why would you kill somebody you don't even know?"

I walk back home, wondering *why me*? Why did our gagster rulers give me neighbors who are multiple murderers? Yeah, I made my wives' lives miserable, but I didn't *take* them.

◆

I shook Ziggy out of a sound sleep and told all, including my miserable miasmic mortifying manhood malfunction.

I told him of my subsequent arousal, concluding, "It's as perverted as it gets, man."

He was sitting up, wide-awake. "She a VC secret agent, Joey?"

"Damn good question, Zig. It's looking to be leaning in that direction. It is. Yes it is."

"If she's VC, it's good you couldn't do it to her. They stick razor blades up their twats, you know, before they take on GIs. That's a known fact."

"A real turn-on, Zig. Yeah, I'm afraid it's not a case of her subscribing to *Popular Science* and acquiring an interest in electrical computing doodads. I do not think that's the crux of her curiosity. The weirdest is that she wouldn't let up on the fifty-first state happy horseshit either."

"Report her, Joey. If she's a commie spy, she oughta be gangbanged by everybody in town, then hung up on a flagpole, and afterwards shot for treason."

"Lighten up, Zig. Nobody's perfect."

He was sitting up in bed now, a fleshy pyramid. His blunt, often frightening features were soft with brotherly concern. Christ, how I loved the guy.

"Her letting you see Lanyard's uniform and quizzing you on the Annex, I don't get it, Joey."

"That bothers me too. The way she had the closet door open, she might as well have had a neon light on his fatigues. If she's a secret agent, she wasn't being very secret."

"Who's that dumb broad, she opened up this box and out flew this shitstorm that messed up the world forever?"

"Pandora," I said, shocked that I knew something that Ziggy didn't. "Pandora's box."

"Yeah, her. That's how come she let you see Lanyard's uniform. Your commie girlie, she was setting Pandora's box in front of your nose and you went and opened it up. Irregardless of why she did it, that's what she did and what you went and did."

"Shouldn't the captain and the colonel be turning her in? I mean, maybe the Cerebrum 2111X is no big deal. If it is, it's not Mai's fault they talk to her and talk in their sleep. They're as guilty as she is."

"You're making excuses for her, Joey. You're pussywhipped and you ain't even got into hers yet. You're a lovesick puppy dog. Lemme get back to sleep."

"Sorry for the wakeup, Zig. Thanks for listening."

"'Things develop ceaselessly.'"

Him and his Chairman Mao. I crawled into my bunk and dreamed horrific dreams.

♦

In the morning, Captain Papersmith was in. Colonel Lanyard was in. We knew this since we overheard Colonel Lanyard in his office. He was reaming Captain Papersmith a new pooper. Coming through loud and clear were "can do," "mission," "behave like an officer in the United States Army," and "you aren't the only swinging dick in this outfit who has personal problems." The colonel had a megaphonic voice when he was agitated. If he yelled "about face," GIs from here to Quang Tri would snap to attention and do a one-eighty.

When Colonel Lanyard said, "that's all, dismissed," we scrambled outside, waited five minutes, and went back in, pretending to just arrive. Saving face wasn't strictly an Oriental notion.

The captain pretended not to notice. He pretended to concentrate on paperwork. He did not appear to have been crying, but his eyes were red and he looked like death warmed over.

♦

The next few days were routine, as routine as routine could be at this goofy time and place. Oh, with the exception of the tarantula. We came home one afternoon and there it was, on the wall above our swelling mound of library books. Ziggy damn near climbed the opposite wall, wearing an unfamiliar visage of fear, eyes widened to fill half his face.

"Relax, Zig. They aren't aggressive, and their bite, while painful, isn't especially venomous, and not fatal."

"You sure? How do you know?"

"One quarter as a biology major was not for naught."

"Maybe your girlfriend and her commie pals who planted it here don't know they can't kill you, Joey."

"Well, while they're common in the tropics, it's odd we haven't seen one before," I conceded.

"Shit, Joey, it's big enough to have tattoos."

I selected a hardcover, John Updike's *Rabbit, Run*, and nudged the novel under the remarkably compliant spider. Amused by Ziggy's seismic footfalls in the hallway, I chucked it out the window.

The subject of critters in the arachnid persuasion did not come up again.

◆

Days passed

July 4, 1965 did, too.

Independence Day of a nation far far far faraway.

In Saigon, it was just another Wednesday. Even if I'd had firecrackers, I wasn't dumb enough to light them off.

I wrote Mother, omitting sidebars on computers and large, hairy spiders. I received a letter from her the same day. Both hers and mine were terse and bloodless and excessively polite.

Mariner 4 was inexorably closing in on Mars. Ziggy spoke of little else. PFC Bierce worked like a dog, laboring ceaselessly and agonizingly on *Jesus of Capri*. Unless it was my imagination, his widow's peak was in full retreat.

Ziggy and I had lunch with Charlie in Dakao. He was running low on Salems. We said we'd see what we could do.

My Dragon Lady was nowhere to be seen except inside my skull. She had become a cautionary tale. If she was a North Vietnamese operative, I was culpable by association. At best, I'd be tagged a commie symp. Dean and Jakie, too. If I were sent to a gallows built for three, it was scant consolation.

I reunited the Polaroid of her with horse-faced Mildred and the urchins. Upside down. Captain Papersmith seemed not to notice.

The oddballs stepped up their pace, to hell with nine-to-five. They came in earlier, left later, and had their meals delivered to the Annex by Tan Son Nhat mess hall cooks. Ziggy and I did our coolie labor, doing what the Vietnamese used water buffalo for.

We unloaded crated Cerebrum 2111X and CAN-DO parts, of which we remained officially ignorant. Each unmarked box that came via military trucks felt heavier than the last. We left them at the door for the oddballs.

As they clumsily schlepped the stuff into their inner sanctum, we'd overhear them chattering their computer gobbledygook. I mean, what the hell were central processors? What were thyratron tubes? They were as excited as if rehashing an important football game. Texas and Alabama in the last Orange Bowl, a topic of that magnitude.

CWO Ralph Buffet did not know us. It was as if we'd been zapped by one of Ziggy's sci-fi invisibility rays. I didn't like the snub. He could've nodded, for Chrissake. I was tempted to loudly inform him in the company of his colleagues that his latest issue of *Pravda* was waiting for him in the mail room.

At deliveries and within the Annex, General Whipple and Colonel Lanyard frequently supervised. Captain Papersmith was the odd man out. Every day at ten, he'd shuffle out of his office, his mind light years in outer space, like Ziggy's. Off he'd go in the deathtrap Jeep the colonel didn't need because he never went anywhere unless he was away on overnight business, the nature of which I knew all too well.

On one such morning our curiosity got the better of us. Ziggy and I flagged down a motorcyclo and said to follow that Jeep. Captain Papersmith drove straight onto Tu Do Street, made a left a few blocks from the Hotel Caravelle, and parked smack-dab in front of the GiGi Snack Bar.

Though "Snack" was commonly in their names, bars in this town that catered to American troops did not customarily serve food, not that you'd care to eat it. Snack, Ziggy and I presumed, was a misspelling of snatch, which they did serve.

That trip with Sally to D.C. and the Vietnam War Memorial? It hadn't been our final journey together. While I was still able to get around unaided, before the morphine and respirator and canes, Sally had surprised me with a trip to Saigon, tickets already purchased, hotel reservations made. I could not say no and I could not love her enough, though I was no longer able to express my affection physically.

As we know, Saigon is now Ho Chi Minh City, and North and South Vietnam are simply Vietnam. The 17th Parallel that separated North and South is merely a dotted line on a map. Americans can ride a train from Ho Chi Minh City to Hanoi. They can tour the Ho Chi Minh Mausoleum. If they don't mind the long lines, they can even have a peek at the old boy preserved under glass.

The GiGi is gone, surely victim of the campaign against counterrevolutionary attitudes that commenced when North Vietnamese tanks rolled into town in 1975. If the GiGi Snack Bar's girls continued cadging Saigon tea

("You buy me drink, GI, okay?") and selling short-times, they did so in a rural reeducation camp.

Sally gave me carte blanche to go anywhere, to do anything I wanted to do. I confined field trips to what I knew and where I'd been in Saigon. Like any city after decades, some things are different, some not. We didn't address it in words, but I knew that carte blanche included a search for my Dragon Lady.

Hell, I didn't even know Mai's last name. Before the trip, I'd Googled Mai and gotten 450 kazillion hits, no help whatsoever. Perhaps if I'd pressed Mai harder for a last name, I could've narrowed it down. She had so many secrets, a significant component of her allure.

Vietnam's population is 85,000,000, greater Saigon's 6,000,000. I don't know what I'd've done if I had her full name and address. And I had Sally's feelings to consider, too.

Another surprise awaited at a two-day Maui layover on the return leg, to buffer our jet lag. In a Paia watering hole, I met an antique hippie, a florid white man in his early sixties. He had skinny arms, a W.C. Fields nose, and a pot gut. He wore a gray ponytail in braids, a tie-dyed shirt, a doo rag, the whole kit and caboodle.

He sat with a woman who wore earrings in her nose. Forty-something, she had abundant tattoos, stringy blond hair, and no bra under her sleeveless T-shirt.

Coincidentally, the hippie had gone to Vietnam, too, in the past year. It was his first visit. He'd been a draft dodger, sitting out the war in Canada. He wanted to see what he'd missed.

As he prattled on about air pollution and food poisoning and pictures of Uncle Ho all over the place, my instinct was to knock him off his barstool. Sally, reading me, stroked my arm, gently biting my shoulder, whispering, "easy, easy." I had neither the strength nor sufficient inclination. We spoke further and he turned out to be a fairly decent person. His woman, too. After a second round (nonalcoholic beer for me), I felt no malice. I even bought them a drink.

Ziggy and I walked into the GiGi and found the captain sulking alone in a corner, his back to the door, not a super-duper idea in that era of *plastique.* He was chasing shots of *Rhum Caravelle* with *Ba-mi-ba.* The girls in their skintight, slit-up-the-side Suzy Wong dresses swiveled at the bar, giving us the onceover. They weren't hustling the captain to buy them Saigon Tea, which was plain bourbon-hued tea in shot glasses that you paid whiskey prices for. They knew him. Our intrepid commander was a GiGi regular.

Me leading the way, we went to him and stood at attention, sort of. The captain finally looked up and blinked at us.

"Private Joe? Private Zbitgysz? Aren't you men on duty?"

"Yes sir. We came by to check on how the papers promoting us to PFC and our MOS change to clerk-typist are coming along, sir."

"Uh," he said, straining his pickled brain.

"Just kidding. We're worried about you, sir."

"Worried about me?"

"Because of your obvious worries. The weight of your responsibilities."

"Oh, yes, thank you, men. Take a seat."

I took a seat. Ziggy headed outside in search of a newsstand and the latest on Mariner 4.

The captain raised his empty glass and two fingers. In ten seconds flat, a Suzy Wong'd cutie-pie had drinks on the table. If the ARVN worked as quickly and efficiently as Saigon bargirls, they'd've kicked Victor Charles's ass out of the South by 1961. The Vietnam domino would be upright, anchored in concrete.

I raised my shot glass in toast. "Thank you, sir."

He drank. I did not, as the locally distilled *Rhum Caravelle* tasted to me like a mix of Bacardi and kerosene.

He stared at me. "I should be a happy man, but I am not. War is hell."

It took a moment for it to sink in that he'd actually said *war is hell*.

"Well, sir, war or no war, you ought to be happy. Shouldn't you?"

He smiled sadly. "Why is that, Private Joe?"

"You're a commissioned officer with an important job, sir. A company commander and unit adjutant. You have a lovely wife and family at home. And you have, you know, the lady in the Polaroid."

"Ah, my assignation. I never did thank you men for your cooperation that day, not to mention your cigarette rations. It's difficult in an inflated wartime economy for a Vietnamese national to make ends meet.

"Therein lies the crux of my dilemma, Private Joe. Mai has forsaken me, a circumstance entirely attributable to rank being pulled on yours truly by an officer of superior rank, although not of superior character. I do not wish to elaborate. My life is going nowhere and I endure a loveless marriage. Those difficulties are relatively trivial. Have you ever had the misfortune to meet the girl of your dreams?"

I looked over at Ziggy, who was still outside, and said, "Afraid so, sir."

He sighed. "I have met my romantic Waterloo."

"Sir, please spit out what's bugging you."

He drank as he pondered my request.

Behind the bar, arms folded by the cash register, was the GiGi's mama-san. The owners and managers pulled sentry duty at the money, that or be stolen blind by the hired help. This mama-san was somewhat older than her girls. She wore heavy makeup and had a beehive hairdo that'd put any sorority girl back home to shame. A little lumpy, she still had a few curves. Mama-san licked her upper lip for my benefit, to let me know the coach was capable of coming off the bench.

Was she the cackler, Quyen, Mai's mysterious sister or whoever the hell she was? The They-All-Look-Alike Syndrome struck again.

I cocked a thumb toward her.

"She's an attractive lady, sir," I said. "The mature ones, they know all the tricks. They've written the book on tricks."

"You misinterpret, Private Joe. I come here exclusively to drown my sorrows. She does not comprehend why I demonstrate no sexual interest in her or the GiGi staff."

I wondered too. "Believe me, lack of interest in nooky happens to everyone occasionally, sir. Unfortunately."

Blearily, Captain Papersmith leaned forward on his elbows. "This is confidential, Private Joe. Classified information. The war is winding down in our favor. There's no guarantee how long any of us will be in-country."

Had he also patronized an opium den? "Won't utter a peep, Captain. Is what's going on in the Annex a factor?"

"Joe. Off the record, there's a new wrinkle. It comes from the highest level and is accelerating the situation. You can say nothing, even to Private Zbitgysz."

"Sir, honestly, you can trust my complete discretion." I lied, such a blatant lie that I crossed my fingers under the table.

He whispered, "One word. Statehood."

Saying "statehood" like the lout and his "plastics" to Dustin Hoffman a couple of years later in *The Graduate*. Bless you, PFC A. Bierce.

I hoisted my eyebrows theatrically. "Wow! For certain, sir?"

"Shh!" he said, giving me a spittle shower. "I don't have the fine details."

"Sorry, sir. Mum's the word."

"The process is so advanced that they've even selected a state gemstone."

"Which is?"

"Sorry, trooper. Classified."

"Of course, sir. But come to think of it, there is a rumor to that effect circulating all over town. Just yesterday, a taxi driver told me that the state insect is to be the tarantula. I thought he was raving. I didn't understand his context till now."

"Poppycock! What would a common cabby know of a high-level Pentagon and White House initiative?"

"Excellent point, sir."

"I require advice, Private Joe. Man to man. I shall elaborate on what I said I did not wish to elaborate on."

Captain Papersmith paused. This was a struggle for him. Me too. I sure as hell was no *Dear Abby*.

"Thank you, sir. I'm flattered."

"You're a man of the world, Private. Lord knows from your personnel jacket, you've lived."

"I have *beaucoup* methods of messing up and *beaucoup* practice at it, if that's what you're driving at."

"Exactly. We learn by our mistakes and we learn from the mistakes of others." He belched softly. "Colonel Lanyard ordered me to report to a senior chaplain he knows, a lieutenant colonel. How the colonel discovered my illicit love, I cannot imagine. Colonel Lanyard said I was immoral, a degenerate. A *degenerate*, Joe! I had no choice but to obey and report to the chaplain. The chaplain ordered me to end my illicit relationship and beg my wife for forgiveness. *Ordered* me."

How slick. Discover his "illicit love." The officer corp's means of eliminating competition. Order the suitor of inferior rank out of the picture. Mai stoking this nutso soap opera, walloping the colonel's bare ass, she was even craftier than I gave her credit for.

"A chaplain can't order you in terms of religion and morality. Can he?"

"It may have been a figure of speech. He did, however, make his views crystal clear."

"Ordering you to behave, sir, I'm not grasping that."

"This is the army. What is there to grasp?"

I'd learned early on from guys who made the error of confiding their indiscretions to the wrong chaplain. You could bank on one-term chaplains maintaining confidence. Lifer chaplains, not all, but a small percentage, ingratiated themselves to their commanders by snitching.

"How did you leave it with this chaplain, sir?"

"I agreed and thanked him profusely for showing me the light. Anything to terminate the session."

I was getting pissed. "Wanna know what I think, sir?"

"Please."

"Basically, sir, the chaplain was telling you to keep your pecker in your pants."

"Crudely stated, Joe, but, essentially, yes."

"With all due respect to this godly, high-ranking chaplain, sir, your pecker is your very own pecker, not his pecker, not Jesus's pecker, not God's pecker. Your pecker is government property only insofar as what it's attached to for a given length of time. Your pecker has Constitution-mandated, inalienable rights that are none of the chaplain's fucking business. He can do whatever he wants with his pecker and so can you within the parameters of the law."

"Quieter, Private," Captain Papersmith said, showing his baby's-ass-delicate palms. "I do appreciate your concern."

"Ever see the flick, *Elmer Gantry,* sir? You don't know that this chaplain isn't a Reverend Gantry. You don't know how he uses his own pecker."

"Granted, but keep your voice down."

I leaned forward on my elbows. "Sir, impending statehood or not, everybody and his brother is saying the war's heating up, so the VC may not surrender soon enough for any of us to go home except in a rubber bag, so no one can blame you for living for today. Piss on Lieutenant Chaplain Colonel Fire and Brimstone, sir. Fuck him and the horse he rode in on."

"Your recommendation has merit, but there is a complication."

"Yes sir?"

"I wrote Mildred asking if I might bring home a Vietnamese woman as a nanny. Our son has behavioral problems and our daughter is a budding nymphomaniac. The children are nearing adolescence. I argued that it might not be too late for the kids if a woman who has endured any number of hardships took them under her firm wing."

I resisted shaking my head in disbelief.

"Yes, yes. I know, Private. Having my cake and eating it too. Our two-story home has a basement with a mother-in-law apartment that is suitable for Mai, and Mildred sleeps like a log. But Mildred immediately saw through my subterfuge and is demanding a divorce. To compound my woes, Colonel Lanyard denied my application for compassionate stateside reassignment to iron things out. I have a quandary, do I not?"

All I could do is confirm that he indeed had himself a moral and practical quandary. A woman he thinks he loves versus the slide-rule heiress, he couldn't have both.

He shrugged helplessly and signaled for refills.

Abby herself couldn't wriggle him out of this one.

Chapter Sixteen

Like Las Vegas casinos, The Great Beyond has no clocks, no defined seasons that I have thus far detected, no encouragement of circadian rhythms. It logically follows that our new life spans are infinite as we've already expended our The Land of the Living life spans.

Make sense to you? I hope so. I hope I'm right, too.

The bad news is that my immediate neighborhood has gone to hell, even if there is no Heaven or Hell per se. Factor in the elevator music (today's selection: "Sloop John B") and the lifestyle jokes that seem to be at my expense, and I am in a state of limbo.

Smitty has become a full-blown pain in the ass. He has come to regard me as his mentor. Whenever he bugs me, I play along, partially because of loneliness--I haven't seen Madge outside again--and partially to get under his skin.

Today, he comes to me and says, "Joe, something is wrong with my television programming. Can you help?"

For Chrissake, I can't even help with my own. The only station running for the past week is Channel 82, the afternoon talk show. LBJ and Ho Chi Minh are having a marathon debate on the War, talking nonstop 24/7. Uncle Ho speaks in Vietnamese, Lyndon in Texan, a drawl that never forms complete words. I have no idea what they're saying, but they understand each other well enough to interrupt and yell and shake fists.

I tell Smitty, sure, and fish a stack of TV dinners out of my freezer compartment. It's time for another food swap anyway.

In his living room, he says angrily, "Look. What is this?"

What the black-and-white footage of deserts and tanks is, I think, a documentary on the Six Day War, which took place in June 1967, when Israel duked it out with Egypt, Syria, and Jordan. It was no contest. The Israelis rolled over them and wound up with a bunch of new territory.

Having to raise my voice because the sound is on so high, I summarize the war for Smitty and say, "Yeah, that was a couple of years after I was in Vietnam. There were jokes about Egyptian tanks having a reverse gear."

He looks at me.

"Where's your sense of humor, kid?"

He holds his remote control like a club. "I cannot turn it off or change channels or even mute the sound."

"I have some maintenance issues with my boob tube too, Smitty."

"What is this language they are speaking?"

Damned if I know. I open his fridge and say, "It's all Greek to me, but it's got to be Hebrew. Hey, how's your bacon and pork chops holding out?"

◆

Ziggy and I were spending our nights in a different breed of limbo. Like children on restriction, we'd been ordered to new quarters: bunks in the 803rd Liaison Detachment's supply room.

It was not punishment for misbehavior, but rather to keep tabs on us and our strong backs, which were often required on minimal notice, as supplies and machines arrived at all hours, at an accelerated pace. The Annex must've been packed to the gills. Cerebrum 2111X and CAN-DO had to be on the verge of being operational.

We were incarcerated slaves, secured by a front-door lock Ziggy could pick in the span of a yawn. The Annex's stepped-up regimen also demanded our scrounging skills to acquire matériel neither shipped in nor previously anticipated. Our leashes temporarily cut, we filled shopping lists. They were eclectic, as if from a frat house scavenger hunt: copper wiring, plastic tubing, adhesive tape, odd-sized light bulbs, a miscellany of screws and bolts. We came through on these special assignments, with and without the aid of Mr. Singh. Brigadier General Whipple personally issued us the piasters I estimated we needed.

"Seed money," he'd quip as I stood in his doorway at the position of attention, palm extended. "It is planting season."

His terrarium/office smelled increasingly pungent and mossy. It was as choked with growing things as the deepest, darkest, triple-canopy jungle. Light from the windows did not filter inward. I swear I heard monkeys and exotic birds.

One evening, Mai knocked on the 803rd's door and called to me. Mai, who I'd tried and tried to make go AWOL from my every thought. She'd slipped a note under it, saying she'd like to see me, friend to friend, an innocent outing, my choice of where and when.

I carefully analyzed this overture, and its possible consequences of dishonor, a general court martial, the death penalty, et al. I analyzed it for at least a hundredth of a second. My trepidation lasted a full one-thousandth of a second longer.

My heart and my groin overrode my brain. I slipped the note to my Dragon Lady, my Mata Hari, saying YES!!! TOMORROW?

She asked when and where. I suggested eleven in the morning and would she like to go to the zoo? I'd been meaning to visit it anyway. Yes, she wrote back, she would love to. She'd meet me there, by the big cats.

When she was gone, I consulted Ziggy.

"Whadduya think, Zig?"

His face was in a story anthology. The jacket depicted a free-for-all battle of flying saucers and spacewalkers brandishing ray guns. A wacky scene then, but commonplace decades hence in video games.

"It's your ass they'll fry."

"I always cherish your advice, man."

♦

The Saigon Botanical Gardens and Zoo, on the northeast edge of downtown by the Saigon River and National Museum, wasn't as rundown as I thought it'd be, but it was getting there. The larger animals, such as the big kitties, appeared moth-eaten and on short rations. Some showed their ribs. I pictured French men and ladies in the 1920s taking their kiddies here, the girls carrying parasols, the boys in knickers, rolling hoops.

I'd halfway decided to bag it, to stand her up. I didn't need her kind of trouble. But when I spotted my Dragon Lady at a distance, my heart rate accelerated to the redline. To hell with the perils of associating with an enemy agent. Fuck it, bring on the firing squad.

"My entire life," she said when we met and shook hands, "I no go to zoo."

Giving her a unique experience in her homeland puffed my chest. "My first time here too."

After the zoo, we both wanted to walk around, and central Saigon was compact. I showed her what was left of the U.S. Embassy. Boarded up and in the process of being cleaned out, it was ugly and chilling. I was gauging her reaction, a half-assed loyalty test. To be a spy was one thing, to wear the sapper's hat quite another. She shivered in real or mock horror and made no comment.

At the Port of Saigon, vehicles and crates and pallets were filling up dockside space, with more ships queued up to unload. We came upon gray waist-high bales of raw rubber that caught my attention. They'd been trucked or barged in from plantations. And I'd thought all rubber was synthetic.

I told her about Ziggy, our bet whether he could sail a rock across the river.

"You were bored?"

"I'm not now."

"Me neither, Joe."

"Too bad it's not earlier. The Central Market is closed for the day and hosed down," I small-talked. "It has it all if you can stand the smell. I once bought a whole pineapple from a lady for three piasters. The lady peeled it for me like an apple and stuck it on a stick."

Mai insisted on my trying an encore performance. We did find a pineapple lady on an adjacent corner, and to Mai's delight, I ate it all and made a sticky mess of myself to boot. As she dabbed me with her hankie, laughing, I fought off wasps and various flying critters on the attack. Great fun.

There were smaller markets and shops on nearby streets. I pointed at cans of cottonseed oil stacked at a sidewalk stall. Below the clasped hands on the label was DONATED BY THE PEOPLE OF THE UNITED STATES OF AMERICA. NOT TO BE SOLD OR EXCHANGED.

"Our tax dollars at work," I said.

Mai didn't get it.

"See, we send Vietnam all these goodies," I explained. "The cooking oil's useful, but it's in gallon tins. I'd be worrying it'd go rancid in the heat. Look beside it. Canned sardines. Catsup. Mustard. I've even seen peanut butter, which the average Vietnamese will upchuck at the sight of. Folks don't always steal this stuff. They buy it from somebody who sells it to buy food they appreciate, like dried fish and rice."

"I buy oil. I no have more oil. I fix you dinner again, Joe."

As if nothing had happened, pun intended. As if our first dinner date hadn't been a fucking disaster (adjective intended). Was I in for an intelligence grilling? Were her espionage colleagues lying in wait in her apartment to inject me with truth serum until I told all? And/or to shove bamboo shoots under my fingernails? I visualized nasty pieces of work who looked like Richard Loo in *The Purple Heart* and an Oriental Peter Lorre.

I recklessly blurted, "Okay, but my turn, Mai. I'm cooking."

She smiled and nodded in acquiescence.

As a food preparation expert, I had one tiny problem. I hadn't boiled an egg before the army made me into a cook. In their cooking school, my skills regressed.

"A gallon's too big," I guessed, delaying the subject by hunting for her oil.

We found a one-liter bottle of sesame oil from Thailand.

"You are expert army cook, Joe?"

"I can cook. Sort of," I said. "Not as well as you, but the army made a cook out of me."

Mai asked, "Have you ever cooked Vietnamese food?"

"No."

"What food you most like to cook?"

"Uh," I answered, stumped.

"When you boy-san, you dream of you a chef?"

Little did either of us know that the chef dream came far later. From this moment to my zenith as an executive chef at swanky downtown restaurants, it was a jump from kindergarten to grad school.

"No, and they don't train chefs in the army, Mai. They train cooks. They assigned me to cooking school after Basic, not on aptitude or personal choice, but because there was a slot. An opening to fill. I was happy because it was preferable to the infantry. Mess halls are warm and have roofs and you don't get KP because the KPs are accountable to you."

"You proud of your work?"

"One time only. It's the highlight of my army career. Have you eaten Italian spaghetti?"

"No."

"I love spaghetti. Not army spaghetti. The way they do it, you have a sauce mix that comes in powder in gigantic cans," I said, stretching my arms, exaggerating slightly. "You cook hamburger in pots. You add water and the powder. You can drain the hamburger grease if you feel like it. Some cooks do, many don't, so what they're ladling up in the chow line is an island of red goo inside a moat of orange grease. It's served on noodles that are either wet and mushy or stuck together like glue from being dried out."

Mai made a face.

"One spaghetti day there was a crate of tomatoes we'd forgotten to cut up into a salad, and they were going overripe. I ran to the post library and checked out a cookbook. I chopped the tomatoes into the standard sauce to simmer. I cooked the hamburger and drained the grease. Added some herbs I found nobody'd touched in years. You had to wipe the dust off the labels and it was hard getting the lids off the bottles."

"GI like?"

"Oh yeah. The troops gobbled it down and asked for seconds. It's unheard of to ask for seconds in a mess hall with the exception of lifers whose taste buds are shot. My timing was lousy. The post mess officer made a surprise inspection. He gigged us, saying my spaghetti didn't follow regulations. He warned me not to do it again, and the mess sergeant chewed my butt royally."

"I am not good cook."

"Yes you are, Mai. You're a wonderful cook. I know that to be a fact."

"Cook Italian spaghetti for me, Joe."

"Today?"

"Yes."

We shopped, improvising: Chinese noodles, a can of clasped-hands stewed tomatoes, mushrooms that looked like eels, a long, skinny loaf of hot-out-of-the-oven French bread, and a jug of Australian red wine.

At an herb stall, the wares were aromatic and alien to me. After I sniffed my approval of a half-dozen of them, Mai negotiated in mile-a-minute Vietnamese, and I paid. In Saigon, shopping was same-same as buying a car at home. You did not pay the figure they wrote on the windshield with shaving cream.

At her place, hers and the colonel's, I didn't beat around the bush. I opened the wardrobe. No fatigues, no sign of "Jakie." For whatever reason, the technical books were gone from her nightstand too.

Were we starting from scratch?

"Just you, Joe," she said, reading my mind and kissing my cheek.

Perhaps it was just *me* now or perhaps Colonel Jakie Lanyard was temporarily unavailable. Everyone at the 803rd was working long hours, as I would have been too today if I weren't presently AWOL.

I could've pressed her for specifics, but I quit while I was ahead. I didn't know what I could believe. I did know what I wanted to believe.

I nuzzled her. She giggled, punched my gut, and shoved me into the kitchen to get to work. Recalling the sequence of my fabulous army spaghetti, I busied myself with the meal. I'd forgotten to buy grated cheese. That was fortunate. Dairy products were as palatable to many Vietnamese as peanut butter.

The dish didn't turn out badly. It was a seminal meal too, a subconscious trigger to my eventual profession. Mai cleaned her plate and proclaimed it a feast.

We left the kitchen mess and made out primly on the edge of the bed, as if we were nervous teens on her parents' living room sofa after the prom. Mai groped my crotch and confirmed that erectile dysfunction was a thing of the past. Mai went into the bathroom and emerged in her red Dragon Lady dress.

Oh, boy, she had my number. Call it a fetish, call it kinkiness. I didn't give a diddly damn. I removed the dress, carefully lifting it over her head, my hands grazing her sides.

In her underwear, she retired to the bathroom. Water ran. I went to the window, to pull the curtains entirely shut and the shutters too. Across the street, sitting at a phở café smoking a cigarette was CWO R. Tracy. I think it was him. *We* were all beginning to look alike to me.

A dim bulb finally flicked on. Tracy and the CID weren't hounding me. Not me individually. Not her individually. Tracy was bird-dogging Mai *and* me, a spy and her stooge. CWO Tracy was building his dossier for my arrest and trial.

Let him prove it, I thought. He was facing our way, L. H. Oswald smirk on his puss. I flipped him the bird. If he saw my middle digit, he pretended not to.

Mai came out of the bathroom, my evil Dragon Lady. I dropped to my knees, lifted her negligee, and kissed her between her legs, tasting honey. If I had it, I'd've given her the H-bomb secret if she asked, not caring if she was Uncle Ho's daughter.

She lifted me by the hair and shoved me onto the bed. I was all over her, she all over me. I was embarrassingly quick. If I wasn't a limp noodle, I was hair-trigger.

I apologized. Mai pinched my butt and said not to. She said we had all night. Sure enough, the second and third times, she beat me to the moon. We fell asleep in each other's arms.

There was no probing on Cerebrum 2111X and CAN-DO and statehood for South Vietnam, then or throughout the night. Nary a word.

Why not?

I'd mull that later.

Chapter Seventeen

Knock me over with a feather, I have a *dream*.

In it, I wander off my cul-de-sac not on to another, but to what can best be described as a Hooverville. It is a filthy dirt street lined with tarpaper shacks with roofs of scrap tin. A ditch alongside the street is a lazy creek of piss and shit.

"Refinance your mortgage?" someone calls out from a hovel.

"Don't have a mortgage," I say truthfully.

"Have you researched gold futures, friend?" a slicky boy across the way asks. "Come on in and we'll talk. We can double your money in fifteen days."

The scent of greed and cologne makes my eyes water. I walk faster.

"By golly, before I repair your TV, the first thing we have to do is fix you up with a service contract."

It's becoming stereophonic. Where is the elevator when I really need it?

"Free investment seminar, lunch on the house, choice of chicken or fish."

"I'm not a spammer. I provide information."

"All we need is a credit card number."

"No, friend, it isn't a time share. It's interval ownership. View of the ocean. This offer is good only today."

The last is the scariest and creepiest of all. A recruiting sergeant in a booming voice: "Mr. Joe, enlistment gets you the school or duty station of your choice. Choice not chance. Get drafted and you're at their mercy."

I run out of there and wake up.

◆

"Your shit is flaky, Private Joe. Get your shit together or I'm gonna jump all over your shit," our Basic Training platoon sergeant had advised me in triple-digit decibels.

This had been directly following a barracks inspection. Our bunks were mandated to be made so tightly that a quarter would bounce on the blanket. My bedding had no elasticity whatsoever. It was the texture of cottage cheese. Forget a bouncing quarter. A Ping-Pong ball would've landed on it with a dull thud.

I'd considered telling the sergeant that housekeeping wasn't my long suit. If he didn't believe me, ask my mother. I'd had the good sense not to, but thanks in large part to my pathetic effort, our platoon failed the inspection. The sergeant had "jumped all over my shit," doubling my KP duty.

I was back in the luxury of our hotel room with Ziggy recollecting that experience. Our room *was* luxurious compared to those World War Two wooden barracks, the worst part being the latrine. Toilets were not partitioned. Of all the indignities to which low-ranking enlisted soldiers were subjected, boys and girls, communal shitting was rock bottom.

I was recollecting communal shitting as I read a letter from Mother, a bland, one-page litany of information, as if a wire service release--the weather, her job, Jack's unsuitable new girlfriend. No mention of Estranged Husband/Stepfather or Wendi with the bubble above her "i." I hoped Mother was starting to recover from the betrayal, but there was no indication in these sparse words.

A Sunday *Terry and the Pirates* strip was enclosed and much appreciated. The Dragon Lady was not featured, but I imagined her behind the scenes, conniving and seducing. I missed my fictional Dragon Lady as if she were real. I hoped she was being careful.

Our superiors were so consumed by their secret computing machine project in the Annex that they didn't notice that Ziggy and I were out scrounging when there was nothing to be scrounged. We billeted in the supply room only when we felt like it. There'd been no shopping list for several days, so I presumed we were at the final assembly stage of whatever they'd wrought. When I wasn't with Mai at 421, I was in our digs with Ziggy, plowing into my newest reading material as he devoured his sci-fi.

I was so irretrievably smitten that trifling worries such as joining Mai as a co-guest of honor at a firing squad for espionage was water off this duck's back. Our lovemaking had blended the cartoon fantasy and the flesh-and-blood woman into one.

Insane as it was, I had no intention of cooperating with snoops and spooks of any flavor, should they contact me. I'd take a midnight swim in the Mekong River before I'd get Mai in a pickle with the higher uppity-ups and anybody's secret police.

Besides, what had we done that was so heinous? What solid evidence was there that she was a commie spy? The one question she'd asked of late came within seconds of my arrival at 421 Hai Ba Trung Street.

"Joe, why do you still have pants on?"

Judging by her actions, Mai wanted my body and she wanted my companionship. Period. That didn't jibe after my third degree on the first date. Over time, I became more and more suspicious and less and less able to let go. Even without my comic strip fetish, ours was not a normal American-Vietnamese romance. The majority of those romances were fraught with non-romantic concessions, usually with a quid pro quo of money and a ticket stateside.

So what did she really, really want? I was sorely tempted to demand she lay it on the line. I mean, how come the skip from unrelenting interrogation to unadulterated intimacy?

But challenging her probably meant the end of extramarital bliss. Sigh. Heavy sigh. If my brain hung between my legs, so be it.

I yawned and looked at the books I'd accumulated from the Tan Son Nhat Library. Piled willy-nilly along the wall as if sandbags, they'd transformed my side of the room from a berm to a full-fledged bunker. I did plan to return them. Someday.

The heftiest volume of all was one of my two latest, a tome known as a coffee table book. Coffee table books were mostly pictorial. They outweighed a cinder block. They were pricey, costing upwards of ten smackers. You gave them at Christmas to loved ones who didn't like to read but wanted others to think they did. You laid one out on your coffee table by the ashtray and candy dish. Instantly, your living room had class even if you didn't.

This coffee table book presented the works of Piet Mondrian in luscious color plates. I'd checked it out in a futile attempt to jog my memory, to dredge from my pickled brain why and how I wore a map of the State of Montana instead of his *Composition 1921*. No luck.

I added it to my literary heap, took a pull of Johnny Red, and delved into my second new tome, *People's War People's Army* by General Vo Nguyen Giap, North Vietnam's answer to Douglas MacArthur. Giap processed into The Great Beyond not long after me, by the way. He was an old timer, over one-hundred.

Vo Nguyen Giap was the architect of Dien Bien Phu, in charge of the ants who humped the artillery up the surrounding hills and pulverized the French. He went on to spring the Tet Offensive in 1968 and remained the military boss when NVA tanks rolled into Saigon in 1975.

I'd hardly begun the book when I realized it was a how-to manual for doing what Giap had done to the French and was doing to us. I wondered if a single, solitary American general or Department of Defense whiz or military intelligence guru had read a single, solitary page of *People's War*.

I tossed it atop a JFK biography, which reminded me of Lee Harvey Oswald cum CWO R. Tracy. It's said that we all have a twin. I was no conspiracy paranoid, but I didn't know anyone who swallowed the Warren Commission Report hook, line, and sinker. As far as I was concerned, those fuddy-duddies and politicians on the Warren Commission had swept the dirty deed under the rug mighty fast.

If you believed Oswald hadn't pulled the job alone, and I had severe doubts, who was he working for? Possibilities ranged from the Mob to the Cubans to the Russkis to LBJ to the CIA. You could make a case for any of them, and who's to say they didn't reward Oswald for his work, by faking his murder, and switching a double for Jack Ruby to plug.

I nudged Ziggy. He put aside *The Devil's Dictionary* by PFC Bierce's granddaddy Ambrose. He'd found it in the Tan Son Nhut "libarry." Grin on his face, moving his lips, turning pages, damned if he wasn't memorizing *Devil's*. At least Bierce's quotes would be jazzier than those in the Little Red Book by that fat ChiCom with the wart on his chin.

And speaking of the devil, where was PFC A. Bierce? His appearance at the Fighting 803rd was now intermittent. Once he'd cranked out the morning report, he seemed to come and go as he pleased.

I asked Ziggy his opinion on the JFK assassination. He sure did have one. Naturally, it was a unique theory.

"Hit squad from the Planet Clarion, Joey," he said. "I seen this story in a magazine and there's no proving it ain't true."

It was my own damn fault for consulting him, toppling him to yet a lower ledge of unreality. "Where's Clarion, Zig?"

"Clarion's in Earth's orbit on the exact other side. You never see it cuz the sun's always in the way."

"Okay, sure, right."

"Oswald was a Clarionite who was teleported here. They was afraid of our space program, the Clarionites were. They listened in to Kennedy saying we'd have a man on the moon before the end of the decade, so they was afraid we'd discover them. Them and the fake Oswald had to do what they had to do to Kennedy. But JFK or no JFK, we'll be on the moon when he said."

"A man on the moon by December 31, 1969? C'mon, man. Fat chance. The odds have to be a trillion to one."

"There's times you don't know shit from Shinola, Joey. You ever hear of them Mercury and Gemini satellites we went and launched?"

"Who hasn't?" I rebutted lamely.

Ziggy then rambled on about Alpha Centauri, our nearest star. At 4.4 light years distant, it was practically across the alley. Little green men in a yarn he'd read lived there. He said Alpha Centauri was actually three stars, one orbiting a second that both orbited the third. He said the Alpha Centaurans were in cahoots with the Planet Clarionites.

I couldn't wait for Mariner 4 to ride into Marsville. Maybe Ziggy would snap out of it. I got off my bunk and said I'd see him at the 803rd, where we were supposed to be anyway.

I walked in as Captain Papersmith double-timed out of General Whipple's office in a frenzy. Before I could confide that a cabby had told me that South Vietnam's state color was gonna be red, Papersmith blurted, "Private Joe, are you familiar with Saigon's finer restaurants?"

Captain Papersmith was irritable and depressed, routine for him. I rocked a hand.

"Can you recommend an establishment that will accommodate a banquet-sized party?"

"How big's banquet-sized, sir?"

"Fifty."

Roughly the number of warm bodies at the 803rd, the oddballs, and cooks and MPs who had lent a hand. "Factoring in security, sir?"

"Pardon me?"

"You know, sir, security against *plastique*. Fifty's an attractive target. Nice round number."

"Security is irrelevant," he said.

Where were we, Elm City, U.S.A.? "Excuse me, sir?"

"Security is irrelevant. Clean the wax out of your ears, soldier."

I described a nice rooftop restaurant a couple of blocks off Le Loi Boulevard. Ziggy and I had eaten there once. It offered a good mix of quasi-American, Chinese and Vietnamese cuisine. In my humble opinion, Victor Charles was not irrelevant, and a roof was safer than street level. You'd have to have Sandy Koufax's arm to sling a satchel charge up to it.

"Is there a separate meeting room with ample space for us?"

"Don't remember. I think they can probably partition off a section."

"Would there be adequate privacy?"

How the hell would I know? "Sure, no problem."

"Are they flexible? Available on a day's notice?"

Did I publish the town's restaurant guide?

"Enough grease on the palm and anybody's flexible," I said, shrugging.

He said to drive him there. So off we went in the rattletrap Jeep. In front of the restaurant, he ordered me to occupy myself while he negotiated with the restaurateur. The captain was gone an hour, came back, and said he had a deal. Then he asked for the name of a reliable printer that did no business with, to my knowledge, any USMACV organization.

A peculiar proviso. Again, I wanted to ask how the hell should I know, but said sure, no problem, pulled over at the next print shop we came to, and said they were the best in town. He told me to wait in the Jeep and was gone half an hour.

On the return trip to the 803rd, I caught a glimpse of a sketch on Captain Papersmith's order that he hadn't completely slipped inside a binder. He'd written in 1965 and left the day and month blank. Also written on it: *USMACV VV Day Celebration* and the name of the rooftop restaurant.

VV?

VV Day?

Later in the afternoon, I slapped my forehead for missing the obvious. We had VE Day, Victory in Europe Day in honor of pounding the Nazis into rubble. We had VJ Day after vaporizing Hiroshima and Nagasaki. No VK Day. The Korean War was a stalemate, a gory zero-zero outcome that could go into overtime any moment.

VV Day.

"Holy Fucking Toledo!" I said to nobody, flabbergasted.

Victory in Vietnam Day.

Was he nuts?

On second thought, maybe we would have the situation mopped up pretty soon. Marines continued to land up north at DaNang. Infantry divisions were coming en masse. The First Airmobile Division was in the Central Highlands, chasing Charlie by chopper. No question, we were kicking ass and taking names.

Secretary of Defense Robert McNamara had stated that most of the military task should be wrapped up by the end of 1965, with a limited number of U.S. military personnel hanging around to train the locals. Since the troop numbers were moving up, not down, the press had been giving McNamara a ration of shit. But what did they know?

Communism in South Vietnam had less than six months before going belly-up. If McNamara and the bigwigs were true to their word, how did the piddly-ass, rinky-dink 803rd Liaison Detachment and their Cerebrum 2111X and CAN-DO electrical computational machine fit in? So what if it would be the size of a barn when it's together and running? That didn't make it miraculous. A dinosaur was as big as a locomotive and had a pea brain.

It may be all over but the shouting, except for one tiny detail.

Had the ants been clued in?

Chapter Eighteen

How many times have I said that the gang that runs The Great Beyond are Pranksters with a capital P. A barrel of laughs. I know, I know, far too many.

I'm talking about filthy lucre here. In The Great Beyond, all our physical requirements are compliments of management. Just like in the army, which provided us with "three hots and a cot." We neither need money for our subsistence--not for discretionary purchases we can't make anyhow.

Suddenly, I have money, U.S. currency. After my morning shower, I try to step into a shoe. I can't. There's a roll of cash inside. It's simply there. In my cookie jar too, the cookie jar I didn't have that is on the counter next to the toaster I've never been able to use because I have no bread to toast. And in a piggy bank from nowhere that's on my bedroom dresser.

I sniff the roll. It smells like money. I hold a bill up to the light. The paper has those little blue and red threads. I do a quick shuffle. The front sides look normal on all, a mix of twenties, fifties and hundreds. Wait, almost normal.

Here's where the fun comes in. They've tweaked our greenbacks a tad. Bill Clinton has replaced Andrew Jackson on the obverse of the twenty. There's a gaggle of nude, frolicking Biblical babes on the reverse.

I pull several *three*-dollar bills out of the roll. They feature Richard M. Nixon's painfully-smiling puss on the front, an engraving of the Watergate Complex on the rear.

My boy Smitty, he comes running as I count.

I answer the door and before I can say hello, he says, "Joe, what is this, please?"

He's holding up a piece of currency that has to be from his homeland. It's colorful, with squiggly writing, guys on horseback, and what looks like a mosque. On the back is 10,000 and oops--

I ask, "What's ten thousand of these worth in real money?"

He's insulted. "If you mean my beloved homeland's money, four U.S. dollars."

"Must be inconvenient having to roll a wheelbarrow full of these around to go shopping."

"This is new," Smitty says. "What is this and why is it on my money?"

The "new" is my "oops." He's referring to a picture of some folks from the olden days sitting at a long dinner table.

It is my great pleasure to inform him.

"Smitty, this is an excellent representation of Leonardo da Vinci's *The Last Supper*. You're seeing Jesus and his Disciples, on the night before Jesus Christ checks out. Jesus has just announced that there's an enemy agent in their midst. Judas, we know, but his merry band, doesn't, not yet. The guys are having a conniption fit and--"

Smitty has about-faced and is throwing a tantrum of his own, speaking angrily in his native tongue. I don't know a word, but I can imagine "blasphemy" and every four-letter word he knows. He's throwing his money around, scattering his lawn with it.

All's still quiet on the Madge front. I'm too curious. I rap on her door. Rap again. Ring the doorbell. Wait. Ring it again. Wait. Walk around the house, looking in every window. To the patio, where the drapes aren't all the way shut. I see no sign of Madge, no sign the house has ever been inhabited.

◆

I was dreaming about money on my supply room bunk, what Mai and I were spending on our honeymoon in Seattle, figuratively throwing money around, too. We were splurging on champagne and a luxurious hotel room, cost be damned. Then I was rudely awakened by CWO Ralph Buffet.

He was bent above me, shaking me, saying, "Wake up, wake up, wake up. We have an emergency."

I whiffed corrosive halitosis. Not that I had room to talk, surely reeking of Johnny Red. "What's up?"

"Sorry to barge in, Joe. Captain Papersmith sent me."

"You won't even say hi to us on the street, Buffet. Remember? He can't send you for us if we don't exist."

"Sorry. Believe me, it's best for both of us if we're strangers. That's your buddy?"

He was referring to the mound in the bunk next to me, pillow over his head, who sounded like a Messerschmitt Bf109 fighter piloted by the German World War Two ace whose biography I'd been reading. I squinted at my watch: 10:50.

I was bone-ass-weary from the manual labor, almost but not quite too exhausted to sneak out to my Dragon

Lady's whenever possible, to cuddle and smooch and snuggle and make love.

Ziggy was semi-morose of late. Current magazine articles on his Mariner 4 reported that it'd flown near enough to Mars to transmit data that said what had been recently said by the scientists, that there likely wasn't diddly-squat on the Red Planet except rock. I'd tried to console Ziggy, telling him to cheer up and relax and wait on the pictures. Besides, VV Day was coming up quick.

"Ziggy doesn't count sheep, Buffet," I said. "He strafes them."

"Joe, could you please wake Private Zbitgysz? We have a crisis and time is critical."

"What kind of crisis?"

"We lack vital supplies."

"What flavor of vital supplies?"

"Electrical."

I yawned.

He took that as a yes. "Thanks, guys. I'll be at the Annex."

"We're not authorized in there," I said, yawning again. "We no can do for your top secret crypto CAN-DO."

"You're authorized now on an emergency basis. That comes directly from General Whipple."

"Why don't you roust the Zigster, Buffet?"

"Please, Joe."

"Shit," I said, tossing a shoe at Ziggy. Waking him up was like disarming a bomb. "Hey, Zig."

He sat up, snorting and coughing.

I summarized.

"What kinda 'lectrical?"

"Whatever it is, I have a hunch we're not requisitioning through channels. Buffet, give us ten minutes to powder our noses."

♦

Colonel Lanyard's and General Whipple's office lights were visible under their doors. PFC Bierce was gone. We were admitted to the blacked-out Annex by CWO Buffet. A cluster of oddballs parted for us, a disconcerting gesture of deference.

Buffet led us to a big electrical box that'd been wired to the local juice and thick cables connected to auxiliary generators. All the computing machinery gizmos were out of their crates, occupying three walls and much of the free space. The thing with the square buttons was on a table in the middle. In the movies, this was where the little green man in charge of cooking us earthlings into burnt toast punched buttons.

Ziggy and I kept a discreet distance from the generators. Ziggy and I liked live electricity as well as we did snakes (me, going back to childhood for no good reason, as western Washington state has only harmless garter snakes) and spiders (Zig), especially when half-assedly jury-rigged like this.

Buffet pulled up a cluster of cables from the floor and showed us the plugs. "The wall sockets are three-pronged. These attached to the Cerebrum 2111X drives and the rest of the gear and the generators are four-pronged.

"They are to connect to our generators and the generators connect to local current in case of overload. The generators are made in Japan, the existing wiring in

France and England, the computer components in America."

"A United Nations of vital supplies. They aren't compatible," I said knowledgably.

"I'm afraid I created unrealistic expectations. We promised General Whipple and Colonel Lanyard that we were powering up and running tonight," Captain Papersmith said, appearing out of nowhere.

"We desperately need adapters," Buffet said.

"Adapters," I said. "No adapters handy? In a parts bin? Anywhere?"

The oddballs responded with a chorus of headshakes.

"How are we supposed to cough up—how many adapters this time of night? There might not be a single one in Saigon anywhere."

"Twenty-eight," Buffet said.

"Twenty-eight adapters," the captain repeated in a six-syllable whimper. "I promised the general and the colonel."

The captain and the oddballs were looking at us as if they were villagers and we were witch doctors who could make the volcano quiet down. They had confidence in us and respect for us. A rare sensation.

I asked Ziggy. "Singh?"

"Nah. He'd be closed by now."

"Charlie?" I suggested.

Ziggy grunted his consensus.

I informed the crowd, "Before we can do, gents, you'll have to pass the hat. Seed money."

They were bunched, reminding me of nature films of penguins on ice floes. To clarify, I rubbed thumb against fingers. They produced three hundred worth of dollars and piasters. Insincerely, the captain told us to be careful.

"We will be in your debt," he added.

"Debt," Ziggy intoned. "'Forgetfulness. A gift of God bestowed upon debtors in compensation for their destitution of conscience.'"

I grabbed a plug and dragged him and his Ambrose Bierce quotations out of there before Captain Papersmith could summon a reply or Ziggy could shift gears to The Little Red Book. We paid a motorcyclo driver a bonus to full-throttle it downtown. Ziggy and I knew a hole-in-the-wall coffeehouse where Charlie and his cowboy buddies hung out when they weren't racing their Hondas, snatching Seikos off GI wrists, and generally raising hell.

We got lucky. Charlie's and his pals' motorbikes were parked on the sidewalk. The only lights visible were cigarette embers and table candles inside the coffeehouse. I whistled and yelled for Charlie.

Nervously, Charlie came outside. He was not happy. We did not visit him on his turf. His draft-dodging buddies weren't partial to Americans. I gave him the plug and told him how many adapters we needed.

"It's a long shot," I said. "We'll make it worth your while."

Charlie eyeballed our wad of green and Ps, then whispered, "Give me money. Then I yell. You speak okay, okay, okay. Okay?"

I said okay and instructed Ziggy to cower without overdoing. Charlie then cut loose in Vietnamese and pidgin, accusing us of doing various disgusting things to our mothers, all the while jabbing a finger in my chest. He said we'd have to come up with a better offer. Ziggy and I said okay, okay, okay, and made a big deal of forking over more cash.

Charlie had saved face and satisfied his buddies that he played cozy with Americans strictly for profit. Swindling the round-eyed butter-stinkers was the name of this tune. Charlie hopped on his bike, and we chased behind in the motorcyclo.

He took shortcuts down alleys I wouldn't enter in broad daylight. They were as pitch-black and narrow as caves. He stopped at a business on a narrow, commercial street. There were no lights and the iron gates were down and padlocked. I knew they were businesses because of the signs, but I didn't know what kind as the signs were entirely in Vietnamese.

Through the bars of accordion iron you could see in windows. There were baby clothes in one. Next door, domed hair dryers like helmets out of the Jetsons: a beauty parlor. With the cyclo and the Honda motors shut off, the silence made my ears ring. An unseen dog howled. I hoped it was a dog, not a VC signaling his colleagues.

Charlie rapped and rapped and shook a set of bars. Eventually it creaked and groaned upward waist-high. He jabbered to someone inside, then came to me with his hand out. I gave him all of the money aside from a small commission I deducted for Ziggy's and my finder's fee.

On his hands and knees, Charlie went into the store. I hoped he wouldn't take long. There was a curfew. You're out in the streets after midnight, you'll do worse than turn into a pumpkin if you bump into a trigger-happy ARVN patrol. But Charlie returned promptly with thirty of the correct adapters, three holes on one side, four on the other.

"Two spare. If some no work."

"You're amazing, man. What is this place?"

Charlie shrugged nonchalantly. "Uncle me. Own and live in hardware store."

We thanked him profusely and parted company. It'd gone so speedily, on an impulse I asked Ziggy if it'd be okay to pay a call on my Dragon Lady. I hadn't seen her since last night and missed her terribly.

He was noncommittal, but I ordered the cyclo to 421 Hai Ba Trung anyway. My best pal and the love of my life, however it ended for us, I thought it was important that they got to meet and like each other.

If Colonel Jakie Lanyard was in there getting his ass blistered, Mai's signal was to leave one shutter slightly cracked. All were latched. Presumably, Lanyard was in his office, shuffling paper. We knocked on her door and knocked. And knocked.

On to Cholon and Quyen, the cackling sister. No answer either and no light showing from within. We rode to the Annex. As Ziggy caught a catnap, I wondered where the hell else she could be.

I wasn't sure I wanted to know.

Chapter Nineteen

We strutted into the Annex and dumped the thirty adapters on a table. A moment of awestruck silence ensued. We had once again utilized a mysterious alternative matériel source, this time outdoing ourselves. No individual I personally know of through strip mall gossip in The Great Beyond walks on water (you'd have to prove it to me), but in the oddballs' eyes we'd accomplished this masterstroke without getting our ankles wet.

"Thirty instead of twenty-eight. Spares," I said. "Close enough for government work."

"You troopers are great Americans," Captain Papersmith said, choking up in gratitude for us saving his career. "I may have misjudged you by not recognizing your daring in the name of a worthy cause and your innate patriotism."

Ziggy said, "'Patriotism. Combustible rubbish ready to the torch of anyone ambitious to illuminate his name.'"

PFC A. Bierce ought to be here, I thought.

"'Patriot. One to whom the interests of a part seem superior to those of the whole. The dupe of statesmen and the tool of conquerors.'"

"Zig, knock it off, okay?"

Good ol' Captain Papersmith. He was inspecting and counting the adapters, to verify our loaves-and-fishes feat.

"Like Joey said, two of them's spares, sir, in case some of them don't work," Ziggy said, withdrawing a magazine from a pocket and withdrawing from group participation.

I stood by as the oddballs plugged the gear together. When they were set to go, Captain Papersmith said, "I'll check if Colonel Lanyard and General Whipple are available."

He scampered to the 803rd HQ and returned with our commander. General Whipple was carrying his olive-drab watering can with the silver star on each side. He was in a distracted hurry, I supposed, and forgot that he had it.

The captain evidently put a bug in his ear about us because General Whipple shook Ziggy's and my hands and said to each of us in a soft drawl, "Nicely done, son."

Son.

I don't recall my natural father calling me "son," but he must have. My pseudointellectual stepdad, never. I was "you" when he wasn't pissed at me. I was "that boy" when he was.

My biological father, Joseph Josiah Joe III, who'd bought the farm at Inchon, had been a captain and a reservist who'd been called up when the Korean War started. He was really too old to be there, as was my grandfather who didn't come home from Guadalcanal. They were gung ho and then some. The family's solemn-military-obligation gene died with them. They would not have been proud of me.

I hazily remembered Father. Not his physical appearance, but the aroma of pipe tobacco and his interaction with us. He'd been affectionate toward Jack and me in a manly sort of way. Roughhousing, tousling our hair, playing ball with us in the yard. He'd been an engineer in a shipyard who'd worked swing shift, so I hadn't seen much of him except on weekends and in the summer.

Did Mother still miss him? When I connect with her here, I will surely ask. It was a question I could not bring myself to ask her in The Land of the Living. I'd known the answer would be a mix of words and tears.

Not only was General Whipple a duplicate of any and all TV dads, he said "son" the way Ward Cleaver and Jim Anderson said it when they gave their TV sons pats on the head for having brought home a B+ on an algebra test.

My dad. My missing Mai.

I can't remember last crying, but my eyes dampened to the point where it interfered with my vision and my dignity, such as it was.

The general snapped me out of it by announcing, "Your attention, please. Colonel Lanyard regrets that he will be unable to witness this historic event. He is facing a deadline on a vital report, so, by golly, let's do our share to fertilize this rich albeit sparsely seeded topsoil called the Republic of Vietnam on the eve of Saigon's worst kept secret, impending statehood. Let us nourish our chloroplast, let us augment the photosynthesis process. Gentlemen, let us push our mission forward, let us get the show on the road."

"The state bird's gonna be the mongoose," I whispered to CWO Buffet, my thoughts centered on my Dragon Lady.

"Be serious for once in your life, Joe," Buffet replied.

Well, I was damn serious on one topic. Was Colonel Jakie (Raw Ass) Lanyard's report deadline a pile of bat guano and was he actually with Mai, getting his ashes hauled?

Mai's baffling whereabouts might or might not be related to her Jakie. The accumulating unknowns were driving me cuckoo.

"Without further adieu," General Whipple said, reaching dramatically to throw the main power switch, as if smashing a bottle of champagne on the bow of a ship. Oddballs fired up the auxiliary generators.

"Pardon me, son," he said to Ziggy.

Ziggy was between the general and the switch. The larger-than-most-earthly-life Zigster was leaning against the desk at the main console, reading his magazine. The tin robot on the cover, bigger than King Kong, seemed bent on eating St. Louis. The only thing protecting the city was a human in a loincloth, who was the spitting image of Jock Mahoney playing Tarzan.

Intensely fixated on a story, Ziggy straightened and shifted out of the general's way. In a clumsy fandango, he brushed buttons and switches on the console, a bunch of them. Ziggy brushing up to something was akin to ramming a '57 DeSoto into it.

"Private!" Captain Papersmith shrieked at Ziggy, who looked up from his yarn, though too late.

The Cerebrum 2111X came to life with a vibrating hum. Air conditioners growled to life. Lights flashed and tape drives spun. Magnetic drums whirred. The keypunch printer started clacking like a jackhammer. The thingamajigging gizmos were at full throttle. These days, you'd say they were uploading and/or downloading.

The beaming general patted Ziggy consolingly as a swell TV father would and shouted over the racket,

"There, there, Captain. Private Zbitgysz merely sprinkled on an extra dose of organic matter. The end result is what counts. Bless you, people, it is electronic music to my ears. Verdant, nutrient-rich growth erupting in fertile loam."

Meanwhile, the oddballs were shaking hands and hugging and jumping up and down like little kids.

The explosions put an end to that.

The first ones were the generators going into spasms, producing foul-smelling backfires. Various lights became strobes. Punch cards sprayed every which way out of a machine.

A far-larger explosion, a genuine *ka-boom*, came from out-of-doors. It gave me a flashback to tales of the VC blowing up the My Canh floating restaurant on the Saigon River. They lit off one bomb. Diners panicked and charged onto the gangplank and caught the second blast from a Claymore, a U.S.-made directional mine aimed at them.

Thirty-one dead. A hundred wounded.

As in that and the Embassy attack, you had to be thinking past the first noise and you had to think in a split second. Ziggy was thinking faster than anybody, shoving down anyone who tried to run by him to the door as if he were flattening tall grass, yelling, "You wanna go and be blowed up?"

A weaker bomb went off, then another. During the chaos, the general finally dropped his watering can. He'd been on his feet throughout and nobody had the balls to throw him to the floor, not even Ziggy.

At the fourth or fifth explosion, General Whipple cried out, "Agents provocateurs!"

The double plural was correct usage, I thought idiotically, me a fleeting English major.

Ziggy held his hands up to dissuade the general, who ignored him and lurched outside.

"Agents provocateurs. Communist agitators. How could they have discovered our timing?"

Colonel Lanyard rushed onto the street from the 803rd in full uniform and steel helmet, cinching his pistol belt. He threw a massive arm around General Whipple. "Sir, back inside, please."

The general stumbling along with him, the colonel marched a swath through the oddballs.

"Agents provocateurs," General Whipple repeated, dazed.

Ziggy and I peeked out. There were more explosions accompanied by lightning-like flashes, but they were increasingly quieter and distant. A smattering of locals on the street carried flashlights and candles. Looking around, mostly in our direction, they appeared to be as pissed as afraid. (Why did Hanoi need the VC when they had the Fighting 803rd?)

Air raid warning sirens were sounding, even though the VC had no aircraft. The few lights still on in the neighborhood were winking sporadically, reminding me of a county fair's carnival shutting down for the night. A nice evening for looting and throat-cutting was upon us.

"Saigon's electricity is antiquated," offered an oddball. "Our generators automatically kicked in to it and overloaded our system and their infrastructure."

I didn't think I wanted be in town for the VV Day hoopla.

"A French system," a colleague concurred.

The unhearing general said, "Agents provocateurs. How could they have known?"

"Agents provocateurs," Captain Papersmith parroted, whether he knew the definition of the term or not. "I absolutely agree, sir."

"The little monkeys would like us to believe it was an electrical malfunction. I'm going out to secure the perimeter," Colonel Lanyard said, drawing his service-issue Colt .45 Model 1911 automatic pistol.

Ziggy and I entered the blackness too, safely to the colonel's rear. We heard vehicles crashing in the distance. Our area already seemed secure. Enemy guerrillas were just as much in the dark as we were and would be as likely to shoot themselves as us.

Some oddballs followed tentatively. Captain Papersmith was the last person out of the Annex, tiptoeing in a crouch.

"Why the hell did you depend on local juice to help power your monstrosity?" I asked Buffet.

"We had additional generators coming. They were stolen from the Port of Saigon. There's incredible pressure by the Pentagon and the White House to finish the project. The general felt we couldn't delay."

"This project, whatever the hell it is," I said, pausing, waiting in vain to be confided in, then continued, "How long ago did you guys know the generators had been poached off the docks?"

"A week. Two weeks. Word came down to get by on what we had. They hoped what we had would handle our needs, but they can barely run fifty percent of the air conditioners, let alone Cerebrum. The brass wouldn't listen to us."

"A whole entire week or *two*?" Ziggy demanded in a tone that made them backpedal.

I said, "Jesus H. Fucking Christ, Buffet. You should've gotten us on the job. That hurts to the core, man. You mistrusting us. Okay, fine. You doubting our scrounging ability, that's un-fucking-forgivable."

"Joe, not so loudly," CWO Buffet said.

"Alternative matériel sources, like we ain't got 'em no more," Ziggy said unpleasantly.

"We could've found out who snatched them and requisitioned them back or we could've requisitioned somebody else's," I added.

"There were security concerns," Buffet rebutted.

"How much harm do you think this is doing to the Saigonese?" I asked. "Zapping their appliances that're plugged in, appliances they can't afford to replace and couldn't afford to buy in the first place?"

"It depends on if they have fuses. It depends on how far the chain reaction goes until it peters out."

We heard fading snaps, crackles, and pops. We saw what resembled flares. I didn't want to know what they were.

"All personnel inside. Double-time it," Colonel Lanyard ordered. "The firefight has moved outside our perimeter."

We did as we were told. We did not have to be told twice. For a split second I thought I saw Lee Harvey Oswald among the curious and angry Saigonese on the next block, his smirking profile a flicker as he lit a cigarette.

The colonel paused and looked up the street, and said, "Victor Charles in to mop up? We'll see about that."

I was halfway through the Annex door when Charlie tooled up on his motorbike. I figured he'd figured it out, having an uncle as a hardware expert. He wanted to see the fireworks' origin firsthand.

Charlie reached us just as the colonel trained his pistol on him and cocked the hammer. "If a foreign national is on a suicide mission, I'll be happy to accommodate the commie punk."

"Friend, not foe," I yelled, diving, grabbing the colonel's arm with both hands as wide-eyed Charlie goosed his bike. It was like trying to bend a thick tree limb, but I did deflect his aim a millimeter or two. The round zipped above Charlie's head by an inch. The colonel squeezed off the rest of the clip into the darkness. I thankfully did not hear screams or the clattering of a Honda striking pavement. But next time we saw Charlie, boy, was he gonna be pissed.

"You had best explain your actions, soldier," said Colonel Lanyard as he slapped in a fresh clip and jacked a round into the chamber.

"I know him, sir. He's not VeeCee."

"Who is he, soldier?"

"He's Charlie, sir, my buddy. Helluva nice guy. Without Charlie, we wouldn't've had those adap—"

"He's a Charlie? A Victor Charles?"

"No, sir, not Charles Victor."

"Victor Charles, soldier."

"Right. Charlie's name is Charlie, not Charles or Victor."

"A Vietnamese national named Charlie who isn't a subversive?"

"He provided the adapters. We couldn't've done this without him."

"Couldn't have done what? Plant explosive devices to sabotage the Saigon power grid and ambush local allies and Americans alike?"

The colonel looked at me in a manner nobody but the colonel could look at you. I shut my mouth and damn near swallowed my tongue.

General Whipple and his watering can rejoined us, sniffing the stink of ozone and burnt insulation.

"Colonel Lanyard, what Private Joe is saying, is that the Vietnamese on the motorcycle supplied the critical parts that enabled Cerebrum 2111X and CAN-DO to commence operation. According to our technical personnel, because of Saigon's electrical inadequacies, perhaps we were responsible for the power interruption, although that cannot be determined without a detailed study."

"In all due respect, sir," Colonel Lanyard said. "There was a fair amount of ordnance expended, far too much for an electrical glitch."

"Be that as it may, visualize, if you will, Colonel, an absence of nitrogen in the soil. The crops emerge, but they're spindly and sickly."

Colonel Lanyard frowned. He was not visualizing nitrogen deficiencies. To everybody's relief, he deferred to his superior, did a Duke Wayne spin of his weapon and reholstered. "Very well, sir."

I saw that the oddballs had kept a portion of their gadgetry functioning and were back at their stations. Weirdly, the machines that sent Saigon city electricity into spasms were not visibly affected by the havoc they'd wreaked.

"We are up and running at reduced capacity, sir," CWO Ralph Buffet said.

In his scariest amped-up voice, the colonel ordered, "Captain Papersmith, you and your computer staff will labor nonstop to complete the mission before the enemy can mount a subsequent attack."

What mission?

"Yes. Sir," the captain said, saluting, heels locked.

Colonel Lanyard said, "You men will work like the very devil. Some men will bivouac in the Annex, on a rotating basis. Captain Papersmith will supervise the duty roster. I will make arrangements at your Tan Son Nhat billets to have necessary belongings transferred. Now, everyone off the street. I'm declaring martial law until I get to the bottom of the situation."

General Whipple didn't object, too worn out by the pyrotechnics to debate. The colonel put an arm around our commander and gently escorted him into the 803rd.

I don't know if Lanyard had martial law authority, or what martial law exactly meant, but Ziggy and I headed into the 803rd. We watched the oddballs as they closed the Annex door. Their faces said there would be no graham crackers and milk before bedtime, if there was a bedtime.

Chapter Twenty

Do I in The Great Beyond experience fear? As in terrified, catatonic, excruciating, quaking-in-your-boots, crap-your-britches fear? You bet your sweet ass I do.

Obviously, you can rule out generic earthly fears of death. I lose no sleep over cancer, fire, clogged arteries, SUVs crossing the centerline, or enraged spouses. Not to mention warfare over the ages, including Vietnam and its 58,000+ American dead who *have* to be somewhere hereabouts. Those perils have already punched our tickets for admission.

Fear of the rumor (that's growing like the fifty-first state fable had in 1965 Saigon) of capital punishment, well, that's a different story. Wouldn't it wreak havoc on the concept of eternal life? Logically it's impossible. On the other hand, our masters can do anything they choose. Anybody who can build a fence around infinity is not to be underestimated.

Since Madge vanished, I'm hanging out more and more at that strip mall, listening. I've developed and discarded theories on what happened to her, most centered on Smitty. To my knowledge, they did not meet during her brief stay. I cannot verify this, however. Maybe he went to her place one evening after seeing her outside having a puff. Maybe they got into a beef. An adolescent boasting match, one-upping each other on the savageness of their life-taking, got out of hand.

The teriyaki joint is the richest rumor mill at the mall. And to tell you the truth, I'm in there at a corner table twiddling my thumbs more than is healthy. By that I mean the little Asian gal behind the counter ready to take orders that are never given from nonexistent strip mall patrons while the cook (her husband?) stands by to prepare the food.

Other mall merchants visit the teriyaki at meal times, but do not order and eat either. What the point of an eatery is, I yet again haven't the foggiest. There are zero calories in teriyaki holograms. No cholesterol, no trans fats.

They come in to gossip with each other and her. They all do. Vietnamese who run the noodle shop and nail salon. The dry cleaner couple; Koreans, I think. The payday loan owner, a small white man of middling age whose small dark eyes do not make contact. A new tenant, proprietor of a tanning parlor; a pert thirtyish blonde whose bronzed skin is sixtyish. The lady with her hair in a gray bun and horn-rimmed glasses held on a chain, the tax preparation professional who prepares no taxes. She, like me, only listens. Perhaps her vocal cords have atrophied from lack of use.

Ms. Teriyaki is the clearinghouse for every story, absurd or not. She's no Dragon Lady, but I am so tempted to move in close, reach out and cop a feel. Not that I'm gonna cop anything but air, not that I am capable of arousal. But you know what I mean.

The rumormongers have no knowledge of anybody re-succumbing, but given our honchos' wit, who can say? That's their argument, a tough one to refute in this structured, irrational chaos. Call it trepidation or apprehension or whatever, but these rumors have created an increasing anxiety in me whether there is an after-afterlife.

Convince me that Madge's disappearance was not in that vein and I'll relax.

Earthly fears of death, circa 1965, yeah, I had a few. You know of my snake hang-up. The prospect of a communist guerrilla around the next corner, sure.

I did not fear being off-limits. I was not fearful of being AWOL, of violating Colonel Lanyard's martial law proclamation. Thanks to the blackout the 803rd had caused, nocturnal Saigon was off-limits to U.S. military personnel.

I cared not.

I was comfortable straying off-limits. In Basic Training and AIT, to discourage us from doing so, they'd marched us into auditoriums and showed films of horrific VD routinely contracted while off limits, of dicks pustulating and putrefying and outright rotting off.

Each unit had nearby off-limits establishments listed on orderly room bulletin boards, with caveats on physical danger and unclean women. They threatened punishment if the MPs apprehended us. Names and addresses of the dens of iniquity were given. Incredibly, some phone numbers, too. We'd regarded the postings as a convenient locater service.

Waiting as a yawning Ziggy picked the front door lock for me to depart the 803rd, I believed I heard more jungle sounds in the general's offices. Vines rustling, coatimundis frolicking in the treetops.

I entered the blackness, a London blitz milieu, with bogeymen on the ground rather than in the skies. I touched an Annex window pane and felt a steady vibration from the uninjured organs of their computational monster. The only visible light in the

803rd Liaison Detachment emanated from vanes of the colonel's window shutters.

I couldn't hike to Cholon, so I made my way to 421 Hai Ba Trung Street. I passed the occasional hibachi burning inside a dwelling for light. I climbed Mai's stairway, fully prepared to curl in the fetal position at her door and await her return, however long it took.

I was not fearful of the consequences of consorting with my Dragon Lady who, if not hardcore Vietcong, was an almost-certain enemy of Truth, Justice, and the American Way. If I was too by association, I took consolation that my immediate superiors were also culpable.

What I did fear, what I was scared shitless of, was Mai's ulterior motives. For the kazillionth time, I analyzed them and drew no conclusion. She fed me and she bred me. I gave little in return but the dubious currencies of passion and devotion.

I feared her eventual demands. I feared they would break our magical spell. She was what she was, and I was too stupidly smitten to care. She had lived up to my Dragon Lady fantasy in every respect.

Mai answered on the first knock.

I damn near jumped out of my sneakers.

"Joe."

Saying my name casually, as if I'd gone out for a quart of milk and a loaf of bread.

"Where the hell have you been, Mai?"

Her face and voice neutral, she said, "You not my boss. You not Quyen."

"I was worried. I didn't know where you were earlier."

Her reply was a step to the rear, allowing me in as she appraised me. "Worry why?"

"I care for you."

"Because it dark out?"

"That too."

"Friend me say Vietcong blow up Saigon power plant."

"Yes, they did," I said, in a Bogart grimace. "The dirty rats."

"No safe for you to come see me in dark, Joe, but you here."

I shrugged in aw-shucks modesty.

"You speak romance? You take chance to come see me. This is romance?"

"Romance is me loving you, Mai. That is romance."

Mai didn't reciprocate verbally, but she hugged me long and hard as I caressed the world's foremost, firmest, most fantastic buttocks. Then instead of going into the bathroom for her customary personal hygiene, she took a handful of shirt and pulled me to her bed. She unzipped me, then herself.

Taken by surprise by her aggressiveness, I flopped on the bed and made an impulsive decision that we'd henceforth have protection against pregnancy and venereal disease. I know, the horse was long gone from the stable, but that's what I decided.

In a clumsy hurry, I fished the gold dollar out of my wallet and the rubber out of its foil wrapper. I dropped it on the floor and fumbled for it on my hands and knees. By then, my naked Dragon Lady was under the covers, wondering what sort of klutz she'd gotten mixed up with.

They sold gold dollar rubbers everywhere. Cheap. At street stalls, in shops, pharmacies. Singh sold them. If you didn't have army-issue on you, you bought gold dollars when you needed them. If you had half a brain you did.

With all the nasty strains circulating in this country and more to come proportional to the buildup, you could have a penicillin-resistant bug and not know. Any fool knew that syphilis could hibernate in your brain for twenty or thirty years until the critters made wormwood out of your gray matter as they'd done to Al Capone's. So safety first it would be.

I'd known GIs who put on two rubbers at once. Patronizing Mama-san's exclusively (prior to Mai), I hadn't worried, as she was a quality-oriented madam.

As far as birth control went, Mai had not confided her precautions with me, if any, and I hadn't inquired. Nevertheless, riding her bareback was no fairer to her than it was prudent for me. If I was carrying some disgusting crud such as blue balls, I'd cut off mine before passing it on to Mai.

My Dragon Lady helped me. She was not clumsy. After gently kissing my organ, she deftly completed the task, rolling on our protection. It was so worldly on her, such a turn-on, yet so affectionate, that I finished nearly as rapidly as our first time.

We lay on our backs, holding hands, in pure paradise. Electricity and the ceiling fan came on.

"You think me not clean, Joe."

"No, no, no. I just thought we shouldn't take any chances. No baby-sans."

"What you want out of life, Joe?"

Normally I hated this line of pillow talk. I'd invariably be pinned in a corner. Judy had been a pro at it. I didn't mind the question from Mai, though.

"I have a buddy who got out of the army. Larry Sibelius. He's gonna be a beatnik. That might be my future too."

"What is beatnik?"

"What my mother thinks I am. A beatnik is a guy who doesn't want to be anything when he grows up except lazy and opinionated. A beatnik is interested only in fulfilling his basic desires and smoking any kind of vegetation that's on hand."

I don't think she understood, but she was up on an elbow. "Your mother no like you?"

"Good question. She loves me, but she doesn't always like me. Not that I blame her. We write letters that are like interoffice memos. We write of my perfect brother and imperfect stepfather. Mai, you'd said your father had been dead a long time. What of your mother?"

"Mother alive. I know not where."

"Why not?"

She lay back down and stared at the fan. End of topic.

Her technical texts. I pawed the nightstand for them. Still gone.

"Mai, your father was an engineer? You didn't really say."

"Yes. Engineer."

"In the north."

"Yes."

"Where in the north?"

"In north."

Okay, fine. "You didn't say why you removed his books. Was it something I said?"

She didn't respond.

"Are the books yours, too?"

That got a rise out of her. "Why you say books mine?"

"Lucky guess?"

She kissed my forehead.

"I'll bet you're good at math, too. Me and exponents, exponents is my middle name."

"You talk crazy."

"So?"

"When you go America, Joe, I no can bear I no see you forever."

At that instant, I seriously considered popping the question. That was impractical, highly impractical. The inches-thick army and MACV paperwork was designed to wear you out and make you forget the idea, which was usually a bad one. The time I had left would not be enough time to extrude it through the bureaucracies.

Then again, I'd run through a blast furnace for her. What's a little red tape? Man, I'm so confused and conflicted. Must be what you call your yin and yang.

Friend or foe, I had to confide in Mai about *something*, to layer our intimacy. I filled her in on my VV Day Celebration Party errand with her Dean, the whole ball of wax. Why the hell not? It was so nutso.

"We get statehood when you win?"

You win? Not us and our valiant South Vietnamese allies?

"Damned if I know. I do know this. The state flower will be the white lily, not the opium poppy."

She squeezed my spare tire. "Oh, Joe."

"If it isn't, it should be, Mai."

I still had marriage on the noggin. Commitment. Commitment I wouldn't give Judy, who if I'd married, would've saved me from the draft, which would've denied me the chance of ever meeting Mai. My head was spinning like it was after our opium den experience.

I pictured Mai and me walking down the aisle, her in a white wedding gown (If you don't like her in white, tough shit).

I pictured Ziggy in a tux, my best man. He looked like the offspring of a rhino and a penguin.

"What's so funny?"

"Life."

She traced the borders of Montana on my arm. "America?"

"An American province. Wide open spaces. Big Sky Country. It's a long goofy tale."

"Tell me."

I told her my long goofy tale.

She giggled. "You drunk as drunk can be, Joe?"

"The one guy I ever met who got drunker than I was that night was a lifer I knew at Fort Ord, an old mess sergeant. After his last hitch, he'd gotten out of the army. For good, he claimed. He'd had a bellyful. But him and his separation pay went on a bender. He woke up two weeks later on a bunk in the Fort Leonard Wood, Missouri reception barracks. He recalled zilch, but he'd taken a Burst of Six, what we call a six-year reenlistment."

"Silly man," Mai said, resuming staring at the fan. "I no see you when you *fini* Vietnam?"

"You might hate America and hate me for taking you there."

"Statehood. We be America, too, Joe."

Bierce and his wild-ass rumor. I was a heel for leading her on. I veered from the subject by telling her more about Ziggy and his Martians.

"He seem nice man. I think he no frighten people on purpose. He believe in Mars man?"

"The first flying saucer that touches down, Zig will be at the LZ, handing out coffee and doughnuts to the little green men."

"I study Mars in school."

"In the north?"

"In north."

"Where in the north?"

"You say you read much, Joe. You and Ziggy."

I gave up on her north. "Yeah."

"What you read?"

"What haven't I read? Even poetry. At least I recently tried."

She looked at me. "You and poem?"

"Yep. For five minutes. *Paradise Lost* is a poem and a big fat book too."

"A book?"

"Actually more than one book. I didn't get far. I checked it out of the library. In a nutshell, *Paradise Lost* was how Adam and Eve screwed up and we've been paying through the nose ever since. Poetry is the art of arranging words so you can't understand them. I looked over a book by Elizabeth Barrett Browning. Her most famous poem is 'How do I love you, let me count the ways.' I wish I'd memorized it all for you."

Mai said I was sweet and wanted to know why I was snickering.

"I do remember this poem I learned in Basic Training."

"Yes?"

"You were not to call your rifle a gun. It was a weapon or a rifle. If the drill sergeant overheard you say 'gun,' he'd have you recite over and over, 'this is my rifle, this is my gun, this is for fighting, this is for fun.'"

I showed her the required hand motions, in which you alternated between pretending to aim a rifle and to masturbate. I went to the fridge for a cold *Ba-mi-ba* while Mai recovered from laughing.

We shared the bottle, and then I said I'd like to write her a poem if I managed to think one up as lovely and wonderful as her. I was stammering when I finished and was rewarded with a lip lock. We had the gold dollar choreography down pat this time, using the second and last I had.

We were long and loving, loosening every nail and screw in Mai's bed. A happy, soggy, sticky mess, we climbed in her shower together. Her hot water was supplied by sunlight on rooftop pipes. We didn't even mind when the water cooled.

Exotic didn't come within a mile of describing tonight. Terry Lee's Dragon Lady, by comparison she was the Little Old Lady from Pasadena. Tonight wasn't *Paradise Lost*, it was *Paradise Gained*.

"I can't stay the night, Mai."

"Statehood is why no can stay?"

"Martial law is why."

"Joe."

"Uh-huh?"

"I lie. Friend me no say Vietcong blow up Saigon power plant. He say 803rd secret building, it do bad things to Saigon electricity."

"Smart friend. Anybody I know?"

"CAN-DO ready, Joe?"

Bingo. Dreaded suspicions confirmed. Let's amend tonight to *Paradise Sort of Gained*.

"My Mata Hari."

"Who?"

I whipped a biographical sketch of the slippery Dutch courtesan on her.

If she was insulted, she didn't say so. "Cerebrum 2111X ready, Joe?"

"Honestly, you know as much about it as I do, Mai. Probably more."

"Statehood?"

"Same same."

It was daylight. I got up and peeked outside. I saw my Lee Harvey Oswald. CWO R. Tracy leaning on a lamppost by a corner *phở* shop, arms folded, looking in our direction, voluntarily or involuntarily smirking. Finalizing his dossier for my firing squad.

"Really gotta go, gotta scoot," I said, putting on my clothes, planning to hustle out there and wrap my hands around Tracy's neck until he spit out some answers. I gave Mai a lunging smack on the cheek, just as a suburban hubby would do when he was late for the commuter train to his office.

I was buttoning my shirt and zipping my zipper when I reached the sidewalk. Lee Harvey had vanished.

I spotted the 803rd's rattletrap Jeep approaching from the next block. I ducked into a doorway and watched Colonel Lanyard pull up to 421. He dismounted and went through the gate. Since Mai hadn't pushed me out the door, her Jakie's visit was probably impromptu, his need for an ass-paddling fervent.

I made a mental note to leave a container of talcum powder on his desk for his inflamed heinie, to make him aware his dirty little secret was out.

Nah. I changed my mind. Mai would take the rap.

The key was in the ignition. I hopped in the Jeep and accelerated from the curb. Stealing it provided lesser satisfaction than a talcum powder stunt, but it did provide a ride home.

Gary Alexander

Chapter Twenty One

My one and only dream in The Great Beyond has come true. In the form of a nightmare.

I'm fixing lunch, improvising a pulled pork sandwich, remembering when I was cutting my culinary teeth at a faux Cuban restaurant. Black rice and beans, plantains, shredded beef in a tomato-based *criollo* sauce. Yum.

The pork part is easy. I'm shredding one of Smitty's pork loins I'd cooked. From the TV dinners I hadn't traded to him, I find a barbecue something and use the sauce. I have no bread or buns to wrap the meat in, so from another TV dinner, I take bread crumbs and layer on each side of the pork. The "close enough for government work" saw is apropos. I remove cooked mixed vegetables from another dinner and have a balanced meal.

A piano rendition of "Shake, Rattle & Roll" plays at half speed.

It's a normally abnormal day in The Great Beyond.

Until I smell the cologne. Remember Hooverville? It's the same potent stuff that stung my eyes there. It overwhelms my cookery.

I hold my nose, yet I can still follow my held nose to the front drapes and see the source. He's outside, hand on chin, checking out his new home, Madge's former home.

I recognize him. Seeing him jogs my memory; I will recognize his voice too. He is every voice calling out from the Hooverville hovels but one.

As I approached the end in The Land of the Living, when pain would not permit me to sleep at night, I'd go downstairs and watch the tube. Infomercials reigned in post-midnight programming and my new neighbor was on often. He sold everything that the Hooverville voices sold. I came to think of him as the King of Paid Programming, the Mother of all Slicky Boys. I don't recall his real name, but to me on the nocturnal tube he was Slick.

Slick is casual in slacks and pullover. He has a ready smile and clean-cut face that makes him easy to trust if you don't know better. He's in his 40s and has the countenance of a former big man on campus.

"Do you like corn dogs?"

I'm used to the cologne now. "Not my all-time favorite," I say.

"Tater Tots?"

"Likewise."

"My freezer compartment is crammed to the gills with them. Where do I get something decent to eat?"

No hello, goodbye, kiss my ass. Slick has no interest in anything or anybody but himself and his problems.

"How did you get here?"

"Here? Where's here?"

"The Great Beyond."

He's quiet for a few seconds, probably a first. "Yeah, where the hell am I?"

"What's your last memory?"

Hand on chin again, he says, "Let's see. I was in the parking garage. I live in a top floor condo."

"*Lived* in a top floor condo," I happily interrupt.

"I'm getting into my SL500 and out of nowhere there's a gun against the side of my head. This deranged old boy said my investment seminar people took him for every cent he had. That's the last I remember."

A pot-bellied guy with a buzz cut and a pockmarked neck comes out the door and says, "Sir, I found some more chow in the pantry and on shelves in the garage. MREs and C-rations."

He's the owner of the other voice I heard in Hooverville, the recruiting sergeant.

"Sarge, keep looking. I can't eat that military shit."

"Sir, this is really good chow if you give it a chance."

"Goddamnit, I said keep looking!"

The old sergeant's face droops. He backs inside.

I ask, "How'd you and him hook up?"

Slick looks at me. He's afraid. "I don't know. I don't know anything. Please tell me what's going on."

"Why is the sergeant here?"

"That I don't know. He's just *here*. He told me he was fragged in Afghanistan by a soldier he'd recruited. He'd promised the trooper he'd have stateside duty if he signed on the dotted line. *Please* tell me what's going on."

Before I walk away, I say, "I'll explain all in my free seminar, lunch on the house, choice of chicken or fish."

I hear Smitty screaming inside his house.

What now?

◆

MPs swarmed outside the Annex, a platoon of them in fatigues, wearing pistol belts and steel pots, carrying M-16s. They'd formed a perimeter, checking and redirecting traffic. Serious business. A routine day was shaping up at The Fighting 803rd.

No PFC A. Bierce. When had I last seen him? If morning reports fail to go out daily, it isn't long before red flares go up. Captain Papersmith was out too. Big surprise there, too, so I took the opportunity to rummage through the papers on and in Bierce's desk.

Nary a scrap of *Jesus of Capri*. His manuscript had gone with him. Bierce kept file copies of recent morning reports in a basket. The latest was several days ago. In the text, PFC A. Bierce had reassigned himself to the 802nd Liaison Detachment at Fort Huachuca, Arizona.

If I recall correctly, my research on the 803rd had proven that there were no liaison detachments, including the 803rd. PFC Bierce, the rumormonger extraordinaire, the rascal had disappeared himself via his typewriter. Bon voyage, Ambrose III.

At the doorway, Ziggy and I watched the MPs. Their jaws were set as if they were guarding Fort Knox. Last night's steady vibration on the Annex windows had powered up to an audible purr. Since juice in the immediate neighborhood hadn't been restored, the Annex had no electrical noise competition.

We watched Colonel Lanyard get out of a taxi, slamming the door hard enough to rock the little Renault. He went into the Annex. A moment later, Captain Papersmith slunk out and hailed a motorcyclo. I told Ziggy about my evening with Mai.

"This romance shit, you love her, Joey?"
"Yeah. I guess so."
"Is she Catholic?"
"Don't know."
"Buddhist?"
"Don't know."

"She VC?"

"Don't know."

"She a spy?"

"Don't know."

"Them technical books of hers, what're they for?"

"Don't know."

"She sharp at math?"

"Not as sharp as you, Zig. What's 49,271 times 1104?"

"Up your nose with a rubber hose, Joey. Your commie girlfriend, where her and her sis, Quyen, come from, how come she won't open up to you?"

"Don't know."

"How many guys is she banging besides you and the captain and the colonel?"

"Jesus H. Christ, Zig. You make her sound like the town pump."

"How many?"

"Don't know."

"You don't pay her shit and you don't tell her nothing and you don't promise to take her home to America like Papersmith does. What's in it for her?"

I almost said she loves me, too, but that'd be stupid, even after last night's unparalleled intimacy. I still didn't have a clue what motivated her, what she felt about me or anybody else.

"Don't know."

"You'd give her the H-bomb recipe if you had it, wouldn't ya?"

"If she asked nicely while unclothed or in her Dragon Lady outfit. Either, or and anything in between."

"You got my blessing, Joey. Ain't nobody perfect."

I'd parked the Jeep around the block. If it wasn't stolen already, we planned to drive it in to Singh and see what he'd give us for it. But curiosity was killing us two cats.

We walked across to the Annex. The MP at the door raised his rifle to port arms. He had a bowling ball gut, buck sergeant stripes (three chevrons), and a strawberry of a nose.

"No admittance."

"You're accusing us of being the enemy? We look like Vietcong to you, Sarge?" I said cordially. "We're assigned permanent party here at the 803rd."

"Clerk typists," Ziggy added, digging at an armpit.

He stared at Ziggy. "You're a typist?"

"This man has the nimblest fingers in the United States Army," I said.

The MP laughed.

"'Accuse. To affirm another's guilt or unworth; most commonly as a justification of ourselves for having wronged him,'" Ziggy droned.

The MP looked at me. "You two drinking this time of the morning?"

"We're teetotalers. Ambrose Bierce the First and my partner speak in tongues. I have a gift in there I have to get. Be a pal, Sarge."

"Sorry, boys. Officers only. Big powwow."

"We're in civvies. We could be captains or colonels. You don't know."

"You two? Whip some ID on me."

"Left it in my other pants. A big powwow on what?"

The MP said, "Me and Westmoreland are tight. He usually clues me in. Not this time. My feelings are hurt. They must've accidentally forgot me. Get lost and go ask Westy your own self."

Once you say I cannot go into X, naturally I need to snoop in X in the worst way. I said, "It's my kid sister's birthday. I forgot her present. It's in there on my desk. A good buddy in there, Chief Warrant Officer Ralph Buffet, wrapped it for me. If I don't mail if off today, it won't make it home in time."

The MP grinned. "She got terminal cancer and won't see another birthday, right?"

"How'd you know?" I said.

"Five minutes and only you, wiseass," he told me. "Retrieve your present and no dinking around. Otherwise, my tit'll be in a wringer. I got ten days and a wakeup before going to the Land of the Big PX, and getting my discharge to boot. They'll cut me some slack if I lose my concentration just this one time. It's no secret I got me a ferocious short-timer's attitude."

"Congratulations on your walking papers, Sarge. How long've you been in?"

"Nine long years. Got a deputy sheriff job lined up in my hometown."

Shades of my former colleague who'd had the same intentions, who woke up two weeks later at Fort Leonard Wood, Missouri. Him and Sarge here were birds of a lifer feather.

"Outstanding. I envy you, man."

"Five minutes and one second, I lock and load, and sashay on in for you."

I hustled through the door and heard hooting and hollering and clapping. It seemed to be an impromptu gathering, the oddballs facing General Whipple, who stood at the main console.

"Hip-hip-hooray," the research botanist said, lifting a paper cup, followed by more hooting and hollering. "It is a record harvest. We have brought in a bumper crop. Kudos to each and every one of you men. You who have toiled so diligently in this fertile field."

Colonel Lanyard was at the general's side, hairy tree-trunk arms folded, not a happy man. If he was brutally pissed regarding the Jeep, too pissed to savor this special occasion, whatever the hell it was, he'd made my day.

Evidently, Cerebrum 2111X and CAN-DO had hatched its golden egg much earlier than expected. I advanced cautiously. Nobody paid me the slightest attention. They were drinking PX champagne. I was tempted to crash the party, which was growing even louder and happier. They were talking computer jargon. I couldn't make out a word of their Swahili.

Not a total loss. I'd flimflammed myself into the Annex, honing my hornswoggling skills. Practice makes perfect, you know.

I swiped a bottle of the bubbly and walked out. The MP checked his watch and said, "In thirty seconds, you were a dead man. Where's your sister's present?"

I gave him the bottle and slapped my hip. "In my pocket. It's small, an engagement ring."

The MP took a swig and laughed. "Pervert."

"Best of luck as a civilian, man, you lucky son of a bitch."

He hoisted his rifle. "Take care. Your day will come too."

Ziggy and I went to the corner *phở* shop and had breakfast.

"The captain," Ziggy said after we'd eaten.

"What about him?"

He said, "Me and you, Joey, we oughta go shake the lowdown truth outta him is what we oughta do."

"Excellent plan, Tonto. Head 'em up, move 'em out," I said, leading the way to the Jeep, discordantly humming the *Rawhide* theme song until Ziggy said he'd hurt me if I didn't quit.

We drove to the GiGi Snack/Snatch Bar. Lo and behold, the captain was at his favorite table.

"Small world, sir," I said, sitting uninvited.

"A world that is crumbling at my feet. Among other things, the colonel's Jeep was stolen and he's on a rampage. You can't trust these ungrateful subhuman little people, them and their petty thievery. We're here at great sacrifice to preserve their freedom, Private, and their hands are in our wallets nonstop."

He said "Private" with such permanence that I knew our promotion to private first class was fanciful. "Sir, your crumbling world? I don't understand."

"Our mission has been accomplished. The data and the personnel responsible for proving it are secured by MPs."

Playing dumb, I asked, "It has? They are?"

Captain Papersmith gave me a basset-hound look, flinched as he gulped a jigger of *Rhum Caravelle*, chased it with *Ba-mi-ba*, and cleared his throat. "A sad tale."

Ziggy had meanwhile wandered off to a newsstand, leaving me to enjoy the captain's sob story all by my lonesome. If it included the scoop on the Annex, it'd be worth the ordeal.

"Private Joe, if I've given you the impression that I actively participate in decision-making or information processing and data acquisition via CAN-DO, it is merely an illusion."

"But you said the mission's accomplished, sir."

"My world is dissolving," he said, his voice fading.

I resisted the desire to wrap my fingers around his pencil neck and squeeze, as I desired to do to CWO R. Tracy. Alas, violence would not accomplish zip except land me in Leavenworth. Fact was, I felt semi-sorry for the captain. Horse-faced Mildred must have been holding a blowtorch even closer to his family jewels.

He finally continued, "Upon restoration of power, Cerebrum 2111X's operation produced grim data. While Colonel Lanyard notified MACV security forces and directed repulsion of the guerrilla attack on the city's utilities, the CAN-DO personnel worked all night. That computer is devilishly fast, faster than our wildest dreams. It is the most powerful electronic brain in the history of mankind. Nothing will *ever* surpass it."

"Wow."

"I attended a fateful meeting prior to slipping out and coming here."

"Oh?"

He sneered. "It degraded into a celebration."

A Suzy Wong served a rum refill to the captain and me a cold *Ba-mi-ba*.

"The documentation has already been routed. To MACV HQ, CINCPAC, the DoD, the JCS, and ultimately—"

He leaned forward. "—The White House itself."

"Double wow!"

"Joe, the war is ending in two months."

"The VC are marching on Saigon?"

The captain slapped his forehead. "No, you dolt. We won."

"Oh. Uh. Good."

"I see you're skeptical, but there is no mistake. We presently have 74,893 troops deployed in-country," Captain Papersmith said. "Cerebrum 2111X and CAN-DO has calculated that the break-even point is 136,812 American armed services personnel, a figure projected to be achieved on 15 October 1965. Victory is assured at that point, on that date. We will have an overwhelming manpower advantage."

Ah, hindsight. Gotta love it. Coincidence of coincidences, the fifteenth of October 1965 was the date of the first arrest in the U.S. of A. under a new law prohibiting burning one's draft card. It wasn't long before Brother Jack incinerated his own.

"Oh, swell, sir. Fantastic."

"The overall force ratios, the ordnance tonnage multipliers, the negative psychological exponents—"

"Exponents," I said. "This is damn serious business."

"—the confrontation vectors, the war-of-attrition efficacy percentile, the escalatory intersects. Numbers don't lie. There is no mistake. You may wonder why the computation was done here instead of in the safe confines of the Pentagon."

CWO Buffet had covered it with us, but I said, "Did cross my mind, sir."

"Because we're ten thousand miles nearer the action. We have insights that can and did fine-tune the raw data."

"Oh, I get it now."

"The statehood situation is the clincher. It remains a top secret to anyone but the highest levels in the White House and the Pentagon, but we've heard the good news through the grapevine."

"Good news, sir?"

"The statehood rumor is no longer a rumor. It is the most prominent negative psychological exponent. It substantially lowered the troop break-even point. Machinery is in progress to make South Vietnam our fifty-first state. Proposals to Congress are being secretly drafted as we speak. A Constitutional Amendment is required. That is icing on the cake, the strongest confirmation of the accuracy of the CAN-DO numbers.

The process is well advanced. I have it on good authority that rice has been chosen as the state grain, we're that far along."

Thanks to one quarter as a Constitutional Law major, I knew that an Amendment *wasn't* required. Article IV, Section 3, if I'm not mistaken. "That's great, sir."

"You're unaware of my background, Private. My prior duty station was as an ROTC instructor at a major university. I have a mathematical background, an MS in it. In conjunction with my ROTC curricula, I taught remedial mathematics, plane geometry and elementary algebra to jocks.

"The 803rd has the highest average educational level of any unit in the army, many personnel with graduate degrees too. Everybody is a commissioned or warrant officer, except you two and PFC Bierce. Incidentally, where is Bierce? I haven't seen him in some time."

I pondered the captain's math skills. A Mai connection there?

"Saw him not an hour ago, sir. Hard at work at his desk."

"Then where are his morning reports? They're days in arrears."

"I'll ask him, sir. That's intolerable. There's no excuse for it. Ziggy and me, after we become clerk typists, we won't shrug our morning report duties. Scout's honor."

The captain didn't respond. He hadn't heard a word I'd said.

"So that's what the celebration in the Annex was for, huh? When's the VV Day party?"

"I did not take VV Day seriously when I arranged for the restaurant and the announcements. How wrong I was.

It is not a unanimous celebration, Private Joe. I could not bear to revel with them. Isn't it ironic?"

"Isn't what ironic, sir?"

"That I did my part to save my Mai from communist enslavement and my success is hastening my separation from her. I don't know how to tell her."

Mai isn't your Mai, she's *my* Mai, I barely resisted saying.

The photo in the Dien Bien Phu book of the French being led off by the ants popped in my noggin. "You're absolutely, positively certain we've won, sir?"

Captain Papersmith sighed. "Private Joe, it is the ironically sad truth. On October 15, the enemy has no choice but to capitulate."

He guzzled his beer. So as not to be rude, I did too.

"Well, sir, that's kind of swell, isn't it? We can go home soon. You can be reunited with your family. Maybe take a shot at bringing whatshername with you."

"Mai."

"Mai. If not as a nanny, well, you'll come up with something," I said, thinking, not a chance, pal; we'll send you a wedding invitation.

The captain blinked, either summoning a reply or stifling tears.

The floorboards creaked. Ziggy lumbered in and sat. He tossed a rolled-up magazine on the table. His eyes were redder than the captain's.

"What's up, Zig?"

"Lookie."

I unrolled the magazine, an August 6, 1965 *Time*, the airmail edition they sold in Saigon, its pages as thin as toilet paper. Ziggy had it open to an article entitled *The Moon-Faced Mars*.

I didn't have to read the piece in toto. The picture of Mars taken from Mariner 4 was worth a helluva lot more than a thousand words. Nothing but craters and rough lifeless terrain. No canals and gondoliers, no vegetation, no Martians. The Red Planet was a meteor-pocked chunk of moonlike rock.

Flippancy may not have been the ideal approach, but I was desperate to lighten him up. "Hey, Zig, that's good news, isn't it? There'll be no invasion from outer space."

The captain was trying to focus on the article. "Invasion? What invasion? I told you, soldier, we've won."

"They ain't there, Joey," Ziggy said.

"What are you babbling about, Zbitgysz? They are throughout the countryside. They have neither the resources nor the resolve to prolong their godless communist aggression against our overwhelming numerical superiority."

A tear trickled down Ziggy's cheek. "Don't you see, Joey? They were and they weren't there."

"Were and weren't?"

"Like I once told you, they're on the street, disguised as humans. Soon as I saw this pitcher they went and started fading and vanishing, Joey. They're going out of existence on account of they never were. I seen some by the newsstand. Seen 'em go *poof*."

Captain Papersmith's head jerked from Ziggy's to mine. "Who, what?"

The Martians winking out before Ziggy's eyes. They weren't tooling toward Earth to herd us into feedlots. I tried to cheer him up.

"C'mon, Zig. No radioactive death beams, none of that conquesting and enslaving shit they do in your magazines. That's terrific. Drink your beer. We'll talk later in length. I know it's a blow, but I'll help you through it. C'mon, man. Bottom's up."

"Death beams," Captain Papersmith said from *his* distant planet. "Ridiculous. The Vietcong don't even possess aircraft."

Ziggy blew his nose. If I'd had any doubts why he was taking it so hard, I didn't now. He'd rather the Martians came in and roasted us than not exist at all. Maybe he didn't deep-down believe they were real. Ziggy's not that loopy.

He did believe they *could* be real. Now, all of a sudden, he didn't and they couldn't be. The insular world in which he was comfortable, within his piles of sci-fi reading material, in which he *was* accepted, was an imaginary one.

In his own way, he was as crushed as the over-religious zealots in the Great Beyond. Fire and brimstone and eternal torture of billions of heretics and atheists and agnostics was preferable to having their convictions dashed.

Ziggy would not give up. "Joey, you think they doctored them pitchers? A conspiracy by the government so people don't panic?"

I shook my head. "Sorry, Zig. I love high-level conspiracies too, but that's a reach."

"Will you men make some sense," the captain demanded. "Am I the only sane and sober person at this table? Am I?"

Ziggy and I didn't answer. I simultaneously saw what Ziggy saw. The captain could not have seen what we saw because his back was to the door.

What he couldn't see, what we saw, was what we didn't see. The bartender and her girls had disappeared.

We were alone, the three of us and the two young Vietnamese males who were riding their motorbike onto the sidewalk. The kid in the rear jumped off. He carried a satchel, as innocuous-looking as a kid's book bag.

We knew what was in the bag. Ziggy rose out of his chair with a banshee yell. I grabbed and shouted at him, "Down!"

Our best chance was to hit the deck, but pulling down Ziggy was like grabbing onto a freight train. He charged to the door, still howling.

The captain stood up and swiveled his idiotic head, asking what Private Zbitgysz's problem was now. Problem was that the satchel was now trailing sparks and the VC was slinging it into the GiGi.

"Ziggy!" I screamed.

His only chance, too, was to dive low and behind something.

"Edward, no! Down!"

Edward was Ziggy's Christian name. I thought using it would trigger an obedience reaction, some dark family demon that'd make him listen. It didn't.

The disoriented captain was between me and the table, standing like a total dipshit. I lunged for Ziggy, but got my feet tangled with Papersmith's. We went ass-over-teakettle, me landing on top of him.

I dug for my peashooter pistol as the satchel bounced off Ziggy's chest. He booted it and kept howling and lumbering ahead. The satchel blew up in midair.

Wanna know what the real deal sounds like? A genuine *ka-boom* at close, close range?

Find an old war movie on the tube, okay? When a scene comes on with big guns firing, crank the volume all the way up, and press an ear to the speaker. It'll be almost as loud, a reasonable simulation. But it cannot simulate the cordite stink that'll burn your nostrils like battery acid. It cannot simulate the screams of the dying and the stink of the dead. All it can do is give you a nasty case of tinnitus.

The shock wave of the explosion slammed the captain and me upward and against the wall. Shrapnel pierced me as if I'd slow-danced with a porcupine. Other than that and gagging on the smoke, I was semi-okay. I was able to stand and move forward.

Captain Papersmith was curled in a ball, his eyes clenched. At a glance, he appeared unharmed, thanks to me being on top of him. I staggered to Ziggy.

The whole front of the bar was blown out. Ziggy lurched like a rummy but, incredibly, he hadn't been knocked from his feet. I recollected his reformatory hack with the Louisville slugger.

The sapper who'd flung the bomb was in pieces on the sidewalk. One of his arms, no longer joined to its shoulder, was twitching. Innocent civilians were on the ground too, wailing and bleeding.

Ziggy playing soccer with the satchel, he'd saved my life and made one of the Cong pay with his. I stumbled outside after his partner. He should've gotten away clean, but the blast had sent him and his motorbike sprawling. He was in the street now, kicking at his starter.

Sweat and blood in my eyes interfered with my vision. I wiped them with a sleeve and, son of a motherfucking bitch, it was Charlie! Had to be.

Blue fumes came bubbling out the exhaust. He took off, weaving into traffic that was pretty well stopped. I ran at him and squeezed off a round. The accurate range of my .25 was ten feet, max. I missed.

I fired again and saw his shirt fabric flutter and perforate at the right shoulder. He winced and nearly dumped the bike, but he recovered. Charlie was gone. I'd be firing wild, into a crowd, so I didn't. We had plenty of bloody innocents for one day, thank you.

Ziggy stood on the sidewalk. He wore a terrible, pained expression. His shirt had turned a solid glossy red.

Ziggy hugged himself, holding his insides in.

"Joey, they killt me."

His legs gave out. He hit the pavement on his knees and keeled over, dead when I got to him.

That's what they told me. They said I was screaming and crying and hugging his corpse. They said I was calling for my mother.

They said that they'd had to peel my fingers straight, one at a time, to pry me loose, even though by then I'd passed out.

Chapter Twenty Two

They flew me in a four-engine turboprop C-130 to Clark Air Force Base Hospital in the Philippines for surgery. I was hurt worse than I thought was, but I did not experience agonizing pain. I felt like I had a hundred bee stings. I felt like I had a mild headache all over my body.

After they sliced into me and I came out of the anesthetic, a nurse gave me a little plastic vial of what the surgeons had tweezered out of my hide and innards, all but that vessel-grazing forearm dollop they didn't remove. Could've been gold nuggets prospectors brought in from panning, but the metal was gray and silver, chunks of nail and pot metal and who knows what else they'd packed in their *plastique*.

The little bastards were masters at improvisation, working with what they stole from us and were supplied by Hanoi and the Bolsheviks farther north. I was an accomplished scrounger, but an amateur in comparison.

The nurse said ten or twelve of those fragments had barely missed something vital. I ought to feel blessed. I pissed her off because I didn't act as if I felt blessed, and I refused to say why. My best friend was dead and my buddy Charlie had turned out to be a commie traitor who'd tried to kill me too. I would've told her, but then she'd've felt rotten and cried, and I'd've felt even shittier.

Or maybe she wouldn't've cried, the way I pouted, behaving like a pussy. For Chrissake, I hadn't been in combat. Not like the infantry troops who were coming in faster and faster, more and more of them airlifted here every day. Some of them were airlifted home in short order, zippered inside body bags.

I'd been at the wrong place, at the wrong time, in a bar, early in the day, malingering, drinking when I should've been working and contributing to the war effort. Hell, I couldn't even give the Intelligence folk who interviewed me anything useful on Charlie, not even his real name. I fingered his hangout with his cowboy buddies, though I supposed they'd moved along. He wouldn't be hanging out much at Mama-san's either.

Nobody at the hospital had heard of VV Day. Nobody had heard that the war was ending any minute, and they looked at me funny when I said it was. To keep out of the psycho ward, I learned to shut my trap on the subject.

Given the tropical climate and the fact that the Vietcong surely didn't bother to wash their hands before assembling their explosives, my doctor said controlling infection as it spread from wound to wound was like trying to eradicate fleas in a kennel. There was a limit to how much penicillin they could pump into me, and they'd already exceeded it. After an onset of diarrhea and a rash on the inside of my mouth, they reduced the dosage.

I was informed that I'd be at the hospital for a while and not to make any plans. My immune system couldn't clobber the germs overnight. I had so much time to spend in the sack, flat on my ass, so much time to think.

Had my Dragon Lady orchestrated the attack on us? Had she been in cahoots with Charlie and his partner? I'd never mentioned her to Charlie, except at the Dakao coffeehouse as a boy-girl hypothetical, and never him to her.

Had Mai ordered our deaths to whitewash our pillow talk?

I shunted aside those paranoid notions to preserve what remained of my sanity. If my obsession with Mai had led to Ziggy's death…

To ease my mind, I let myself worry about VD instead. After all, if Mai could orchestrate a bombing, she might have liked infecting stupid-ass GIs like me. I ran into a medic buddy of Larry Sibelius's, so I had him rush a blood test on me. The medic said it came back negative and I shouldn't worry, as the syph didn't capitulate to penicillin as easily as the clap did. It would've shown up and I was as clean as a whistle. My Dragon Lady and I had not exchanged virulent critters before I'd used gold dollars. Leaving that worry behind didn't provide much relief. It just let the other bad thoughts back in.

Brigadier General Whipple came by very late one night and awakened me. He was wearing a second star, now Major General Whipple. He was en route stateside for a new assignment that he did not reveal to me. The general sat at my bedside, like Ward Cleaver if The Beav was in bed with the mumps. He called me "son" and tried to whip a Bronze Star on me (à la Larry Sibelius at Nha Trang). Hearing "son" didn't choke me up this time. Thinking about Ziggy did.

After him reading a peculiar citation describing how I'd seen the sappers and warned off passersby who were able to duck to safety, I politely declined. I told him emphatically that Ziggy had been the hero, not me.

I asked about the 803rd and Cerebrum 2111X and CAN-DO and VV Day and the war in general. He shushed me and changed the subject to injured plants.

How when diseased or suffering a broken stem, they needed rest and additional nourishment and the proper medication. Us mammals were analogous.

When I woke up in the a.m., I thought I'd hallucinated his visit, but there was a potted plant at my bedside (plenty of green leaves and tangled vines, genus unknown). A Purple Heart and Bronze Star were pinned to my hospital pajamas. I kept the first piece of hardware. The latter went out with the trash that also contained my pus-stained dressings.

I had dreams by the shitload.

I constantly dreamt about Mai. They were the most exotic and erotic dreams I'd ever had. If my skivvies weren't wet when I woke up, my body and eyes were.

Many dreams were of Mai in the Dragon Lady dress in the cartoon panel from my wallet she'd wadded up and contemptuously discarded. My Dragon Lady had the cartoon Dragon Lady's face. She dressed per my fetish. She held an ivory cigarette holder that fizzled like a Fourth of July sparkler. She pitched it to me, and it became a satchel charge when it struck my chest.

During a feverish catnap, after rerunning Papersmith and I hitting the deck in the GiGi Snack Bar, a variation of my life flashed before my eyes. Not events, but an amalgam of people promenading across the stage adjacent our grade school gym, participants in a spring pageant: Judy, Doug, Mother, Father, Jack, Papersmith, Lanyard, Whipple, Step-Pappy, PFC Bierce, CWO Buffet, Mama-san, and cackling Quyen. Even Wendi with the bubbled "i" and horn-rimmed glasses, and Mildred Papersmith, neither of whom I'd met.

Ziggy was notably absent.

I never ever dreamt about Ziggy. If was as if he'd evaporated with his Martians. Asleep, he was illusory.

And when I was awake, I couldn't bear to think about him standing outside the GiGi holding his insides in. Yet I couldn't stop.

Why haven't I mentioned Ziggy in the post-death present? He's with us somewhere beyond my Vietnamless quarantine. Of course he is, though he's not in my useless The Great Beyond phone directory. Some folks are probably unlisted.

I have an incredible coincidence to tell Ziggy, should we meet again. There were a dozen patients assigned to our hospital bay, always coming and going, bound for return to Vietnam or to home, dead or alive. A guy in the bunk next to me had superficial leg wounds. He was in for minor surgery and a trip back to his unit. He wasn't especially talkative. Nor was I.

He came out of the shower one morning, towel around his waist. I damn near fell out of bed. He wore a tattoo of Piet Mondrian's *Composition 1921* on an arm. It nearly wrapped a biceps.

I managed to ask, "You dig modern art?"

"Yep. Flames painted on a car."

"That's it for art?"

"Art pictures that look like something, I guess I like. You know, that one that was on the *Saturday Evening Post* cover where they're sitting at the table at Thanksgiving with the turkey in the middle of it. I forget the guy's name who did it. That's art. This modern abstracted shit, you can shove it."

"Then why this tattoo?"

He looked at his arm as if it were gangrenous and asked, "That's what this is? Art? Nobody in my family knows what it was. Nobody I met knows what it is. We thought it come out of the tattooer's head, like, you know, a kid with crayons."

I told him what it was and who Piet Mondrian was. He replied with a so-what look.

"Why this tattoo?" I asked again.

"Damned if I remember."

"Where're you from?"

"Billings, Montana."

Bingo. "Ever stationed at Fort Ord?"

"Yeah, and Ord's where the tattoo come from. I was on pass, a weekend in town. Monterey, Salinas, maybe Frisco, too. Dunno. Had some drinks and don't remember shit except waking up in an alley with a brutal hangover and a sore arm."

I rolled up my sleeve, flexed Big Sky Country, watched his eyes bulge, and told my story. For a couple of fellas who didn't talk much and had nothing in common except Uncle Sam and defaced skin, we yakked and yakked and yakked. We presumed we'd met in a bar and had gone pub-crawling together. We must've had quite a time.

His unit was an aviation company in Qui Nhon up on the South China Sea coast. He was a mechanic and crew chief on a twin-engine Caribou, and got down to Tan Son Nhat once or twice a month.

I gave him directions to the 803rd. He promised to look me up next time in Saigon and I promised if I was transferred anywhere, I'd write him. We'd connect and tie another one on.

Didn't happen. It usually didn't in the service. Not because anybody's insincere. It's just that things and people change so damn fast.

I'd already forgotten his name, but I missed him when he checked out of the hospital. I was lonely. No familiar faces, no mail. I'd written Mother and I knew she'd written me immediately after she'd received the telegram they sent when a husband or son was wounded or killed. I knew she had, but my mail hadn't caught up to me in this pre-Internet, pre-cellular eon.

Captain Papersmith had been taken to Clark, too. I didn't know that for a week. He hadn't visited me. This hurt my feelings since I figured he'd be ambulatory. Other than me falling on him, he couldn't've been bunged up too severely. I'd taken shrapnel with his name on it.

Being an officer, Papersmith was in a different wing, in a four-man room, not packed into a bay as I was. I found his room as a gaggle of brass was going into it, including two generals and a bird colonel. I hung around in the hallway and saw them huddled at his bed. They stayed fifteen minutes. I waited till they were long gone and went in.

On his nightstand were the reasons the brass had paid him a call. There were gold oak leaves on it. Captain Papersmith was now Major Papersmith. The major had tubes in his nose and was dozing. Besides the promotion, there was a medal case and a citation for bravery. I saw the Silver Star pinned to his pajamas and read the citation.

Then-Captain Dean J. Papersmith had been cited for heroism in the face of a Vietcong guerrilla bombing attack in a Saigon civilian recreational establishment frequented by MACV military personnel. Disregarding his own safety, he'd shielded a fellow soldier, an enlisted man, in all likelihood saving his life when the communist bomb explosion had occurred. He'd unsuccessfully attempted to prevent the death of a second enlisted man, whom he'd heroically administered first aid to following a firefight in which he'd mortally wounded one fleeing perpetrator and killed the other.

I stood there a moment, breathing deeply, to regain a modicum of self-control.

I gently nudged the major, then smiled and whispered hello into his ear, as not to disturb or attract the attention of his roommates or the medical staff.

He gave me a sidelong glance and a weak nod.

"Congratulations on your battlefield promotion, sir."

An even weaker nod.

"What's wrong, sir?" I whispered. "Nothing too serious, I trust."

"They're running tests," he rasped. "They'll know soon."

I gave his Silver Star a tug and said I knew one thing that was wrong. "Do I have to spell it out, Major, sir?"

He shook his head.

"Isn't the Silver Star the third highest heroism award, sir? The next higher being the Distinguished Service Cross? The first is the Congressional Medal of Honor."

He nodded.

I moved in against his ear. Speaking as congenially as a Red Cross Donut Dolly wheeling a coffee and sweets cart, taking requests, I said, "Fine, what's done is done. I personally didn't give a damn about medals, but if you don't put Ziggy in for a DSC, I'm gonna shove your Silver Star up your ass. Sideways. Give you a legit reason for being in your deathbed here. Do you understand, you miserable craven despicable useless sneaky worthless chickenshit rancid lying ass-licking piece-of-bat-guano douche-bag motherfucking cocksucking dildo of a cowardly peckerhead cunt? Sir."

He nodded.

"And slip in here in the dark of night and take those fucking tubes out of your fucking nose and make them into a fucking tourniquet for your family-fucking-jewels."

He flinched.

"And strangle your scrotum with it like I'd twist a chicken's neck."

Another flinch, bordering on a spasm.

"Good afternoon, sir," I said, straightening up and clicking my heels. I saluted and did a snappy one-eighty.

◆

Two days later, a MACV awards and decorations clerk came by and asked me to verify the major's narrative on Private Edward N. Zbitgysz, a true version of events. I said it was correct to my recollection. I added that Private Zbitgysz was the bravest man I ever knew. My tears made the clerk uneasy, so he scribbled notes fast and bugged out.

Later in that day, while I was on the terrace, enjoying the sun and reading, Lee Harvey Oswald came up to me. They brought books on carts for us and the selection was slim, but I was halfway through a dandy, a recent bestseller set in Paris when the Germans were bailing out in 1944. To torch the city or not to torch the city, as mandated by the Führer, that was the question.

I didn't realize he was there till he was five feet from me, clearing his throat to get my attention. He handed me picture ID that identified him as Chief Warrant Officer R. Tracy of the CID, the Criminal Investigation Division.

"In case you've forgotten, Private Joe," he said, smirking.

I looked at the ID, looked at him, looked at the ID. I thought of the cartoon Dick Tracy's powerful, square jaw, in contrast to CWO Tracy's weak Oswaldian counterpart. "Oh, right. I vaguely remember you chatting with Sergeant Rubicon. How's Rubicon doing?"

"Better than his wife is."

"Nice guy. It's a shame."

His smirk tilted but didn't widen. "Go ahead, take your time. Everybody does."

"I'm dying to know what the R. stands for, Mr. Detective R. Tracy."

He snapped his fingers, and I handed him back the embossed plastic.

"What'd I do for you to follow me throughout Saigon and hunt me all the way here to Clark?"

"I think you know."

Me and my Dragon Lady/Mata Hari. Not to mention dealings with Mr. Singh, the stolen M-14 and ammo and Jeep we sold to Singh, various and sundry shenanigans at the 803rd, ad infinitum. After I break every rock inside Leavenworth's walls, I'll build my own gallows.

Proactive was a future buzzword we'd been mercifully spared in the 1960s. But proactively, I laid my best hard-ass stare on the CID agent till he averted his beady eyes, and said, "Don't have the foggiest what you're talking about, Mr. Tracy. The army must not have much crime for you to investigate for you to harass a wounded soldier who, incidentally, was awarded a Bronze Star for valor."

"If you want to play dumb, Private, it's your funeral."

He pulled stapled sheets of paper out of his briefcase and rattled off familiar titles of books, beginning with *People's War People's Army*. It took him five minutes to finish.

"Ring a bell?" he said.

My overdue library books. I was stunned. I didn't know whether to laugh or cry, to shit or go blind. Immensely relieved that we weren't on the subject of black marketeering and/or high treason, I exhaled and said. "Most were damn good reads."

"*Good*? If you have a taste for seditious communist filth, they are. Half these books you stole raise a stink in respect to the status quo," CWO Tracy said. "Why would you care what the Vietminh did to the French army at Dien Bien Phu? *The Quiet American* by some anti-American limey named Greene Graham too. Were you gloating?"

"Are you a literature critic, sir? Some of these are classics. And, hey, they were in the Tan Son Nhat library."

"I'm expressing my opinion as a good, loyal American."

"Opinions are like assholes," I said. "Everybody's got one. Last I heard, America's a free country based on a piece of paper that includes the First Amendment."

CWO Tracy laughed. "Not when you're in the army is it a free country. You're government property. Not when you've stolen that many books from military-operated libraries at Tan Son Nhat."

"How many?"

"I've tallied two-hundred-and-thirteen books. A sizable percentage are subversive, written by artists, communists and faggots like those weirdo Spaniard painters."

"What faggot weirdo Spanish painters and what have they got to do with books?"

"Paul Picasso and whatshisname Daley."

I had to laugh. "*Pablo* Picasso and Salvador Dalí weren't fairies, Tracy. They got more ass than a toilet seat. You and I should be so lucky. You want subversive, you should see *Dr. Strangelove*—"

"I walked out halfway through. Antiwar propaganda."

"The ending where the world's one big mushroom cloud farm, yeah, it might be considered propaganda. Irrespective of your movie review, Tracy, *Dr. Strangelove, or How I Learned to Stop Worrying and Love the Bomb* is the greatest movie ever made. Know where I saw it? The Ft. Ord post theatre."

Note: I also saw *Strangelove* on DVD toward my earthly end when the chemo and meds failed to conquer the pain. Over and over again. Gave me a chuckle or three.

"Let's stay on the subject, Private Joe," CWO R. Tracy said. "You have in your possession two-hundred-and-thirteen pieces of stolen government property."

I thought the total might be closer to three hundred, but, hey, who's counting?

"I didn't steal them, I borrowed them. I had every intention of returning them, but I've been busy taking on more responsibility, on special assignments involving alternative matériel sources. Plus assisting in repulsing a communist attack on the 803rd Annex and sustaining injuries, from which I am slowly recovering."

"Spare me the bullshit, Private Joe. A number of the books have been overdue for months. Did they go on the black market?"

"Oh, I get it now. You're the library police."

"Don't get smart, soldier."

"I didn't think books were a hot item on the black market unless they're photos of naked ladies or the Gutenberg Bible."

"That's how much you know, Joe."

"You'll find them all in our hotel room if it hasn't been cleaned out."

I was confident the books would be untouched, as I was the only person I knew who would steal a book. I asked Tracy if he knew who he looked like.

He said he'd been reminded five million times and that he was saving up for plastic surgery the army wouldn't pay for.

"I don't deserve this," he said bitterly. "My career was on the rise until November 22, 1963. On top of the teasing about my name, I'm reduced to petty theft investigations of smart-mouthed pinko punks like you."

"I'm awfully sorry," I lied. "Your talents are being squandered."

"Are you patronizing me, Private?"

"Not me, sir. I do wish you'd tell me what the R. stands for."

He ignored me and said since I cooperated and was wounded in action and had been under a Vietcong attack at my unit, he'd drop charges if the books were where I said they'd be. I suspected he was making a bigger deal out of me than he had to.

If he'd followed me to the 803rd and Mai's, he sure as hell knew where I lived, where the books were. I had a sneaking hunch that Tracy didn't mind being tied up in a long-term library book caper. He wouldn't have to go nose-to-nose with hardcore criminals, tough customers of both the American and Vietnamese variety.

Regardless, I never saw CWO Tracy of the CID again. Nor, alas, the books.

◆

By and by, they C-130'd me back to Tan Son Nhat, where I got a final check-up at the field hospital. The airbase was Grand Central Station. Uniformed U.S. units and their vehicles and equipment were arriving in droves. Weeks away from Saigon seemed like years.

I was itching to go into town to find my Dragon Lady and get the truth out of her, but the hospital kept an eye on us. Everybody was going by the book about everything, no exceptions. This war was getting beyond serious.

I was sitting on my bunk in the transient hootch, waiting for my reassignment orders when in walked Charlie. I'd been reading the Nazis-in-Gay Paree book I'd totally forgotten to leave behind at Clark. Charlie jolted me out of my literary trance a helluva lot quicker than CWO R. Tracy had.

Reflexively, I slapped my pocket for the pistol I no longer owned. My sudden action puzzled him. His baggy ARVN uniform puzzled me.

"What the hell?" I said.

"What the hell you," Charlie said. "Tell me, Joe. Why you shoot me when electric pole blow up?"

"I wasn't shooting. I prevented a Looney Tunes colonel from drilling you, pal. I grabbed his arm or you'd be dead."

"For sure?"

"For sure."

As it wasn't clear if Charlie was unarmed, I played it cool. Though I was aching to, I didn't inquire why he'd slung a satchel charge in the GiGi Snack Bar, killing Ziggy and almost me, too. I didn't want a repeat performance. I wanted justice. And some truth, too.

With all the cool I was able to muster, I swallowed, then asked, "So how are you?"

"Not for shit, Joe. They grab me off street two week ago. Take me to Quang Trung."

"Nice of you to drop by. How'd you get away?" I spoke slowly, as if to a child, attempting to read him.

"They give me pass. Liberty."

An outright lie. Unless he'd signed his own pass. The South Vietnamese Army did not let fresh meat out of their sight.

"Me sorry for Ziggy. You too, Joe."

Charlie was deadpan, eyes glazing. Damn good acting on his part. I gritted my teeth. I didn't say a word.

"Joe, why you look at me how you look at me?"

Enough beating around the bush. "Charlie, there's a hitch in your shoulder. You get hurt recently?"

He lifted a leg and showed me a skinned knee. "No shoulder. Leg. Me ride Honda on Tran Quy Cap Street. You know Tran Quy Cap, Joe?"

"Yeah. Parallel to Hong Tap Tu. Isn't there an Italian restaurant there?"

"Traffic slow. ARVN, they pull truck in front me, yell to show ID. I try go by. Guy in truck have pole he stick out. Knock me off bike."

"You're in the army now," I sang badly. "Sure you didn't hurt a shoulder?"

"No shoulder. Knee."

"Raise your shirt and turn around. Lift it high," I said, as if I were Colonel Lanyard giving an order. My eyes didn't leave him.

I went through the hand motions, so there'd be no misunderstanding what I wanted him to do.

Charlie smiled nervously and palmed his crotch. "They operate on you in hospital? Cut prick off? You go queer, Joe? Your hands on me when we go see them shoot rich Chinaman, go too late. Too many people to push through."

"It's a game of inches."

"Then we go Dakao. You ask me about boy and girl. You bullshit and say girl not for you."

"C'mon, Charlie, humor me. They're having a mosquito problem here," I said, changing my tone. "They've got long stingers and carry malaria, yellow fever, all that nasty shit. It's for your own good. I can get you treated here if you have it."

He did humor me, exposing a smooth brown back. No scars, no bullet holes, nary a pimple.

"Okay?"

"Okay," I whispered, lacking the gonads to confess my suspicions.

Lesson learned: We all look alike to him and they all look alike to us. A Vietnamese Charlie his size and age on a motorbike in the heat of bloodletting was therefore a Charlie of the VC persuasion.

His friendship was pure, mine racial and tentative.

"Anything I can do for you, man?" I asked, feeling lower than snakeshit.

"No, Joe."

"Cigarettes? I got a brand-new ration."

Charlie shook his head. "No time."

That was when I knew Charlie was saying goodbye. He was going over the hill. The only reason he hadn't ditched the uniform yet was to get in to see me.

We small-talked on the good times. The drinking and carousing with Ziggy. The pussy at Mama-san's. The execution we barely missed (no sweat, Charlie had said, plenty more greedy Chinamen). Our long talks. Coffee and pastries at Dakao. Him acquiring the vital electrical plugs.

"I like you, Joe. Mama-san, you good to her."

"She was nice, Charlie. Despite her profession, she's a good lady."

"Mama-san, she my mother me."

That was a bulletin. I could not summon a reply.

We had a big hug and Charlie left.

It was my turn for glassy eyes.

◆

Kind reader, I am so sorry. Remember when I walked away from Slick after my chicken or fish wisecrack and heard Smitty scream inside his house? And left you hanging?

Well, this is what happened....

Smitty comes flying out his front door, legs pumping, still screaming as he sees me and angles in my direction.

"Whoa Nellie," I say, palms up.

He skids to a stop on the slippery grass and nearly takes a tumble.

"Joe, they invade. All over my house. I don't know. I never see them before. I cannot turn without one in my face."

"Who? What?"

"I don't know. They have these uniforms on."

He's gasping, incoherent. "Okay, okay. Go in my place and watch some TV. The Vietnam War is on. It'll settle you down."

He obeys and I walk into his place.

"Hello, young man."

"Uh, hi, Sister."

The nun in black-and-white habit is gray, bespectacled and plump. I shake her proffered flesh-and-blood hand.

"I'm Sister Agnes. And you, sir?"

More nuns are behind her, busying themselves with dust mops and lemon-scented waxes. The aroma of baking dominates.

"Er, um, I'm Joe."

"It's very nice to meet you, Joe. Would you like a chocolate chip cookie? Sister Mary Jean is a wonderful baker. They'll be done shortly."

I hear more activity upstairs. "I would very much, Sister. Thank you. May I ask where you came from?"

Sister Agnes frowns. "That's the strangest thing, Joe. I know that I'm in The Great Beyond. My fellow sisters do, too. But we cannot recall the circumstances that brought us here nor the acquaintance of one another."

"Very peculiar," I say. "How many of you are there?"

"Seventy of us. We counted."

I smile, but do not reply. Bingo. Smitty's promised seventy virgins.

"The young man who lives here, he is troubled."

I nod. "He sure is."

"He's messy. We'll clean up after him and cook, and try to be of comfort to him."

"He'll appreciate it when he calms down. I know he will."

"Joe, I hear the oven door open. The cookies should be ready."

"Lead the way, Sister Agnes."

Chapter Twenty Three

Next morning, I see no activity at Slick's. I check the house out as I did upon meeting Madge. Gone. Him and the old sergeant both. What the hell is this place, a halfway house?

I'm sitting on that porch, searching my brain for some logic in this. Yeah, our ringmasters have off-the-wall funny bones, but I'm failing to capture their reasoning. Is there reasoning?

I am in the midst of sadistic and well-planned chaos.

There is a relatively-new science in the Land of the Living known as chaos theory. Where things are chaotic, except they really ain't, something like that.

Whichever, it's all about tormenting me and me tormenting Smitty. I can think of no other reason why he's still around.

An hour ago, he came out to bitch about today's elevator-music tune: "La Bamba."

"Mr. Joe, what is this they are playing? It has a--how you say?--tempo, a beat that does not let me relax."

I've been letting him stay with me in a spare bedroom, as the seventy nuns seem to have staked a claim.

"It's Israel's national anthem," I tell him. "Catchy, huh?"

"Are you lying to me again, Joe?"

"Smitty, I'd never lie to you," I lie.

He cocks his head to his place. "Please, Joe, when will they leave?"

I smell baking in the air. Oatmeal raisin. I'll have to mosey on over. "No time soon, I hope."

He pouts and goes back inside.

The mail truck pulls into the cul-de-sac. TGBPS (The Great Beyond Postal Service) drives red, white and blue trucks like American USPS trucks in The Land of the Living. They're also right-hand drive, so the driver can stick mail in mailboxes without getting out.

Problem is, drivers and vehicles are holograms. I proved this once by laying down and letting one pass over me. Nary a scratch. TGBPS delivers lots of mail, much of it junk. As the mail is also air, our boxes are empty even when they're stuffed.

I cannot stop myself from writing letters to family and friends, dead or alive. I realize it's a waste of time, but I have time to waste. I seal them inside envelopes that, like my food, are simply there, usually on the dining room table beside the paper napkins.

The first-class postage on the envelopes is entertaining if useless. The stamps are decorative, many quite attractive. Those with portraiture do not depict world leaders or achievers—this is where the fun comes in—but notorious mail robbers.

Black Bart, who robbed a number of Wells Fargo coaches in the 1800s. Notorious 1930s outlaw Alvin Karpis. Principals of England's 1963 Great Train Robbery. And more obscure scofflaws.

The best depicts a stand of bamboo, a professional-looking piece of artwork. The caption: SOUTH VIETNAM'S STATE GRASS.

I put the letters in my mailbox with the flag up. The mail truck comes by. Of course nothing happens. Until I stop looking for as short a time as an eyeblink. Then the flag is down, my mail gone, presumably dispatched to a black hole.

◆

My 1965 hospital postal adventures were almost as bizarre.

Being wounded and hospitalized in order to increase one's mail volume is to do it the hard way, but it sure as hell worked. My mail finally arrived. Volume had quintupled, from loved ones and from people I hadn't seen in ages. I reciprocated, banging out four or five letters per day, a frenzy of communication.

In response to a bland, no-class telegram from the Department of the Army announcing that her son (name, rank, service number) had been "slightly" wounded, my mother wrote, *I LOVE YOU!!! I pray for you and your speedy recovery. Your loving mother.* I don't think she'd prayed once in her life, so I was really moved.

I know Ziggy's mother got a telegram, too. I know she received the same message, with the omission of "slightly." As they say, there's the right way, the wrong way, and the army way.

I initiated contact with Ziggy's mom. It didn't end until her death in 1988. I hope she's been reunited with the Zigster. In her first letter to me after my first to her, she wrote that her Edward considered me the brother he didn't have. She said she loved and admired his interests such as astramony (sic), literature, science, and the solor (sic) system. She was as heartfelt as she was unschooled. My stepfather would've flunked her in a blink of an eye.

Step-asshole did not write me, but his Wendi sent me a get-well-soon card on behalf of them both. I wrote her to thank her for the card. She wrote to thank me for thanking her. I wrote to thank her for thanking me for thanking her.

We exchanged photos. The horn-rimmed glasses Mother had described were gone. Her permanent wave was gone, and her hair was long and straight. There was something unscholarly in her eyes. When I asked if I could bring home a gift from the exotic Orient and what would she like, she requested in detail a set of lingerie that'd drive any man out of his mind.

Our correspondence had moved to another level.

My brother Jack did not write. Mother had to spring it on me that he'd taken part in a campus anti-war demonstration and that a bad situation was brewing with unkempt new friends of his, including the girl he's gaga over, who was totally unsuitable. A girl who had hair longer than Cher's. A girl who wore dresses that were either too short or too long, and bracelets that jangled. A girl who did not shave her legs and armpits, for Heaven's sake. Mother said that while Jack would never admit it, she felt that he was ashamed to write me.

If you can believe it, they're planning to burn their draft cards in front of God and everybody. I swear, darling, I don't understand either of you kids.

Jack enjoyed 2-S draft status. I knew by experience that as long as he was in school he'd retain it. They'd call him up after the women and children. I wrote him a postcard telling him that for a grad school prodigy, he certainly could be a dumb shit. Burning a 2-S draft card was like burning a one-hundred-thousand dollar bill.

Ten feet from the mail room, I stopped and tore it up.

I wrote him a four-page, single-spaced letter, pouring my guts out.

Chapter Twenty Four

October 15, 1965, the day that there were 136,812 American troops in South Vietnam. Make that 136,811.5. While exiting a stairway from a 707 at Tan Son Nhat, a guy who'd been nipping on a pint of 151-proof rum fell down and broke his crown. He was loaded into an ambulance, condition unknown.

Pope Paul's visit to America was the cover story on *Life* magazine's October 15, 1965 issue. The front page of the October 15 *Los Angeles Times* celebrated the return home of their World Series champion Dodgers, after they'd defeated the Minnesota Twins, four games to three. It shared the page with a banner that screamed DRAFT CALL REACHES NEW HIGH.

October 15 was the birth date of Barry McGuire, who sang one of my all-time favorites, *The Eve of Destruction*, the *Dr. Strangelove* of tunes. October 15 was the birthday of Olympic gold medalist sprinter Bobby Morrow and actress Jean Peters and Arthur Schlesinger and Friedrich Nietzsche.

October 15, 1965 was not VV Day. There was no dancing in any street, no horns honking, no confetti snowing from windows.

My medical release was held up until October 15, but not for medical considerations. Earlier in the week the generals who ran South Vietnam had a spat they settled with another coup d'état. Our MACV bigwigs were running out of patience. But what the hell were they gonna do? Send the Saigon generalissimos to bed without their supper? Life quickly resumed Saigon's version of normality and I was free to go.

The War was building steam. "Escalating" would soon be the operative buzzword. "Imbedded" applied too, but the term wasn't used until decades later in a similar clusterfuck on the opposite end of the Asian continent.

There were tanks and trucks and Jeeps and GIs in Saigon, an olive-drab gridlock, an increasingly volatile environment. I was amazed that the Paris of the Orient simply didn't blow up like a cheap firecracker.

On October 15, 1965, I had fifty-two and a wakeup, fifty-two days in Vietnam to break the Joe family tradition of croaking in a war.

I had fifty-two fleeting days to find my Dragon Lady. Each passing day doubled my panic that I wouldn't. I knew if those fifty-two passed and no Dragon Lady, I'd be a nervous, agonized wreck.

I doubt if I could step on that homeward bound 707. I'd go AWOL and door-to-door searching for her. Friends, that's what equal overdoses of lust and love will do.

I took two days leave before reporting to my new unit. First stop was 421 Hai Ba Trung. Mai's apartment had been rented to an American civilian bureaucrat, no forwarding address of prior resident given. Her Cholon digs were occupied by nobody familiar. None spoke English or admitted to. I wandered aimlessly to places my Dragon Lady and I'd been together—the zoo, the market, the riverfront, the Conti *terrasse.*

No dice.

The 803rd Liaison Detachment had been disbanded. The day the ding-a-ling outfit sent CAN-DO's good news to the Pentagon and White House, the Vietcong overran a provincial capital by Tay Ninh. They also captured three town potentates and beheaded them, and cut off several major highways too. We bombed North Vietnam and had four planes shot down. We'd yet again forgotten to warn the ants that their efforts were futile and they'd lost the war. The Vietnam domino was tumbling to earth.

The 803rd's computer's proclamation (ordnance tonnage multipliers, confrontation vectors, escalatory intersects, et cetera) might've been forgiven if they hadn't inserted a narrative with their numbers that South Vietnam's impending statehood was validation of their conclusions. They thought it added a rich context.

It sure as hell did.

They said you could hear President Lyndon Baines Johnson from the D.C. Beltway, reaming every VIP from McNamara to the Joint Chiefs to MACV HQ.

"What kind of locoweed were those boys smoking? Did they pull this fifty-first state shit out of their asses?" LBJ was quoted as bellowing. "I'm gonna have somebody's pecker in my pocket."

The fifty-first state rumor petered out on its own. Our powers that be threw a bucket over the looniness, including VV Day. The cover-up was masterful. How CAN-DO stayed out of the press and remains hush-hush to this day is beyond me. Woodward and Bernstein types dug into it and hit a brick wall. Same with folks like Mike Wallace and his *60 Minutes* bulldogs.

There was new furniture and new personnel inside the Fighting 803rd, but the Annex wasn't guarded, as there was nothing to guard, no magical automatic brain, not even our scrounged plug adapters. The new lumber and new lumber smell was gone, too, replaced by mildew and a faint electrical stink.

The Annex and the 803rd offices were slated to become an information agency. The one six blocks away had been vandalized into rubble. A mob of neighborhood people still without electricity had objected to the information with which we were endeavoring to inform them. It was deemed that the change of informational scenery would give the locals a change of heart.

Yeah, right.

I made friends with the info agency's morning report clerk, an authentic, genuine, bona fide, school-trained clerk who actually knew how to type. I innocently inquired on the whereabouts of his predecessor, PFC A. Bierce, who was an occasional former lunch companion of mine.

He had the answer at his fingertips, in a cabinet, precisely filed. For whatever reason, a copy of Bierce's separation papers had been mailed here. Ambrose, father of the fifty-first state rumor, had received an honorable discharge from the nonexistent 802nd Liaison Detachment of Fort Huachuca, Arizona.

I pictured him now in a Nogales apartment, the aspiring novelist practicing the loneliest of crafts, pushing *Jesus of Capri* onward, a fitful keystroke at a time.

I wanted to learn where my other 803rd colleagues had gone. My new pal made a phone call to a MACV buddy who handled personnel records. Suspicion confirmed: the brass had promoted the entire gang to sweep the debacle under the rug.

Major Papersmith went berserk at Clark and had to be shipped to Japan to dry out. Electrodes were attached to his temples to quiet him down.

Colonel Jake Lanyard was Brigadier General Jake Lanyard. He commanded an infantry brigade. He was in the field where he belonged, kicking ass, and taking names. He was reputed to take enemy ears, too, charms for a necklace. I wondered who paddled Jakie's pooper now. Female Cong POWs in tight black pajamas lashing him with fronds?

Major General Whipple commanded a National Guard armory in Turpentine Springs, Arkansas. He had been bound for there when he visited me in the hospital. He'd been booted upstairs where his career would not see the light of day. But the growing season in the South was long, and that should agree with him.

Ralph Buffet resigned his warrant. The rest of the oddballs did likewise. Not one uttered a peep about Cerebrum 2111X and CAN-DO. Ever. I presumed their severance packages cost a considerable chunk of taxpayer bucks.

Our hotel room hadn't been rented out. It was empty, though. There was no clothing or toilet articles, no wilted lily, no Johnny Red, no books.

I moved back in, halfway afraid of the memories. Without Ziggy and my books, it was damn near haunted. After an hour-long crying jag, I felt better. The dump became livable.

My gecko hung out on the ceiling. I stared at it for hours before conking out.

◆

I was assigned a bunk at Tan Son Nhat that was to gather dust. I had to wear fatigues, on which my brand-new PFC stripes were sewn, to go with my freshly-minted clerk-typist MOS. I wondered how long either would last.

I reported to my new unit there—USMACV-SHUFO. SHUFO stood for Strategic Headquarters Utilization and Flow Operations. They pronounced it shoe-full. It was "shuffle" to me, for we did that to vast quantities of paper. We cranked out even more reports and documents than the 803rd had. Man, did we pump out that paper.

I didn't know why USMACV-SHUFO was formed or what we accomplished, and nobody else did, but, were we busy. SHUFO had no shortage of shavetail draftees who could type. We had first-rate equipment, too. We had a telex, and I had my own wooden swivel chair at my own desk and my own *electric* typewriter I didn't know how to operate, though I could switch it on and off.

Mother and I continued to write regularly. Jack, too. And Wendi, our correspondence increasingly salacious. I spent my work days hunting and pecking replies on my new machine, getting to be semi-proficient with two fingers. Ziggy's mom wrote me a letter, her excitement rendering it nearly illegible. Bigwigs were coming to her home to award her the Distinguished Service Cross for her son. They'd be bringing reporters. Her baby boy was going to be in the paper, on the front page. There'd be a photo, too, one taken when he was a sophomore in high school, his last year of formal education.

She asked me what Edward's last words were.

I whipped the most commendable lie of my lifetime on her: "I love you, Mom."

Joey, they killed me would not do.

Paying homage to Ziggy, Sally's and my last trip was to the Lowell Observatory at Flagstaff, Arizona. We covered the grounds slowly. The altitude (7246 feet) was tough on a dying geezer. Sally, bless her, indulged me, lending an arm when necessary.

The observatory was founded by Percival Lowell. In his twenty-four inch telescope, he saw Mars, its canals, its polar ice caps and oases. The telescope was inside a wooden dome that rotated using electric motors and tires-and-wheels from 1954 Fords. Very cool.

I tingled. At this site, Lowell saw what Ziggy saw through his mind's eye.

◆

My USMACV-SHUFO boss was Major Blue, SHUFO's Administrative Officer. Behind his back, they called him Old Blue, because he was. Old. And blue too, on most mornings when he was gruesomely hung over. Jowly and balding, he was my height and twenty pounds heavier. He was among the saddest-appearing persons I'd ever known.

A lifer and a Midwesterner, Major Blue was ancient, age forty-two, an eon older than me. A boozer and skirt chaser, he wasn't around the office much. If it weren't for the Vietnam War, Major Blue would be going nowhere even faster.

One day, the major invited me out for noon chow. Major Blue was a decent guy, but we hadn't exchanged fifty words. Surprised, I said, yes, sir, my pleasure.

We rode a taxi to a hole-in-the-wall eatery two streets off Tu Do, for tasty roast pigeon that was served whole, head and neck too; noodles; and ice-cold *Ba-mi-ba*. Major Blue used chopsticks like a native and conversed in Vietnamese with the waiter. Real Vietnamese words and sentences, not just slang and pidgin and obscenities and propositions. This was his second Vietnam assignment. Stationed at Fort Riley, Kansas, in the process of his fourth divorce, he'd volunteered to return.

"From the fire into the frying pan," Major Blue said.

We walked along the Saigon River while our "noon chow" digested.

"Joe, a little birdie told me you got things done at that screwball 803rd unit you were in, you and your late buddy. My condolences, by the way. He sounded brave."

I nodded. "Yes sir, he was."

There were barges on the river, a floating caravan. Air conditioners were stacked on one, the same model Ziggy and I had requisitioned from that Air Force flatbed in the deep distant past of not so many months ago. If they were piled any higher, they'd eclipse the sun. Can't win a war without air conditioners, I thought. Things were getting crazier by the day, imploding into sheer chaos.

"Chaos," I say absently.

"The whole shiteree, you're saying?"

"Yes sir."

"Joe, I've been around long enough to know that any master plan that comes out of the Pentagon and the White House, one hand often not knowing what the other's doing, is certified to be a--I'm searching for the right word."

"Clusterfuck," I said.

"Couldn't've put it better myself."

A couple of GIs passed us. They had muscles, haircuts, and slick, embroidered shirts.

"Special Forces," Major Blue said.

"Green Berets?" I said. "How do you know?"

"Check out the lettering on the back of the shirts. They come out of whatever godforsaken place they're serving at on R & R and get those shirts made for them at Cheap Charlie's, a couple of blocks off Tu Do. Cheap Charlie can and does anything you want stitched on caps and shirts."

Before they were out of range, I turned and read: *Special Forces Prayer. Yea, though I walk through the valley of the shadow of death, I will fear no evil, for I'm the baddest motherfucker in the valley.*

I smiled. "I like it."

"They're in a bar and somebody *doesn't* like it, they are highly capable of backing up those words."

"I'm a believer."

"First-rate scroungers you were, so the legend goes," Major Blue said out of the blue.

An affirmation that there was no such thing as a free noon chow.

"Yes sir. Private Zbitgysz and I frequently embarked on special assignments, employing alternative matériel sources."

"I don't know about your 803rd Liaison Detachment except its newfangled computing gadget. Didn't work out, did it?"

"No sir, it didn't."

"That situation has been classified top secret."

"Yes sir."

"That rumor that South Vietnam's to be our fifty-first state is dead as a doornail." He jabbed a thumb upward. "If the wrong people hear you even mention it, you might get your tongue ripped out."

"Not me."

"What we've got is a war of attrition we'll be living with indefinitely. Uncle Ho up in Hanoi, he's in no hurry. He'll wait us out and wear us down to a nub, how he did it with the Frogs."

"Yes sir."

"Those computers, like you had in the 803rd, they're novelties. They're a fad. You don't win wars with snazzy new inventions. You win wars on foot, Joe. Rifle, bayonet, shoe leather."

"Yes sir."

"That's the deal about wars. They say life's short, but you don't know how short till you've been in a war."

"No sir."

"I've been in three of them, beginning with the last good war," Major Blue said. "I enlisted on 8 December 1941, bright and early Monday morning. At the recruiting office, I stood in a line that went around the block. I joined the Navy thinking I'd be killing Nips the soonest, doing my share to sink their fleet. I was a senior in high school and figured I'd learned all school could teach me. I figured wrong on both counts.

"They shipped me out on a heavy cruiser for Atlantic convoy duty. The seas in the North Atlantic in winter, you might as well be in a rowboat running rapids. I puked my guts out for days. I almost wished a U-boat would put me out of my misery. I wangled me a transfer to the army. Landed in Sicily as we were chasing the Krauts up the Eye-talian boot.

"I was a first looie when the war ended, but when they demobilized, I was busted back to corporal. I wised up and got my GED and a few junior college credits for good measure. When Korea came, I won back my commission and it stuck.

"I'd planned on staying in and retiring after thirty. You put in your thirty years, you retire at three-quarters of your base pay. I wouldn't have had it made in the shade, but I could get by on less of a civilian job. I could be an usher in a movie theater or some such if my ex-wives didn't find me. I'd make a couple of bucks and catch the films. Not the worst way to live."

The major was perspiring from the heat and humidity and exertion of walking. He stopped to catch his breath and light a cigarette with a Zippo.

"I'm finishing up my twenty-fourth year and that might be all she wrote," he went on. "I was passed over twice for lieutenant colonel and if I'm passed over a third time, I'm in mandatory retirement. See what I mean about life being short?"

"I think so, sir."

"There you are, Joe. Live for the moment. The Armed Forces Television Network has arrived in-country, you know."

"Yes sir."

"They say if we're here long enough, they'll be transmitting in color, too. Same same computers. I'll believe the newfangled when it functions on an everyday basis."

Will he ever get to the point? "Yes sir."

"Top-quality black-and-white TV sets are expensive and scarce even if you're prepared to shell out," the major said. "Big-screen, twenty-one-inchers are the scarcest."

I watched the mountain of air conditioners drift lazily along and said, "There are always scarcities, sir."

"Truer words were never spoken. Supply and demand, they make the world go 'round and 'round. My first Vietnam stint was in '63, advisor to the ARVN out of the MAAG compound up in Pleiku. That's Military Assistance Advisory Group. MAAG merged into MACV in '64. We were advising things the little guys didn't care to be advised about since we were starting to take over the war anyhow. I didn't have the opportunity to make the connections you have in this burg.

"What it is, I have a sweet lady friend of the slant-eyed persuasion who'd dearly appreciate to have in her possession a Philco or RCA console. If a twenty-one-incher could be arranged, I do believe she'd worship me to death."

"I'll see what I can do."

"You'll be performing a miracle, Joe. I'm what you call financially embarrassed. Major's pay doesn't go far when you're being circled overhead by embittered gals you once loved, by them and their shyster attorneys. I think I could cough up a bottle of Jim Beam, along those lines."

"Sir, I'd prefer to spare you any out-of-pocket whatsoever."

"That's kind of you, Joe. It is. I'd be grateful."

"There is a favor you could do for me instead."

"Name it."

"You're an admin honcho, sir. You know plenty of people in the army and in Vietnam. You could probably trace someone."

"An individual on active duty?"

"No sir. A Vietnamese civilian." I told him about Mai, playing it cool, confining information to what I thought would be helpful in locating her.

He saw right through me. "Son, you got it bad. Her too?"

So much for cool. "I think she does. I hope so. Yes sir."

"You are aware of the problems in permanently fraternizing with these indigenous gals, aren't you, Joe? I mean desiring companionship and nooky with one following your standard twelve-month tour."

"Yes sir, I am."

"One of life's dilemmas, Joe, is how us menfolk get romance and lust all tangled up. Like a spastic retard and his feet. As often as not, you hit the deck in a heap. I'm not criticizing you, Joe. It's just how it is."

Romance. "No argument there, sir."

"Lord knows I'm no authority on love, Joe," Major Blue sighed and flicked his cigarette into the Saigon River. "You do what you can do, I'll do what I can do."

For my end of the bargain, I requested that the major turn a blind eye to SHUFO's surplus equipment that wasn't shortening the war in any case and to give me access to the unit's Jeep. I cleared space in a storage closet by surplussing seven still-in-the-box IBM electric typewriters. I swapped them to a helicopter mechanic at Tan Son Nhat who was rotating soon and didn't need his twenty-one-inch console. He didn't tell me his plans for the typewriters, and I didn't ask.

Major Blue was so happy he glowed. He said that if there were any more television sets where that came from, him and I, we could work something out. His lady friend's lady friends would be envious and who could say where that'd lead.

"Ladies and their catfights," he said, winking. "There's nothing like competition for a male of the species to inspire bedroom creativity."

"Yes sir. Uh, my Mai?"

"I'm working on it, PFC Joe. I promise I am. It is a challenge, a real bearcat, a bitch and a half, complicated by no last name. Mai's as common here as Mary or Jane."

I accepted his word and paid Bombay Tailors a call.

"I trust you're as prosperous as usual, Mr. Singh."

"A businessman must adapt to volatile circumstances, Mr. Joseph. I am charmed and honored. Please allow me to offer my condolences for Mr. Zbitgysz."

Wondering how he knew about Ziggy, I thanked him and initiated a conversation regarding TV sets.

Mr. Singh said, "Excellent-quality giant-screen televisions are available. Please be advised, however, that premium models involve additional logistical impediments."

I braced.

"Accordingly, Mr. Joseph, do you know where I might obtain New York strip steaks, 35-millimeter cameras with integrated light meters, Vat 69 Scotch, lubricated prophylactics of U.S. manufacture, transistor radios, Christian Brothers brandy, rum crook cigars, phonograph player needles, truck tires, fingernail clippers, Brylcreem hair lotion, and Worcestershire sauce?"

"I'll see what I can do," I said.

♦

A dreamy "Unchained Melody" wafts as I watch Dien Bien Phu and the ants on Channel 668, sound muted. Smitty and his fifth helping of mac and cheese are upstairs. He's increasingly withdrawn, which is fine and dandy with me.

I am enjoying the richest, tastiest brownies I've ever eaten. Sister Mary Jean could work for me as a baker in any kitchen I ever ran in The Land of the Living.

I am recollecting word for word this post-noon chow conversation with Major Blue. The memory intrudes and meshes as I continue to ponder my cul-de-sac anomalies when a light bulb goes on.

I have found a pattern and a solution to the enigma.
There is no pattern and there is no solution.

Chapter Twenty Five

A week passed without a hint of progress in tracking down my Dragon Lady. I thought Major Blue stiffed me, so I had an excuse to put Singh's shopping list on hold. Also, if additional television sets meant additional nooky for the major with television-crazed ladies, I did not want to be responsible for him, at his advanced age, suffering a coronary while in the saddle.

In his defense, the major did ask me into his office, said he was sorry, and made excuses for how hard it was to locate Mai.

"These mysterious little Oriental ladies, Joe, they're here, there and everywhere in this pretty pussy paradise of a town. None of them have last names of colleagues they willingly share, let alone their own."

"Nice alliteration on the Ps, sir."

He looked at me. "Private Joe, how you talk, there are times when you can be as inscrutable as any Chinaman. These gals aren't listed in the phone book, if there even is a phone book. They don't have Social Security numbers. If they own motor vehicles, they're likely not registered with the DMV, if there is a DMV. It's like that series, *Naked City*, where the background voice says, 'There are eight million stories in the naked city.' We got a bundle of them in Saigon, too. See what I'm driving at?"

"Inscrutable as any Chinaman" was the Zigster's reference to Chairman Mao and his *Quotations from Chairman Mao Tse-Tung*. Should I take it as a compliment or insult?

"I guess so, sir."

He had framed pictures all over his desk, exclusively of women. Some old, some young. Each was slim and appealing. They could've been any Caucasian females in the universe but his four exes. I didn't ask who they were. If he cared to tell me about his photographic harem, he'd tell me.

When I think of Major Blue and those photographs now, I'm reminded of the train ride Sally and I took in conjunction with our Lowell Observatory visit. A touristy affair, the train traveled on trestles and wound through Arizona mountain passes. The scenery was spectacular, the wildlife abundant.

There were two fortyish couples in the seats ahead of us. The men were florid and sported pot guts. They frequently slipped out to the deck to have a puff. The women were fit and vivacious. They chatted nonstop, obviously bored with the train trip and their hubbies. They'd be attractive widows in their fifties, hot to trot after a suitable period of mourning.

◆

Thereafter, Major Blue reported to me daily, "No luck, Joe. None. I have feelers out. I've called in *beaucoup* markers. Your sweetie vanished into thin air. But I'll keep working on it. My middle name is tenacity."

Frustrating as it was, I attempted to remain patient.

The Tan Son Nhat library had expanded, spilling into converted hootches. On the off chance my Dragon Lady miraculously turned up, I browsed their poetry section. I'd write Mai a poem if I could script one as perfect as her.

Yeah, correction. I know she isn't perfect, likely being a Commie spy and guerrilla and so forth. But you know what they say about absence making the heart grow fonder and the memory grow weaker.

I was going to give it a whirl, even if I didn't see her again. I'd use the books as inspiration, not to copy verbatim. Well, okay, semi-plagiarism. I'd be a poet of sorts, a half-assed bard, and she'd swoon. It was probably as close as I'd ever gotten (or ever would get) to a non-sexual fantasy inspired by a woman.

The handful of poetry books did not circulate. My *Paradise Lost* was there. The other volumes were dusty and moldy. The problem was how to obtain them. I couldn't check them out. I'd tried earlier with a recent best-seller, a biography of Queen Victoria. Request denied. Thanks to CWO R. Tracy, crackerjack library shamus, and my prior history of overdue books, I was at the very top of their shit list, capitalized and underlined in red.

The poems I wanted were written by sensitive and romantic chicks. Their names were Bronte, Dickinson, and my gal, Elizabeth Barrett Browning. I knew the names, but with the exception of Browning, very little of their work. My myriad college majors did not include flowery literature. In retrospect, I should've majored in verse that disastrous quarter I plunged into pre-veterinary medicine.

I decided to try an old reliable method, a bribe. I asked the clerk at the counter, a listless specialist-4. "How much to buy these?"

He sniffed the fungus and examined the yellowed, curled edges. "They're ours?"

"Yep."

"You wanna buy *these*?"

"That's what I said."

"Where'd you find 'em?"

"On the shelf next to astrology."

"You like poetry?"

"Sure do."

"They're yours. Merry Xmas."

"Really?"

"Really," he repeated, eyeing me tentatively, suspecting that any GI keen on poetry was light in his loafers.

"Thanks, man."

"Don't mention it. Gotta make space for the Mickey Spillanes arriving soon."

I left with my poetry, legal as could be. I felt upright, virtually civic-minded.

My plan adjusted to having that Browning one translated into Vietnamese and elegantly bound. Me and my horny, rose-colored memory, I'd just whip it on Mai and enjoy her reaction. It was the thought that counted.

I didn't follow through. Browning's antique style represented a challenge, regardless of one's English-Vietnamese proficiency. I worried that something would be lost and/or gained in the translation. I worried I'd come across as a dope. Like the dope I was wasting all this time on poetry.

In addition to my Dragon Lady anxiety, I was developing a case of short-timer's paranoia. I had what I thought of as The Triple S: Scared Shitless Superstitious. A real soldier, a grunt in a paddy, *knew* he was slated to catch a bullet the day before he was due to rotate. That was understandable.

In my duties as a desk jockey at USMACV-SHUFO, it'd be my luck to croak from an infected paper cut. They had all manner of bacteria in tropical Asia. Or I'd succumb to melancholia and ennui and the vapors, pining for my Dragon Lady.

Thanks to the TV I'd acquired for him and his companion, Major Blue was living in a state of unmarital bliss. His lady friend treated him like a maharaja.

"It's enough to make a man go *engagé*," he told me.

"Awn-gaw-jhay?"

"*Engagé*. That's a Frog word for going native." He held thumb and forefinger a quarter of an inch apart. "I'm that close to *engagé*, Joe. That close."

Major Blue appreciated my efforts and empathized with my short-timer jitters. He did not push me to stretch my neck any farther onto the chopping block by dabbling in the black market. Sorry, Mr. Singh.

The morning I had thirty-nine days and a wakeup, per that calendar in my head, Major Blue came to my desk, winked, and casually tucked a folded piece of paper into my shirt pocket. It was a note in Mai's handwriting saying to please be at the Continental Palace *terrasse* at high noon.

I came out of my chair as if shot from a cannon. My unintelligible shout startled everyone at USMACV-SHUFO within a one-hundred-decibel radius. Needless to say, I complied to her request, stopping en route at a flower vendor for a single white lily.

◆

It took a moment to recognize Mai. She sat by herself at an interior table. She wore an *áo-dài* and big dark glasses that nearly covered her stratospheric cheekbones. Compared to her, Mata Hari and the Mona Lisa and the entire Hollywood stable of starlets were a kennel's worth of bowwows.

She stood and held up a single white lily. I reciprocated. Without preamble, my Dragon Lady and I kissed lightly and exchanged lilies cross-handed. If anybody on the *terrasse* snickered because we were as saccharine and maudlin as any scene in any Rock Hudson-Doris Day flick, it'd be pure envy.

I could barely breathe, let alone talk. I stared. I wanted info. I wanted something. I wanted *her*. I was at the seventh grade sock hop.

She said, "Your people clumsily searched for me. They made my neighbors and friends uneasy. To put a stop to it, I left a note under your office door. I wanted to contact you, Joe. I wanted to so much, but I had not generated sufficient nerve."

So much for Major Blue's ace detective squad.

We sat and I said, "I've had sleepless nights over you, Mai. I can't stop thinking of you."

"I came to say farewell."

Something was wrong with her English because nothing was wrong with her English.

"Farewell. As in for good?"

"Regrettably, yes."

"No."

She lifted a delicate palm. "Yes. *Fini*. It is unavoidable."

"*Fini* to where? And why are speaking like a Stanford grad in English lit?"

"I cannot divulge where. I shall explain later."

"You're American, not Vietnamese, aren't you?"

"No, Joe, I am Vietnamese."

"North Vietnamese, huh?"

"*Vietnamese.*"

"Level with me, Mai. C'mon, who are you? Why and where do you come and go? The night I couldn't find you at either of your places and you evaded me on the subject, which was and is fishy."

She bent forward and squeezed my wrist. "Joe, please, no."

"Why not, Mai? Talk to me, love of my life."

This was as close as I could come to asking her if she'd known about the satchel, asking her why she wanted to kill me and the best friend I'd ever have. I was a chickenshit, not wanting to know, because if I heard the truth and it was the wrong truth, I'd have to get up and walk out before I wrung her neck.

"I simply cannot."

She seemed sincere to a degree. Frightened too. I approached her obliquely. "Okay, who's Quyen the cackler? Truthfully, Mai."

She straightened as if slapped. "Why do you ask again? I have told you."

"Big sister disappears when you do. Big sis bossed your Cholon neighborhood around. The first time I laid eyes on you, Sis pinch-hit for you with Papersmith, for whatever reason."

"I asked her to. When Dean drinks like he does, he is so, so repulsive."

"Who is Quyen? Who is she to you? Who are *you*? C'mon, Mai."

She removed her shades. I saw something new in her eyes. Resignation?

"You will keep whatever I say in strict confidence, Joe?"

"You know I will, Mai."

"Absolute secrecy."

"Scout's honor."

"Quyen is a high-ranking officer in what you refer to as the NVA."

"The North Vietnamese Army?"

She hushed me with a hand on my mouth and said, "Quyen is a colonel in the PAVN, the People's Army of Vietnam. She most decidedly is not my sister."

"Who the hell is she?"

"You might tag her a watcher, a handler, a minder."

"A professional chaperone, like in a spy movie?"

"An apt definition."

"She's from the north, you're from the north."

"Yes."

A waiter came for our orders. Mai wasn't hungry, and my appetite had taken a hike. She asked for a glass of white wine. I went for a double Scotch-rocks. My nerves required medication.

"You probed me about the technical books on my bookcase."

"Books that belonged to your late father. You moved them out of sight after I did."

"I secreted them from Dean and Jakie. Why did I allow you to see them? I shall explain that too."

"They're yours, aren't they?"

"They are."

"Yet another facet to my exotic Dragon Lady."

It pleased me that she couldn't suppress a smile. "I was good at mathematics in school and in pre-engineering classes too. Boys were supposed to excel at mathematics, not girls. It was unnatural. The other students made fun of me."

"Same same in the States."

"I refused to hide my abilities. Joe, you once alluded to Dien Bien Phu."

"Bad joke."

"You were accidentally accurate, more accurate than you could have dreamed. I was in secondary school during the French War. I was recruited and brought to Dien Bien Phu. As a result of heavy casualties through years of fighting, there was a dearth of surveyors and math-related specialists. Whether I was unnatural or not, our leaders were pragmatic. When we moved the big guns up the hills surrounding the French garrison, my job was to calculate artillery coordinates."

The *Terry and the Pirates* Dragon Lady could not have been a fraction as complex as mine. Could not. Not that the comic strip counterpart was a dummy, but c'mon. No way was she a math whiz, a teen prodigy at geometry and trig and algebra and drafting. *Terry's* was no ant either.

I sucked in a deep breath. "You did one helluva job. Why the hell are you telling me this, Mai? I am your enemy."

"Not personally an enemy. I like you, Joe. I may love you."

"I know I love you, Mai. You drive me crazy, whoever and whatever the hell you are!"

"You suspected I was a communist spy, but that knowledge did not dissuade you from climbing into my bed at every opportunity. You are so devoted and courageous."

I had no reply but a neck-scorching blush.

"I came to Saigon months ago when the 803rd began operation."

"From *the* north."

"Yes, Joe. From the north. Again, utter secrecy?"

I raised my right hand. "Mum's the word."

"I am a native of Haiphong, where I continue to reside. Until I was conscripted into this duty, I taught algebra and calculus at Haiphong University. I learned rudimentary English in secondary school. They enrolled me in advanced English classes at the university. The bar-girl pidgin was a ruse. As was my concomitant promiscuity. It was loathsome to me, but necessary for access to the American serviceman."

"Thanks a bunch."

"Joe, you are again behaving like a spoiled adolescent. It is beneath you. What was I to do, 'accidentally' bump into my targets and discuss quadratic equations over coffee, then segue to secret projects on the second cup?"

"I know, I know, I know."

"You and I are different, Joe."

"God, how I wanna believe that!"

"I did what I had to."

"Who's this 'they'?"

"Use your imagination."

"I'm afraid to. Our boy Dean-o taught math too. Was that a factor in zeroing in on him?"

"We thought so at first. But no. His expertise was levels below mine. He was not helpful in those disciplines nor in computer science, which is in its infancy at home. It and the machines themselves are spoon-fed to us by our benefactors in Moscow."

She shifted to a whisper. "Do you know what we call the Soviets?"

"No."

"Americans without dollars."

I laughed and said, "Mai, let's talk about love. Romance. Why me?"

"I was not to you merely a surrogate in an unhappy marriage or an ejaculatory depository. Your longing, your passion for me. Your idealization of me. The allurement of you being smitten by me as a result of a fantastical cartoon. Your attraction to me was beyond exceptional."

"There are kinkier fetishes. I know there are," I said in my own defense. "Did Lanyard, like Dean, have an unhappy marriage?"

"Jakie's wife was a penitentiary guard before they wed. He did not complain constantly about his Helen as Dean did about his Mildred. I drew some disturbing conclusions from snippets. Helen knows how to use her baton, but the marriage is barren otherwise."

"Wow. To be a fly on their bedroom wall."

"To paraphrase our Mrs. Browning, Joe, let me count the ways I love you."

"Take your time. Don't leave anything out."

"Brazenly letting you see Jakie's uniform in my wardrobe was a test. If intimidation overruled affection, you would be out the door, as you would when you discerned my political allegiance. A roll in the sheets would not be worth the risk to you, when sex is available on numerous street corners and in the numerous bars of this decadent cesspool of a metropolis."

"I was intimidated, if you'll remember. At least a part of my anatomy initially was."

"You are a loyal if misguided American. You and yours have not an inkling why you are here, only the domino theory propaganda. Forgive my redundancy on this, but you risked and continue to risk your freedom and even your life to be with me. I cannot emphasize that too often."

"Don't remind me. In retrospect, I guess I'm finally realizing that my subconscious mind told me I could reform you, and we'd both be in the clear. My heart and my, you know, overruled, as they so often do. One thing I really really need to know," I said, having a harder than hard time spitting it out. "Mai. In a word. Ziggy."

"I am so sorry you lost your best friend, Joe. I swear it was not my doing. Yes, the NLF, the National Liberation Front, the Vietcong as they are to you, is a close ally. We do not always agree and one is not always informed of what the other is doing. Friction between us is commoner than your side realizes."

Office politics, I thought, giddily speechless. I was so relieved, she could be Ho Chi Minh's mistress

"If I had known what was planned and that you and Dean and your Ziggy were going to be in that bar, I would have insisted that Quyen use her influence to put a stop it."

"At one helluva risk to yourself, Mai."

"Perhaps, but there is no shortage of Americans to kill."

I shivered at her matter-of-fact statement. "A couple more questions. Your full name?"

She smiled. "Sorry, Joe. I must be a Jane Doe."

"Where were you the night I raised a fuss when I couldn't find you?"

"A cell meeting, endlessly rehashing the 803rd."

"And what did you decide?"

She looked at me and put on her shades. "I do not want to talk now, Joe."

I caught her meaning and gulped down my Scotch. "Me neither."

We got a room upstairs. Sans a gold dollar, we were all over each other the second the door shut. With apologies to Sally, Mai and I made the most intense, ferocious, gratifying love of my lifetime. I held her so tightly I feared I'd cracked her ribs. Her nails raked my back so relentlessly I feared I'd lost a quart of blood. No matter. We could not restrain ourselves. I licked and kissed and nibbled and bit every square millimeter of her flesh.

In the middle of the night, she said, "Joe, you have not questioned in detail my interest in the 803rd. In you and Jakie and Dean and General Whipple."

"General Whipple too?"

"You and your dirty mind. With profound apologies, he professed such love for his wife, Katherine, that chastity was his only alternative."

"All outfits have weirdoes in them."

"Adultery was as toxic as a DDT dusting on a food crop, the general said to me. I rarely fail in seduction. I was trained well. I was at once charmed and insulted. Once more, why have you not relentlessly demanded an explanation of my interest in your liaison detachment?"

"I thought it was obvious. You were spying on us because of Cerebrum 2111X and CAN-DO."

"At the outset, yes. But early on, my superiors discovered the mission of the computer was to predict the end of the war. They deemed it ludicrous. Hilarious. They felt that when the computer's conclusion did not come to pass, it would demoralize your generals and political leaders."

"In hindsight, you were very correct."

"Joe, we have been fighting the same war intermittently for two thousand years. Only the invaders are different. The Chinese, the French, and the Americans, among others."

"Yeah? Your Russkis, your Americans without dollars? I bet they're getting more and more like a snoopy, bossy mother-in-law."

"In 1945, Ho Chi Minh was quite amenable to being allies of the West, but you gave us back to the French."

I shook my head. "Trying to debate politics with a commie is like debating religion with a Southern Baptist."

"May I return to the issue at hand, Joe? I related to Quyen what Dean said drunk, what Jakie said in his sleep, and what you said voluntarily about Cerebrum 2111X and CAN-DO."

"As Ziggy once said, I'd've given you the recipe for the H-bomb if I had it and you asked nicely. Slight exaggeration, but you get the message."

"To become the most reviled traitor in American history because of me, that is so sweet of you, Joe," She kissed my cheek. "Quyen and her superiors thought the 803rd mission was hilarious. We have people on Saigon's docks who knew exactly what the components were. They took pains to ensure that the machinery wouldn't be stolen or destroyed in an NLF attack. Quyen had a terrifying tantrum when you almost did it yourselves that night you damaged the power grid. She can be indiscriminately murderous when she is in a rage.

"They were ready to withdraw me and bring me home when a serious problem occurred. A growing initiative for South Vietnam to be America's fifty-first state. Your 803rd Liaison Detachment seemed at the center of it in a secret function we are still unable to determine. Oddly, when the 803rd was disbanded, the statehood talk faded and quickly fizzled out. Was it a coincidence, Joe?"

I wondered if Vo Nguyen Giap's *People's War People's Army* dealt with outrageous rumors of enemy annexation. If it did, I missed it.

I grinned. "My turn for hilarity."

"How so?"

I gave her a complete rundown on PFC A. Bierce and his rumor-mongering, tossing in his exponents primer for validation.

She breathed heavily. "That is a sigh of relief, Joe. It never was, never will be anything but a practical joke by an aspiring novelist?"

I kissed her cheek. "You got it, kiddo. President Johnson went apeshit when he heard."

"You have madman generals who would bomb Hanoi and Haiphong with nuclear weapons if we occupied American domestic soil, which the State of South Vietnam would be. This was our primary concern."

"You're on the mark. You and Bierce."

"So I have to go home, Joe."

"No you don't. Piss on them. Stay, Mai. Please. If they discover who you are, I'll try to arrange amnesty, I'm a great negotiator."

"I cannot, Joe, and this is why. I lied to you about my mother and father. They are alive. They live as man and wife. I have three brothers and two sisters. We live within a block of one another in Haiphong. There are veiled threats what would happen to them if I did not explicitly obey orders. Quyen was here to keep me on the correct path."

I didn't know if I was relieved she wasn't a gung-ho commie spy or devastated since the heartless bastards had her over a barrel, extorting her. Whichever, I was euphoric.

"Hold me, Joe."

I held her, gradually admitting to myself that I could not take her to the Land of the Big PX. We fell asleep clinging.

How she slipped out of my arms and out of the room before morning I'll never know.

I had thirty-eight and a wakeup.

Chapter Twenty Six

The Land of the Living is gorged with surprises. The Great Beyond is, too.
Today in the latter is a stunning example.
I call Smitty down for breakfast. He doesn't answer. "Rocket Man" is on, and maybe he's stuffed toilet paper in his ears. I go upstairs. His room is littered with empty mac and cheese cartons, but he's not there.
I scramble eggs and eat alone.
On my way out for a walk to the strip mall, I check my neighbors. To my left, the door is ajar. I go in. Smitty's not there either. The nuns are gone, too. I don't smell baking and there are no cookies or brownies set aside for me.
I go to the other place. No Slick. No nothing. I find a large rock in the landscaping, between a couple of shrubs that could use water. With all my might, I throw it at a side window. It breaks, glass tinkling inside and out.
This is a surprise, a vulnerability, albeit a trivial one. I go around the house, find more rocks, and break each and every downstairs window. I have proven nothing. I have behaved like a "baby-san." It feels damn good.
I walk on to the strip mall, which is no longer there. It's been replaced by another deserted cul-de-sac.
I head home, feeling so fucking alone.
All windows remain broken at my neighbor's. Good.

A red, white and blue The Great Beyond Postal Service (TGBPS) truck pulls in. I stand in front of my mailbox to play my little hologram game. The truck does not run through me. It stops five feet away, bad brakes squeaking.

The blue-uniformed driver is redheaded and weedy. He leans out and says, "What's the matter with you? I run you over and I lose my job."

I smile and crack the corniest of jokes. "I have a death wish."

He does not smile. "That's your problem, man. I got a schedule to keep."

I salute and step aside.

And touch the side of his box as he passes.

And feel a slipstream and smell exhaust when he accelerates away.

With a shaking hand I reach into my box and pull out material addressed to: OCCUPANT THE GREAT BEYOND

It's all printed matter--books and paper-clipped studies on chaos and the chaos theory.

I am in the midst of sadistic and well-planned chaos.

I have found a pattern and a solution to the enigma. There is no pattern and there is no solution.

I sit cross-legged on the soft grass on this perfect San Diegoesque day and browse the materials. Chaos theory, I read, is a newer science that permits us to see order in what we previously thought was erratic and random.

Weather in The Land of the Living is a prime for-instance. In our day and age, if a meteorologist in temperate zones can accurately predict weather four days in advance, that is an accomplishment.

Let's say it's January 2041 and computers are a trillion times more powerful than they are now, powerful enough to implement a program that accurately converts chaos into reality. The weather bureau can then inform you that Hurricane Sadie is going to come ashore where you live in September 2045. You can start stockpiling plywood to board up your windows. Look for sales on it.

Smitty and Madge and Slick and seedy strip malls and vacant cul-de-sacs and the rest are chaotic elements that are steps in a procedure. Will I ever be able to figure it out, to project what is ahead in my life after death? I have all the time in the netherworld to try.

I've told you this often and it bears repeating. Our honchos are antic and not always in an unkindly manner. They are playful, and their occasional largesse can be touching and flabbergasting.

I go inside and find on my dinette table a stack of blank invitations and a recommended guest list. Unbeknownst to me, a reunion has been arranged. For me. It will take place two weeks from today at our neighborhood cabana. We do not have a cabana, but I'm sure one will exist then. Punch and cookies will be served. If I can connect with whoever decreed my party, I'll lobby for baby back ribs, cole slaw, garlic bread, and potables with a stronger zip than the punch.

A typed and unsigned (of course) note atop the tastefully engraved stock requests that I handwrite my signature to each and whatever else strikes my fancy.

I hear hammering. I look out a window and see a cul-de-sac halfway down the block that did not exist ten minutes ago. Workers are pounding nails on the wooden skeleton of a townhouse condo complex. I open the window and whiff fresh lumber. There is a sign at the curb: VIETNAM VET ESTATES. OPENING SOON.

I return to the table and the guest list, which includes:

My mother. We'll hug and I'll listen when she speaks to me and treat her with respect. I'll try to atone for all those days and weeks and months and years that I didn't as a child who knew everything.

My father, late of Inchon. Him and his pipe smoke. We'd roughhouse some and play a little catch.

My mother and father. Shouldn't take much to match-make that pair.

Ziggy and his mom. Where do I start with the Zigster and his mom I at last get to meet? I can hardly wait!

First Lieutenant Ron Gibbs, our ROTC antagonist who arrived here far too early because of that Bouncing Betty. No hard feelings about our frat house stunt on his part, I trust.

Chief Warrant Officer R. Tracy, a 1974 suicide by gunshot. Poor bastard, I hope I hadn't contributed to his depression. I'll be a good host and let him bring it up if he so chooses.

Tom Backstrom, my all-time favorite sous chef, a genius with sauces and stocks. He was a 2006 auto accident, victim of a drunk in a Cadillac Escalade crossing the centerline. Wrong place at wrong time for Tom. He had no luck even when he was lucky.

Further, Tom was in his red Pontiac convertible he'd just won on that game show where a blonde makes letters appear. He'd found out he had to pay income tax on the car. I'd offered to help by using my pull with the restaurant owner to give him salary advances, but it hadn't been enough. The IRS lien sent him over the edge into bankruptcy. No luck, no luck at all. I'll ask Tom if he'll assist me with the ribs. His barbecue sauce is to die for (pardon the pun)

Stepdaddy and Wendi too, her of ovarian cancer, much too young. When I came home from Nam, she and

I did connect. It wasn't me seducing her to spite her hubby. It wasn't that she had grown to hate her hubby as much as he hated book editors.

We'd moved far beyond that. One thing instantly led to another, an up-close and personal extension of our correspondence. We got into her car and swerved into the parking lot of the first motel we came to. We fucked each other's brains out. Lordy Lordy, Wendi with the bubble over the "i" was so sweet and needy. Last I saw her was when she dumped me, weary of my boozing. The only good thing I did for her was encourage her to unload Stepdaddy. I'll graciously welcome them to my home, even him. Yeah, we'll be an awkward trio. Should be interesting.

Larry Sibelius. No explanation other that he's amongst us. Hopefully there'll be time to take him aside and help him get his feet on the ground, so to speak. Am dying (no pun intended) to give him a blow-by-blow of Ziggy and me in the opium den. Am dying to hear about his lady poets. Were they all that he expected?

Former PFC A. Bierce too, the scalawag.

I should tell you that in The Land of the Living, Ambrose eventually finished *Jesus of Capri.* It went through four agents who flogged it for six years to fifty-four different houses before it found a home at a small press who released a dinky number of copies. Didn't sell many initially, but got terrific reviews, the publishing version of good field, no hit. Then, fortuitously, a foaming-at-the-mouth televangelist got his hands on it. This self-righteous, big-haired ol' boy was nationally known and syndicated. He prayed on his knees with presidents and senators, and influenced their policies, so afraid were they of his public disapproval.

He noisily proclaimed *Jesus of Capri* as perverted, lecherous, sacrilegious smut, the handiwork of Satan, Zionists, and the Vatican. Fortunately for Bierce, this was accomplished not long before God's representative was nabbed in an airport restroom, inappropriately wagging his weenie.

A bidding war by big publishing houses ensued. *Jesus of Capri* made every best-seller list and made Bierce a zillionaire.

My notable army superiors, Major General Whipple, Brigadier General Lanyard, and Majors Papersmith and Blue succumbed to various and sundry geezerhood-related maladies. Prostate cancer, hardened arteries, strokes, advanced liver disease--the usual. Also amongst us are high school classmates and members of the Draft Board who saw through my professional studentship. Won't have time to do more than shake their hands, say hi, and gesture to the self-service bar.

I continue reading. The roster is long. I myself was a geezer, so it ought to be. Ah, Mr. Singh of Bombay Tailors, too. Remember when I told him he should've been running a car lot? Talk about self-fulfilling prophesies.

After Singh skipped to the States just prior to Saigon's fall, he settled in Southern California and became one of the nation's largest car dealers, with a string of sixty stores. Singh's ubiquitous TV commercials featured himself and his gleaming white smile, standing beside his special of the day, speaking sincerely into the camera with his clipped colonial accent that car shoppers inexplicably deemed irresistible. I wonder how he's handling The Great Beyond without money to change or cars to sell. I'll give him a little good-natured teasing. Next to last is the cackler, Quyen, the NVA colonel, nonsister of my Dragon Lady. Quyen bought it during the 1968 Tet Offensive, where she'd been sent back south to lead an assault. Cut in two by a GI's machine gun. Can't imagine what we'll have to converse about, though I'll always be grateful for her subbing for Mai with Papersmith.

On the bottom is Mai Le Truong Johnston. Cause and date of death not specified. She'd been married over forty years to a GI, a lifer sergeant last stationed at Fort Lewis, Washington. They resided in Lakewood, in south Tacoma, near the post, a mere thirty miles from me. For all those years.

How can this be? Had she had a bellyful of Quyen and her commie dogma, and her and her family being virtual prisoners in Haiphong? Had she gathered them up and sought political asylum or gone south after the 1975 collapse of South Vietnam under some pretence and become boat persons?

And what of Sergeant Johnston? I read the list again. His name was not on it, just hers.

If it *is* her. If it really is, perhaps she hadn't returned to North Vietnam after all. I'll have so many questions for her.

If it isn't my Dragon Lady, well, our masters' sense of humor can be cruel. I'm already quite aware of that.

To say I have mixed emotions is the mother of all understatements.

I get to work on the invitations. I shall invite everyone on the list.

I can't wait for two weeks to pass.

Can't.

About the Author

Gary R. Alexander enlisted in the Army in 1964 and served in Saigon. When he arrived in country, there were 17,000 GIs. When he left, 75,000. *Dragon Lady* is Gary's first non-mystery novel. He is the author of several mysteries featuring stand-up comic Buster Hightower--*Disappeared, Zillionaire* and *Interlock*--published in hardcover by Five Star/Cengage and in ebook by Istoria Books. He has had short stories published in *Alfred Hitchcock's Mystery Magazine*. He resides in Kent, Washington.

An excerpt from an interview with Gary Alexander
(Read the entire interview at the Istoria Books blog: http://istoriabooks.blogspot.com/2011/03/interview-with-irreverent-goldbrick.html)

IB: Because you served before the big troop buildups, did you experience any of the fighting?
Gary: Like Private Joe, I still have a piece of shrapnel in my arm and a Purple Heart. But I'm no war hero. I was minding my own business, sound asleep on 2/7/65 when the VC mortared our compound. I was damn lucky. Two guys on the other end of our hootch were killed and a mortar that didn't explode landed two feet from my head. They were aiming for the guard tent, where troops not on guard duty sleep. It was across the sidewalk from us. The absurdity of *Dragon Lady* was partly "inspired" by the fact that our M-14 rifles were chained and locked under our bunks. The powers that be felt we were more dangerous to ourselves than the enemy was. Victor Charles could've walked in and slaughtered us. That attack was kind of Vietnam's Pearl Harbor; it snapped everybody out of their complacency.

IB: Could you tell us about some of the men and women with whom you served -- do you stay in touch with any of them?
Gary: This was not an all-volunteer Army, so we had plenty of folks like myself who were civilians at heart. My best buddy throughout the Army and I kept in contact for years afterward. We lost touch about 20 years ago. I regret that.

IB: Have you visited the Vietnam Memorial?
Gary: I did. I saw the name of a kid I'd known before Vietnam, but hadn't known he'd died there. I broke down.

Other Istoria Releases by Gary Alexander

Disappeared (ebook)
Zillionaire (ebook)
Lunch Reads Volume Two:
Two Mystery Short Stories
Skullduggery Stew
and
Roswell Girl

About Istoria Books

Istoria Books is a boutique publisher handling only fiction, selecting books we consider to be "good stories, well told."

All our books are very competitively priced, and we run many discount specials.

Visit the Istoria Books website (www.IstoriaBooks.com) and sign up for the mailing list to learn of special discounts and deals.

Literary, Mystery, Romance, Women's Fiction, Short Stories, Historical and more…

Istoria Books
www.IstoriaBooks.com

Printed in Great Britain
by Amazon.co.uk, Ltd.,
Marston Gate.